MW01036058

THE
LIAR'S
DAUGHTER

BOOKS BY RONA HALSALL

Keep You Safe
Love You Gone
The Honeymoon
Her Mother's Lies
One Mistake
The Ex-Boyfriend

THE
LIAR'S
DAUGHTER

RONA HALSALL

bookouture

Published by Bookouture in 2021

An imprint of Storyfire Ltd.
Carmelite House
50 Victoria Embankment
London EC4Y 0DZ

www.bookouture.com

Copyright © Rona Halsall, 2021

Rona Halsall has asserted her right to be identified
as the author of this work.

All rights reserved. No part of this publication may be reproduced,
stored in any retrieval system, or transmitted, in any form or by
any means, electronic, mechanical, photocopying, recording or
otherwise, without the prior written permission of the publishers.

ISBN: 978-1-80019-284-3
eBook ISBN: 978-1-80019-283-6

This book is a work of fiction. Names, characters, businesses,
organizations, places and events other than those clearly in the
public domain, are either the product of the author's imagination
or are used fictitiously. Any resemblance to actual persons, living or
dead, events or locales is entirely coincidental.

For my lovely husband David, who has the patience of a saint and the heart of a warrior.

PROLOGUE

The ambulance rocked as Ifan negotiated the stony track.

'Oh my God, I'm feeling seasick,' Ann said, clutching the door handle. 'Are we even going to make it?' She peered ahead through a low tunnel of trees.

'Looks like it evens off up here.' Ifan swung the vehicle round a tight bend, his manoeuvre accompanied by the screeching of branches as they scratched along the paintwork. 'But this is what you call seriously remote.'

They were attending a call at a farmhouse situated in a high valley that ran along the mountainside at the back of Beddgelert, in the heart of northern Snowdonia. As locations went, it was a nightmare to get to. Ann always dreaded calls to the area because the single-track roads weren't designed for four-ton ambulances. There were no landing places for the air ambulance, and often the first responder would be sent out in their smaller vehicle. However, with a massive area to cover and limited resources, it was a matter of who was available to take the call. Ifan had a different mindset to her; he fancied himself as a bit of a rally driver and saw it as a challenge.

Ann held the door handle tighter, her body thrown from side to side as Ifan negotiated the bend. 'I hope this isn't a hoax,' she murmured, looking through the windscreen for signs of a house.

'The dispatcher thought it was genuine, but I suppose there's no telling. The woman just asked for help, managed to give her address and said she'd had an accident. Then said she felt faint and went quiet.'

Ann grimaced. 'They're always the worst calls. You just don't know what you're going to find: dead or alive?'

'Here we go.' Ifan hunched over the wheel, peering under the branches. 'House up there in the trees.'

'Thank God.' Ann could see it now, the hulk of a stone building looming through the foliage. 'Can't say I'm looking forward to going back down that track, though.'

The ambulance pulled to a stop and the paramedics climbed out. Ann shivered. 'Someone just walked over my grave,' she said, glancing around. 'It's a bit creepy up here, don't you think?'

Ifan laughed as he jumped in the back to get their bags of equipment. 'You're a right townie, Ann. I'd love to live somewhere like this. Peace and quiet. No bloody neighbours playing loud music at two in the morning.' He scowled as he passed her the bags. 'They were at it again last night; seems like party night every night with that family. Mind you, even I wouldn't fancy going up and down this track too often. No handy shops if you run out of anything.'

The farmhouse sat squat in the landscape, nestled against the slope of a field at the back and protected by woodland on either side. Handsome and well proportioned, it was a nice-looking place when you got up close, if a bit run-down.

They were at quite a height, and a cold wind whipped Ann's fringe off her forehead. She shivered again and zipped up her jacket as they hurried towards the front door. Red paint curled away from the woodwork. Ifan banged the knocker, which was brass and shaped like a lion's head. They waited for a moment. The assumption was that the woman was on her own, but you never knew. They couldn't go barging in.

'Ambulance,' they both called. When there was no reply, Ifan tried the door. It was open. He called out again as he went inside, Ann following.

They entered a well-proportioned hallway, stairs ahead of them, a door to either side at the bottom. With a practised routine, they checked the place. Two reception rooms, as an estate agent would call them. One formal, with a dining table at the far end and a couple of armchairs by the window. Bookcases stuffed to the gills, and an old-fashioned bureau in the alcove at one side of the fireplace. The other room was obviously used as a sitting room, with a battered leather sofa in front of the inglenook fireplace, which housed a wood-burning stove. A scattering of mismatched chairs. An old TV in the corner. Family photos on the walls.

They hurried down the hallway to the kitchen. It was a big room that ran the width of the back of the house. Old-fashioned units lined the walls, probably put in twenty years ago or more. The floor was quarry tiles, worn to the sort of smoothness that only happened over many years.

A woman lay sprawled across a large kitchen table that stood in the centre of the room. Her dark hair, streaked with grey, tumbled over her shoulders. As they got closer, Ann could see a patch of scarlet on the back of her head, blood caked in her hair, glistening as it oozed from a long, jagged wound.

'Nasty head injury,' Ifan said, bending closer to give it a proper inspection.

Ann put two fingers against the woman's neck, glad to feel warm skin, the throb of a heartbeat. 'Definitely alive,' she said. 'But her pulse is a bit thready. She might be in shock.'

Ifan bent to look at the woman's face, which was turned towards the back door, her head resting on a handbag, her hand curled round a phone. 'She's breathing.' Gently he rubbed her shoulder. 'Hello. Can you hear me?'

They were both still, listening. No response.

'Hello.' He tried again. 'You called an ambulance. Can you hear me?'

'Possible fractured skull, I would imagine, with a wound like that,' Ann said, studying the back of the woman's head. 'What do you think? Has she been attacked? Do we need to get the police up here?'

Ifan took a moment to reply, scanning the room as if he might see someone crouching in the corner, ready to pounce. A loud bang made them both jump, followed by a whoosh of cold air. He gave a nervous laugh. 'Must be the door.' He looked towards the hallway. 'I don't think I closed it.'

'This looks suspicious to me.' Ann could feel her own heart racing, adrenaline coursing round her body. She'd been attacked recently when trying to help a patient and the fear was fresh in her mind. That time they were on the street, though, and it was Saturday night, the remnants of a party breaking up in a nearby pub. She'd been a bit jumpy ever since; now she was feeling increasingly uneasy. 'Whoever did this might still be here.'

Ifan was already busy putting a bandage round the woman's head to keep the wound clean. 'Let's move her to the floor, get her stabilised.'

'Okay. Then I'm calling the police. No way she did this to herself, is there?'

'Nope. Definitely a non-accidental injury.'

The woman murmured something, her words thick and indistinguishable.

Ann bent towards her. 'Hello. We're paramedics. Can you hear me?'

The woman was trying to speak, her mouth pushed up against the handbag, making it tricky for her to move her lips.

'We're just going to make you a bit more comfortable,' Ifan said, taking up his position at the woman's side as he and Ann prepared to move her to the floor, where they could do more thorough checks. It was imperative to make sure that her oxygen levels were okay and get a cannula in. The woman grunted and tried to move, but it was obviously a struggle.

'It's okay,' Ann murmured, reassuring her as they manoeuvred her out of the chair. The phone fell from her hand onto the table, but her other hand remained clasped round the strap of her bag.

'Can I just take this and put it on the table?' Ann said, pulling at the bag. But the woman became agitated, her hand tightening round the strap. Ifan shook his head and Ann let the bag rest on the woman's stomach as they laid her on the floor.

'There, you just relax. We won't be long, then we can be on our way to hospital.'

The woman's eyes opened and she mumbled something that sounded like *thank you*.

'How did this happen? Were you attacked?' Ann asked as she found a vein for the cannula.

'Accident,' the woman managed to say, before leaning to the side and vomiting on the floor. No food as such, just bile.

'Concussion at the very least,' Ifan observed, passing Ann the bag of saline. 'Blood pressure is low, so we'll get this going, see if it helps. I'll nip out for the stretcher.'

'It was definitely an accident?' Ann asked, doing what she could to wipe her patient's face clean. 'Because I can get the police to come and check the house if someone attacked you.'

'Accident,' the woman repeated, her voice coming in breathy gasps, face screwed up in pain. 'In the barn. Floorboard went.' She gave a low moan. 'Tools fell out of the loft.'

'You live alone?' Ann asked, following her own line of logic as she set up the drip. Her eyes scanned the room, noting the boots beside the range. Different sizes. There could be an abusive partner around and the woman was too frightened to point the finger. You never knew in these situations, and her explanation didn't really fit with the injury.

Ann was sure there was more to this than a blow to the head. There might be other injuries they couldn't see and the low blood pressure could be a sign of internal bleeding.

The woman muttered an inaudible reply before her eyes fluttered closed and her head flopped to the side.

Ann glanced up as Ifan hurried through from the hallway, pushing the stretcher.

'Quick! She's gone again. Lost consciousness. Pulse is still there, but erratic. We need to get a move on.'

They lifted her onto the stretcher, gathering their bags of equipment and checking they'd got everything. The woman's fingers were still hooked round the strap of the handbag. Ann tucked the phone inside.

They were just by the front door when another loud bang made her jump. Ifan glanced over his shoulder. 'Got to say, this place is giving me the creeps now.'

'Do you think there's someone else here?' Ann asked as she guided the stretcher towards the back of the ambulance.

'Who knows? Not our job to find out, is it? We need to focus on getting her to hospital.'

The wind rushed through the trees, sending branches clattering against each other, boughs creaking and squeaking. They both looked round at the sudden surge of noise.

'She said it was an accident. In the barn. But I'm not sure.' Ann scrunched up her nose. 'What do you think? Call the police?'

'Can't do any harm,' Ifan agreed as they pushed the stretcher into place. 'I'll make the call if you want to get sorted in the back here. Get ready for a bumpy ride back down.'

Ann's stomach rolled just thinking about it. She set to work getting the drip set up and making sure the woman's airways were clear, her breathing settled ready for the journey.

'Police are on their way,' Ifan said a few minutes later, before shutting the back door. She heard the driver's door slam, then the engine thrummed to life and they were off.

She studied the woman's face, thin and angular, like her body. Almost malnourished, she would say. It wasn't unusual on these remote farms, where it was impossible to make a proper living off the land. People scraped by with what they could grow, selling a bit, doing another job to bring in some money.

She'd noticed the woman's ear lobes were torn, as if earrings had been ripped out at some point. A sign of abuse?

'You're safe now,' she murmured, sure that her own conclusion was correct. This was no accident.

PART ONE

Now: Eva

CHAPTER ONE

Eva stroked her dad's hand and felt his clasp loosen, his head lolling back against the headrest of his chair. She studied his face, his mouth dropping open as he gently snored. It was a struggle to come to terms with his transformation. He'd lost all his bulk, and his balance wasn't good these days, so he shuffled rather than walked, a dimness in his eyes signalling that he wasn't really present.

It had happened so quickly, her dad morphing from an action man who'd think nothing of going rock-climbing in the Peak District with his mates to a frail shadow of his former self who appeared to be edging closer to death by the day.

Her heart clenched at the thought that he might soon be gone from her life, a realisation that was only now starting to sink in. She'd always been his greatest fan, so proud of his daring adventures. They even looked alike, sharing the same dark hair, brown eyes and long face. The same rangy build. Part mountain goat, part monkey, he'd always joked.

There were no jokes anymore.

Dementia had taken hold three years ago, not long after Eva had graduated from university with her degree in wildlife conservation and plans to save the planet. Or bits of it, anyway. She'd imagined travelling all over the world, from project to project, but once her dad had become ill, she'd decided to stay closer to home. Fortunately she'd done voluntary work with the local nature reserve while she was at school and was lucky enough to secure a ranger post during the spring and summer, helping to organise volunteer groups to undertake maintenance tasks. By the time that contract ended, the post office were recruiting seasonal workers to cover the Christmas mail. Between the two, she more or less had work all year round, switching from one contract to another with maybe a month's break in between.

This year, though, once the postal contract had finished, she hadn't taken on the job at the nature reserve, staying at home instead to help her mum. It was clear Linda was struggling, and with the two of them as carers, it spread the load. As an insurance salesman, her dad had an excellent policy which was paying a decent income and with their savings they could just about manage.

Her mum had visibly aged in the last year, her blonde bob neglected and in need of a cut, more lines on her face and a permanent sadness in her eyes. She was Mike's second wife, quite a bit younger than him, the age gap even more noticeable now. Although technically Eva's stepmum, she was the only mother she'd ever known. She'd been their next-door neighbour when her parents had lived in Blackpool, and when Eva's mum died, on the day Eva was born, Linda had stepped in to help.

By his own admission, her dad was hopeless with babies and scared witless by the idea of coping with a newborn on his own. From Linda's account, she'd fallen in love with Eva the minute she saw her and had been only too happy to help out. Over time, romance had blossomed between her and Mike, and two years later, they'd got married and moved to Nottingham, to the house where they still lived.

During Eva's childhood, her birth mother was rarely spoken about. There was only one picture of her in the house, taken on her wedding day. A picture Eva treasured and kept in her bedside cabinet. Her mum looked nothing like her – petite, with dazzling blue eyes, pale skin and a mane of red hair. To Eva, she would be forever a mystery, someone she could never know, but that didn't stop her thinking about her. She wondered what she was like as a person, what they might have in common, whether she'd be proud of the daughter she'd never seen.

But Linda was a wonderful mum and they'd always been close. Now it was time to step up and look after Linda and her dad for a while. Her own plans would have to wait.

Linda had got to the point where she was clearly exhausted, already grieving for the loss of Mike, no longer a partner to her but increasingly like a child. Eva knew her life was going to change in ways she could hardly imagine, with a dying father and a grieving mother to care for. It was going to take a bit of getting used to.

She stroked her dad's hand again, glad to be able to spend this precious time with him, determined to savour all the lucid moments. He'd been quite an athlete in his day, his rock-climbing feats legendary in the sport. He had shelves of climbing magazines going back years, and every day now they looked through his collection together, stopping when a picture jogged his memory. Eva enjoyed seeing his eyes light up, hearing the laughter in his voice as he recounted stories, giving her an insight into a life she'd never been a part of. His life before she was born.

She'd started to shoo Linda out of the house, making sure she had time for herself to do a bit of shopping, or meet up with friends, or go to yoga, so she could at least relax for a little while. When her mum was out, Eva would pore over the magazines with her dad, or she'd get out the photo albums and they'd chat about the places they'd gone on holiday, or favourite memories that the pictures sparked, just letting the conversation wend its own way through his disparate thought processes. Sometimes he'd recount tales from his own childhood, his eyes sparkling with the memories. She lived for those flares of animation. It struck her that there were so many things she'd never known about the man she'd lived with for most of her life. Now she felt closer to him than she had for years. An irony that fed the sadness in her heart.

It wasn't just her father who was living in the past; she found that she was doing a lot of that too. She supposed it was part of the grieving process with a degenerative disease, as you watched the person you loved getting further away from you, the things you used to enjoy doing together no longer possible. There were no more games of cards, something they'd always enjoyed, the rules now forgotten. No teasing, because his sense of humour had shrivelled to nothing. No conversations about friends and neighbours, their names too hard to recall.

She held his hand a little tighter. 'Love you, Dad,' she whispered, aware that she probably hadn't said it enough, hoping he knew how important he'd always been to her. How she wouldn't have been brave enough to follow her passion and go off to university if it hadn't been for his encouragement.

Linda popped her head round the door, just back from a yoga class. She held up a bag from the local bakery. 'I got us a couple of pains au chocolat, if you're ready for a coffee.'

Eva smiled and gently placed her dad's hand on his lap before following Linda into the kitchen. She stretched and yawned, amazed at how taxing it was keeping an eye on him, his conversation hard to follow when his thoughts zoomed off at a tangent in the blink of an eye.

Linda put the mugs of coffee on the table and handed her a plate for her pastry.

'Thanks for dad-sitting, love. I can't tell you how much better I feel now I can get out a bit more. Being able to do yoga with Dee again is such a treat. Honestly, I go for the relaxation at the end, but I'm sure my body appreciates the stretching, and my mind definitely enjoys an hour and a half without wondering what your dad's up to!'

Eva bit into her pastry, her favourite. Her mum was lovely like that, always buying her little treats. She was lucky, she knew, that they had such a strong bond. So many of her friends had clashed with their parents and couldn't wait to move out when they went to university. In contrast, Eva had needed quite a bit of persuading to go away and study, her father insisting that it would widen her horizons and be character-building. He'd been right, and once she'd settled into her course, she'd loved every minute of it. She wondered when she'd get to use her skills again. All that knowledge sitting in her brain, desperate to be applied. It could be months before she could go back to her passion. It could be years. There was really no telling and the not knowing was difficult, her life in limbo.

'I'm glad to be able to help,' she said, licking crumbs from her fingers. 'You should have said something sooner and I would have stopped work.' She glanced at Linda. 'You know that, don't you?'

'Oh, but I couldn't spoil things for you. I just wanted you to be young and free and do all the things I should have done at your age but never did.' Linda sighed, stirring milk into her drink before passing the carton to Eva. 'Anyway, it wasn't too bad until he had that mini stroke a few months ago. That's when we started to struggle, wasn't it?' She reached across the table and rubbed Eva's arm. 'I appreciate you being here.'

'Love you, Mum.' Eva caught her eye. 'And I want to be here. You and Dad have always been so supportive, it's my turn to give something back.'

Linda blinked and took a sip of her coffee, a sheen of tears in her eyes.

They sat in silence for a little while, eating their pastries, Eva thinking about how hard it had been for Linda this past year, having to cope with a series of unfortunate events. Her dad had managed to scald himself with hot water from the kettle and had been rushed to A&E; his legs were still scarred from the accident. Then he'd set the kitchen on fire, leaving a chip pan on in the night after he'd got confused and thought he was a student and had been out with his mates. Another time, Linda had rung Eva at work, absolutely frantic because he'd disappeared. A neighbour brought him back a few hours later, having discovered him sitting in her garden.

Since then, they'd kept the outside doors locked all the time to stop him wandering off, even though he'd seemed to have forgotten now how door handles worked. He couldn't be left on his own because his behaviour was so unpredictable, and he wasn't allowed in the kitchen. Linda said it was worse than having a toddler. Especially when he got frustrated and angry with himself, or confused about things. Then he'd start throwing stuff around, lashing out. Eva had only seen it happen once, but it had been pretty scary and completely out of character. Linda had soldiered on, dealing with things on her own. Always insisting she was fine. No wonder she looked so frazzled.

'I'll make tea tonight if you like,' Eva said as she picked up her mug and cradled it to her chest.

'I've been thinking about things.' Linda looked serious now. 'While I was supposed to have an empty mind for the meditation at yoga, all I could think about was putting a rota together for us. Then you can have time out as well. At the moment, it's all about me, but if we're going to be doing this for a while, it needs to be fair.' She caught Eva's eye. 'We've got to look after ourselves and that's not selfish. It's just good practice. That's what they said at the carers' support group yesterday and it's been on my mind ever since.'

Eva smiled, glad that Linda was starting to think about loosening control over the household chores. But she was also happy that she'd be able to plan some time out for herself.

'Good idea. I'd like to catch up with Holly. She's just moved back home, between jobs, she said, so it would be great to organise a meet-up.' Eva hadn't seen her school friend since they'd headed off to different universities six years ago, and although they chatted regularly on social media, it would be lovely to see her in person.

Linda's phone started singing 'We Are the Champions' from somewhere on the worktop. She got up to answer it.

Eva watched, curious, as the expression on her mum's face changed and her hand went to her chest. 'Nancy? Are you sure it's Nancy?'

The only Nancy Eva knew was her paternal grandmother, but she'd died years ago.

Linda frowned as she listened to the other person speak.

'Right… Right… Yes, of course. Um… well, I'd like to help, but…' She pulled at her hair. 'Look, I'll have to ring you back… What?… Yes, today. I understand that it's urgent. I just need a moment to gather my thoughts. Okay?'

She ended the call and turned to Eva, her face deathly pale.

'What is it, Mum? For God's sake, come and sit down. You look like you've seen a ghost.'

Linda walked back to the table and sank into her chair. 'You're not far wrong there,' she said, her eyes staring into the distance, not focused on Eva at all.

'Come on, Mum. What is it?'

She sighed, resting her elbows on the table, her head in her hands. Eventually she spoke.

'I don't really know where to start. Everything's happening at once.' Her voice cracked. 'I'm not sure I can cope with this on top of your dad.'

Eva's heart gave a little skip. It was clearly bad news. 'You're scaring me now, Mum. What's happened?'

Another big sigh, and when Linda spoke again, her voice was thick, as if she was trying not to cry. 'It's just one thing after another.'

Eva reached out and rubbed her mum's arm. 'I'm here now. I can help. Whatever it is, it's not all on you anymore, okay?' Linda nodded, but still wouldn't look at her. 'A problem shared is a problem halved, isn't that what you always say to me?'

Silence. A few sniffs.

Eva waited, her whole body tense and her mind screeching at her to stay calm. She really wasn't great when people were emotional. It tended to set her off as well and that was the last thing they needed.

Finally Linda took her hands away from her face and rubbed the tears from her eyes. 'Look, I hardly know how to tell you this.' She paused for a beat. 'The thing is… you had… well, you have… an older sister.'

CHAPTER TWO

Eva gasped. *A sister?* Had she heard her right? But before she could say anything, Linda carried on speaking. 'I really don't want to go into all the details. It's a long story and it all happened when you were born—'

'Wait, what? A sister?' Eva's heart flipped in her chest like a gymnast doing a tumbling routine. For a moment, she felt dazed, thoughts spinning round her head, and she clung to the table as if that would help to steady her world.

'Yes. You have a sister.' Linda let out an enormous sigh and leaned back in her chair. Her eyes squeezed closed for a moment, as if she was fighting against the revelation. Eva stared at her, willing her to carry on. Finally Linda continued, her eyes fixed on the table. 'Nancy. She was sixteen when you were born. And when your... your mum died, Nancy took it really badly and she... Well, there was a note.' She stopped and swallowed, her voice hardly more than a whisper when she spoke again. 'The police found her clothes under the North Pier at Blackpool. She'd brought nothing with her, no bag or anything. There was evidence that she'd...' Linda's eyes met Eva's, 'taken her own life.'

'Just a minute.' Eva put a hand to her forehead, her mind refusing to absorb what she was being told. *How could I have a sister and not know?* Her chest felt tight. 'I don't understand.'

'Well, I can't be any clearer.' Linda glanced up at the ceiling before her eyes came to rest on Eva again. 'I don't know how else to say it. We thought your older sister had committed suicide when you were a baby.' Her hand clasped her cheek. 'God, what an awful time that was. It was too much to take in.' Her chin quivered. 'The police investigated; we looked and looked for years. In the end we had to accept that she really had done what she said she was going to do and killed herself.'

Eva knew from the shifting tone of Linda's voice that there was something not being said. She was familiar with all the nuances, how her mum's words didn't always match the truth. She'd seen her do it with her dad loads of times, but understood it was Linda's way of avoiding arguments. She liked to keep everyone happy, did Linda, and she never let the truth get in the way. Just a little white lie, she'd say with a wink, if Eva caught her out. It was funny, though, that Eva had believed it was only her dad Linda lied to, which was understandable given his tendency to flare up at times. She'd always thought her mum had been honest with her. Apparently not.

Her jaw tightened as anger burned in her chest.

'Why didn't you tell me?' Her voice rose an octave. 'You knew how much I wanted a sister! All my life spent thinking I'm an only child and I'm not.' Her hand wrapped itself in her hair and pulled. 'I can't believe you kept that from me,' she hissed as she glared across the table at her mum.

In the silence, the new information circled around Eva's mind, looking for a place to settle. *A sister.*

Linda's voice broke into her thoughts. 'They want us to go and pick her up.'

Eva frowned, really confused now. 'Pick who up?'

'Your sister.'

'She's not dead? I'm pretty sure you just said she committed suicide.'

'You're not listening again, Eva. I just wish you'd bloody listen!' Linda's voice was so loud it made Eva snap to attention, sitting bolt upright now and bristling. It wasn't her fault she didn't absorb information verbally. She'd been born like that. She was more of a print person. Liked to see things written down. It was probably the only thing Linda got cross about.

'Sorry, Mum, it's just a bit of a shock. I mean, wow. A sister? You're going to have to explain exactly what is going on.'

Linda squinted, fingers rubbing at her temples like she had a headache. 'Right. Right.' A frustrated huff. 'That phone call was from a hospital in North Wales. Your sister Nancy is a patient there. Anyway, she wants to discharge herself, but she has head injuries. Concussion, I think the woman said. They don't want her going home if there's nobody there to keep an eye on her.'

Eva's anger smouldered in the background as her curiosity took centre stage. Her sister was alive and injured. This was getting more surreal by the minute. 'Did they say how she got hurt?'

'An accident. That's what she told them. Something about tools falling out of the loft in the barn.'

A barn? Now this was sounding intriguing. Her sister lived in a house with a barn. That implied land. Countryside. Wildlife. Nothing like this. Here, the semi-detached houses were organised in neat rows, all the same, interspersed with cul-de-sacs of detached dormer bungalows, with larger gardens and garages to the side. The development had been built in the 1990s and had settled into its place, just off a main road into Nottingham. It was tidy and civilised, but you could hear the hum of traffic in the background, a world away from the wildness of nature where Eva longed to spend her time.

She thought for a moment, her mind joining the dots.

'And she was sixteen when she disappeared?'

Linda nodded. 'That's right.'

'Okay…' Eva did the maths in her head. 'So she'll be forty now?'

'Hmm. Yes. Christ. Forty.' Linda blew out her cheeks. 'I can't believe it all happened so long ago.' She blinked. 'And now she's turned up.'

Eva studied her mum's face, her mind humming with questions. *Is she pleased Nancy's alive?* It didn't look like it. If anything, Linda appeared more despondent than usual, the corners of her mouth turning down, her shoulders slumped as though she was being pressed beneath heavy weights.

'I wonder what happened in those twenty-four years.' Eva caught Linda's eye, a new question on her tongue. 'Why didn't she come home?' She frowned. 'Had there been a row or something?'

Linda's mouth dropped open, then closed again. 'I don't think you quite understand, love. Nancy's mum had just died. She had a baby sister – you – who screamed practically non-stop, and her father was emotionally absent. Poor girl, she'd had her world ripped from under her.' She tutted. 'I don't think there's any mystery about why she might have run away.'

They were both silent for a moment. Eva's heart hammered in her chest as she tried to subdue her mounting anger, waiting for an explanation that would make sense. She'd hated being an only child, but however much she'd expressed a need for a sibling, one never materialised. Later, she'd found out her father had a vasectomy. Linda, she knew, would have liked children of her own, but it wasn't to be.

Why would they keep this a secret?

Linda interrupted her thoughts, coming straight to more urgent practicalities.

'The hospital wanted to know if your dad could go and stay with her. She had his contact details, you see, though where they came from, I don't know, because we moved here after she disappeared.' She took a breath. 'Anyway, that's obviously out of the question. None of us can go, can we? Not with your dad to look after. And we've got appointments with the stroke clinic and the physio next week.'

'I'll go,' Eva said, before she'd even assessed if it was a good idea. She was too angry to stay here, too fired up with a sense of betrayal for it not to come out at some point. And if Linda was going to dodge the questions, maybe Nancy would be more forthcoming. Somehow, meeting her sister seemed more important than anything else. 'I'm sure you can manage for a few days without me and it sounds like Nancy really needs a bit of support.'

Linda looked appalled. 'I don't think that's a good idea, love. Oh no. That won't work. She won't know you, will she?' She ran her tongue round her lips. 'And you don't know her.'

Eva wasn't really listening, her mind already made up. 'North Wales, you said?' Her heart did a little skip at the thought of an adventure, a release from the pressure of caring for her dad. A perfect place to go and think and work out how she felt about this bombshell – the fact that she'd been lied to her whole life.

Her mind was starting to catch up, the shock morphing into curiosity. What would it be like, having a sister? They might bond. Nancy might be lovely, someone she could be friends with, close to. A fizz of excitement bubbled in her stomach.

Linda glared at her, then gave a shake of the head. 'I can't even pronounce the name of the hospital, but it's in Bangor, opposite Anglesey. On the edge of the Snowdonia National Park. That's how the woman described it to me.'

'Snowdonia? Isn't that where we went on that camping trip when Dad hadn't told us he was meeting up with his climbing mates and we hardly saw him for a week?' It was the hottest summer there'd been for years and some of the climbs he'd wanted to do were up in the mountains and hardly ever dry enough to tackle. Linda hadn't made a fuss at the time, but Eva could tell she was annoyed. She had a way of silently seething, her shoulders drawing up a bit, her chin jutting out as she forced a cheery voice.

Now she gave a distracted frown. 'Oh God, yes, I must have tried to blot that out of my memory. You and I had a nice time, though, didn't we?'

Eva remembered long days on the beach, playing in the sea with Linda, building little shelters out of stones to protect the barbecue. Visiting castles, which had been a bit of an obsession at the time. Going up Snowdon on the train. Visiting the Sea Zoo and nature reserves. Yes, they'd had a lot of fun, just the two of them.

'It was a great holiday,' she said, with genuine enthusiasm. It was the first time she'd been to such a wild and magnificent landscape, and it was where her passion for conservation had been ignited.

She caught her mum's eye.

'Why didn't you just tell me I had a sister? All those years I spent badgering you for a sibling...' She shook her head, still unable to comprehend.

Linda pulled a tissue from her pocket and dabbed at her eyes. 'Honestly, love, we thought it was for the best. If she was dead, you didn't need to know. You didn't need to have that sadness as well as losing your mum. We were always going to tell you when you were old enough, but then the years went by and you were such a cheerful child it never seemed the right time.'

She blew her nose and looked thoroughly defeated. Eva relented a little. She could sort of understand her parents' reasoning, but still...

She stood, desperate to get out of the room and have some space to think.

'I'll go and stay with her until she's better.'

Linda pulled a face, the one that said she thought Eva was making a mistake. 'I really don't think it's a good idea. Please, Eva, don't go.'

Eva's jaw hardened; she was in no mood to be persuaded. 'Somebody has to go and help her. It might as well be me.'

She narrowed her eyes as she tried to visualise her sister. Perhaps they wouldn't even look similar. Would that feel weird? After all this time, would she feel a connection, a genetic bond?

Now that she'd started thinking about it, she wondered if she'd been a bit impulsive, deciding to go and stay with a stranger. Especially one who'd left the family and had never been in touch.

That's strange, isn't it? Why now? But she'd watched the TV programmes – long-lost relatives finding each other again – and knew families became estranged for all sorts of reasons. If Nancy had their current address, maybe she'd been planning on getting back in touch.

'I really don't think it's a good idea,' Linda repeated, her voice disturbing Eva's thoughts. 'I'm going to ring and say we can't help.'

'What? No, don't do that.' Eva glared at her mum. 'Why wouldn't I go and help? She's my sister.'

Linda pursed her lips in a familiar expression of annoyance before she spoke. 'She walked out twenty-four years ago, let us believe she was dead.' Her hand closed into a fist round the damp tissue. 'Your dad has lived with that. The guilt. Blaming himself for focusing on your mother rather than his daughter.' She returned Eva's glare. 'Do you think he needs all that dragging up again?'

Eva's mouth dropped open, hardly able to believe what she was hearing. 'But Mum, don't you see, it might be good for him. If he knows she's not dead, he can let go of that guilt, can't he?' It made so much sense, one last thing she could do for her dad. Give him some peace in this twilight period of his life. *Perhaps I can bring the family back together.* Surely that would please him, give him a lift? She was clear now that it was the right thing to do. 'When she's better, I'll bring her home.'

'Oh God, no.' There was fear in Linda's voice, horror in her eyes. 'She can't come here. It would kill your dad to know she's still alive.'

CHAPTER THREE

Eva frowned, trying to work out if that was a rational response. *Why would it kill him?* You'd have thought he'd be delighted. There was a chance that he might not recognise her, she supposed, and he did find new things unsettling. *Is that what Mum means?* Or was there something else?

The whole thing was utterly confusing and her head was pounding, her thoughts galloping around like a herd of animals. *I don't think I can talk about this now.*

'Right, well, I still want to meet her. Whether I bring her back here or not, I'm going,' she said, a determined tone to her voice. Would her mum really stop her? She didn't think so.

Linda stood and moved towards her as if to give her a hug, but Eva swerved out of the way, holding up a hand to make her keep her distance.

'Sorry, Mum. I'm just…' Emotion filled her throat, threatening to spill out in an unseemly rush. 'Later,' was all she could manage. She reached the door and turned. Linda looked completely dejected, and Eva wavered. 'I just need a bit of time to process everything. I can't believe you didn't tell me before.'

She turned and ran up the stairs to pack a bag, anger still rumbling like a summer storm in her brain.

Bloody parents. They always thought they knew best, constantly filtering life to sieve out the unpalatable lumps. Her dad liked to ignore things, pretend they weren't there, while Linda liked to cover things up and smooth them out, ironing life's creases. No doubt they'd thought they were doing what was best for Eva, but would it really have harmed her to know the truth?

The older she got, the more she understood that her life was built on a foundation of secrets, which didn't become obvious unless she did a bit of digging and made an effort to uncover them. There were still whispered arguments and cryptic comments that remained a puzzle to this day. Now that her dad had dementia, she supposed there was a lot she would never know. But it was the present he struggled with and on a good day he would happily chat about his own childhood. Perhaps she could get him to tell her more about their family. Her sister.

She thought again about Linda's comment – that it would kill him if she brought Nancy home – and her internal chatter fell silent. It was a strange thing to say. Why wouldn't he want to know that his daughter was alive? More to the point, why had Nancy pretended to be dead and stayed away? Was it just the death of their mum, or had something else been going on? Had there been some sort of falling-out between Nancy and her dad?

Linda had swerved that question.

Or was it to do with our mum?

As a child, she'd been conditioned not to ask about her birth mother, understanding that her questions caused her parents distress. Instead, she'd created her mother in her mind, a fairy-godmother type of character, and fantasised that she wasn't really dead. That there'd been a mistake somehow and one day she'd come back. It was a stupid idea, but it had helped when Linda and her dad were having one of their tense days, as Linda liked to call them, which involved no conversation and an atmosphere so thick you could hardly breathe. On those occasions, Eva would retreat to her room and conjure up her dead mother, who would keep her company until relations between her parents had gone to back to normal.

Now that she was an adult, her curiosity about her birth mother was stronger than ever, a constant itch that she tried not to scratch.

What characteristics had she inherited from her? Would they have had shared interests? Were they similar in any way? She liked to think so, because apart from a love of travel and the outdoors, she had very little in common with her dad.

She smiled to herself. Surely her sister would be able to answer all her questions. *Our mum.* She might even have photos. Eva only had the wedding photo, which was formal and staged; she wanted more now – more information, more pictures, actual memories, things her mum had said and done so she could get to know what she'd been like as a person. With an older sister, this all seemed possible and she couldn't wait to get going.

She googled hospitals in North Wales and found there were only three. It was easy to identify the right one. She checked the route and estimated driving time, then set up her sat nav app. With that done, she hurried downstairs, bag in hand, crammed full of clothes to suit any weather, hardly able to believe what she was doing. Normally she liked to think about things for a little while before committing herself, making sure it was the right decision, but there was no doubt in her mind about travelling for three hours to meet her sister. No doubt at all. And once she got an idea in her head, Eva would admit to being stubborn.

Linda was still in the kitchen, putting the finishing touches to a quiche. 'I'll just stick this in the oven for lunch and throw a salad together and that'll be it.'

'I'm going to Wales, Mum. I told you. It's a bit of a drive and I don't want to get there too late.'

Linda's face fell. 'Oh no, love. Please don't. Just… Wait until after lunch and we can talk about it.'

Eva gritted her teeth. 'I'm going and you're not going to stop me.'

Linda went back to crimping the pastry round the side of the dish, her shoulders hunched as she worked.

'Anyway, I thought the hospital said someone had to go and collect her?'

Linda pulled a face. 'Well, they thought she'd just discharge herself and were worried about her being on her own. She lives on a farm, apparently.'

A farm! Even better. Eva could feel her heart being wrapped in the romance of it, her mind already conjuring images of flocks of sheep, herds of cattle and chickens pecking round a cobbled yard.

She turned down the volume of her excitement, trying not to get carried away when Linda was so obviously disapproving.

'Look, I'm sorry you don't think it's a good idea, but you must be able to see it from my point of view. I *need* to meet her.' She grimaced, nerves tugging at her belly. 'It's going to be odd staying with someone I know nothing about, though. What can you tell me? Anything, doesn't matter what, just so I feel more prepared.'

Linda blew out a breath. 'Hmm. I didn't really know her, to be honest. She was a teenager when I moved next door. I hardly saw her. Typical youngster, out with her mates or stuck in her room. I'd only been there a few months before your mum…'

Eva's shoulders tensed.

'Died. She died. You don't have to tiptoe around it.'

'I'm sorry.'

'No, don't be sorry, I know you're just trying not to upset me, but honestly, it's fine. It's not like I ever knew her, is it?' She was aware she sounded sharp, but her anger at Linda's deceit was pushing to the surface.

'Sorry.'

She moved towards the door. 'Okay, well I'm off.'

'Are you sure you don't want some lunch first?'

Eva's hand tightened round the handle of her bag, aware that Linda's delaying tactic was a precursor to persuading her not to go. 'I'll get something on the way.'

She marched out of the kitchen, closing the back door with an emphatic thump, threw her bag onto the back seat of the car and slid into the driver's seat. It was her dad's old car. A battered

Citroën Berlingo that had been on many adventures with him all over the UK. Now it was hers, a belated birthday present. It smelt of sweaty feet and it still had a bundle of his outdoor gear in the boot that she hadn't got round to sorting out.

Wasn't life strange? she thought as she drove down the road. The way it lobbed these grenades out of nowhere, little explosions that rocked your world and sent you spinning in a new direction with consequences you could never have foreseen.

CHAPTER FOUR

Eva sang along to the radio as she drove down the A55, the sea sparkling to her right, the sun picking out the limestone cliffs of the Great Orme, jutting into the sea in the distance, Llandudno nestled alongside. An army of wind turbines spun lazily out at sea. Ahead of her she could see the jagged outline of the peaks of Snowdonia, clouds skimming the highest summits, casting brooding shadows.

The journey had been quite straightforward once she'd got onto the motorway, then it was dual carriageway all the way down North Wales to Bangor. Three hours in total and her sat nav now told her she'd be there in exactly thirty minutes. For the last hour, her emotions had ping-ponged between delight at the idea she had a sister and fear that they'd have nothing to talk about, making the whole expedition really awkward.

If Nancy had run away twenty-four years ago and they hadn't heard from her since, presumably she hadn't wanted to be found. But then… why did she have her father's contact details? Not the house that Nancy herself had lived in as a child, but the one the family had moved to once she was gone. There were so many questions Eva wanted to ask, and she knew she'd have to rein herself in lest she overwhelm the poor woman. She didn't want to come over as an excitable puppy, but that was exactly how she felt.

She'd rung ahead to tell the hospital she was on her way and the person she'd spoken to had sounded pleased. 'I'll let her know,' he'd

said. 'Then maybe she'll stop asking for a taxi to take her home.'
He laughed. 'Your sister is one determined lady.'

Eva liked the sound of her already.

The hospital was situated on top of a low hill on the edge
of Bangor and could be seen from the dual carriageway as she
approached. Squat and grey and forbidding, it could be mistaken
for a prison if you didn't know better. She hoped it was more
welcoming inside, and it was. Although there were several levels
and it was quite a walk to the ward.

She arrived at the reception desk and asked for Nancy.

The nurse, a young man with a round face and a thatch of dark
hair, smiled at her. 'Oh good. It's been quite a job persuading her
to stay until you came, to be honest.' He lowered his voice. 'I have
to warn you, though… she got a bit agitated when we told her
you were coming. She was quite cross that someone had made
contact with you, said it was a complicated situation.'

He hesitated, Eva's cue to fill in some of the blanks, but she
wasn't going to launch into explanations, not when she didn't know
the full story herself. She gave a tight smile and after a moment
he carried on. 'Thing is, she'd given her permission, you see, so
we hadn't realised there was a problem.' He shrugged. 'Obviously,
with a head injury, memory and confusion can be an issue for a
little while, so just bear that in mind. Anyway, I think she's okay
about it now.'

Eva's heart filled with trepidation, her hands clammy. The idea
of being with someone who didn't want her help changed things,
but she supposed if Nancy had run away and been hiding, she
wouldn't be delighted that someone had blown her cover. Animosity
had to be expected at some level, given the circumstances. *And
I wonder what those circumstances really are?*

With her curiosity piqued, she took a deep breath and followed
the nurse into the ward, determined to be charming and patient
and kind. And if that didn't succeed in winning her sister over,

she'd look after her until she was well and then be on her way. A different outcome had taken root in her mind on the way down to Wales, though, one where they just clicked and Nancy asked her to stay longer and said her home would always be Eva's home.

She shook her fantasy world from her head as the nurse stopped by a bed. In the chair next to it sat a skinny woman with jutting cheekbones and eyes as blue as the summer sky. Her wavy brown hair had an auburn tint, streaked with grey. She had a strong face, Eva thought. A warrior's face, which was totally at odds with the pale grey tracksuit she was wearing and the blinding white trainers.

Alternative. Eva gave a tentative smile. She liked alternative.

The woman's eyes travelled up and down Eva's body, resting on her face, assessing. Eva shifted her weight from one foot to the other, wondering how to greet this woman.

'Look who's here, Nancy,' the nurse said. 'She's come to take you home.' His eyes dropped to the handbag at the woman's feet. 'Have you got everything?'

Eva realised with a jolt that the nurse would expect them to know each other, would have no inkling of the history. *Does Nancy know who I am?* She wasn't sure what she'd been told and as Eva had been a newborn when Nancy had left there was no way on earth she'd recognise her. She was trying to cobble together an opening gambit when Nancy spoke, her voice full of rounded vowels and proper diction. Unlike Eva's Nottingham accent or her parents' flat Blackpool intonation. She'd obviously been mixing with well-educated people. Eva's curiosity clicked up another notch. *What has she been doing all these years?*

'I didn't come with anything, if you remember. Just my handbag.' Nancy smoothed the fabric of her joggers, a pained expression on her face. 'Even my clothes seem to have disappeared.'

'That's because they were torn and covered with blood. Like you'd been dragged through a hedge.' The nurse gave Eva a look, rolled his eyes, as if to say, *I did warn you.* 'At least we managed to find some clothes to fit you. I think Sandra did a great job kitting you out.'

Nancy sighed. 'I look ridiculous.'

Eva smothered a giggle, because her sister was right. She did look mismatched, to say the least.

'Well, it's only something to wear for the journey. You can change as soon as you get home.' The nurse sounded defensive, like he'd had enough of his difficult patient. 'Mind you, the doctor said you'll need to take things easy, with plenty of rest, and joggers are very comfy for lounging around.' He gave a broad smile. 'So then... if you're ready, I'll just get your meds to take with you.' With that, he hurried off, leaving Eva and Nancy alone.

Eva swallowed her nervousness and smiled. 'I'm Eva,' she said. Then added: 'Your sister,' in case Nancy hadn't worked it out. Or hadn't remembered who the hospital had organised to come and collect her. They could be confusing places, hospitals, as she knew from experience with her dad. Staff were so busy and patients and their visitors weren't always listening. Consequently, messages didn't always get communicated or received correctly.

Her eyes met Nancy's and she glanced away, intimidated by the force of her sister's stare. She started gabbling to fill the silence. 'The hospital rang and asked if someone could pick you up and stay to keep an eye on you.' She smiled again, not feeling quite so confident now. 'They were worried about you being on your own. I volunteered.'

Nancy's frown suddenly disappeared and her face broke into a broad smile. 'Eva. Little sis!'

Eva grinned, relief sweeping all her doubts aside. 'You're not going to believe this, but I didn't know I had a sister until today.'

Nancy's jaw dropped. 'They didn't tell you?' she said, incredulous. 'Dad never mentioned me?'

Eva bit her lip, shook her head. It sounded really bad spoken out loud.

Nancy laughed then, a low chuckle that started in her belly, then shook her shoulders, until she was bent over, her body rocking. Eva wasn't sure why it was funny, but at least she'd inadvertently broken the ice. She felt her own lips twitch into a smile, an instinctive reaction, because when somebody was laughing that hard, it was nigh on impossible not to join in.

The nurse came back while Nancy was still trying to get her laughter to subside. He handed Eva a paper bag. 'Here's the meds; there's labels on everything telling you how many and what times of day, et cetera.' He looked at Nancy, who was wiping her tear-stained face, then turned and raised an eyebrow at Eva, who shrugged. 'If you'd like to come with me, I'll get you a wheelchair. She's still wobbly on her feet.'

Eva followed him into the main reception area, where he pulled a wheelchair from an alcove. 'This should do. You've got brakes here, to secure the wheels when she gets out, okay?'

She nodded. 'It's fine. My dad's been in hospital. I've got a bit of experience with these things.'

'The doctor just wanted to have a word before you go. You know, to brief you on the situation and what to look out for.'

They walked back to the desk, where a young woman with a messy bun was studying a computer screen. She glanced up as the nurse spoke. 'This is Nancy Gordon's relative. Eva, isn't it?'

Eva nodded. 'I'm her sister.'

The woman stuck out a hand which Eva shook. Her fingers were slim and cool against the sticky warmth of Eva's skin. 'I'm Dr O'Brien. I've been looking after Nancy.' She frowned. 'I'm not sure if anyone's told you how she came to be here?'

Eva shook her head. 'It was my mum who answered the phone. Head injuries. An accident in the barn or something. That's all I know.'

'Nancy is adamant it was an accident. But we're not so sure. The paramedics brought her in as a non-accidental injury. They thought there might have been somebody up at the farm who'd attacked her. Anyway, the police have been there and had a look round and have spoken to Nancy but she's sticking to her story. So there's nothing more to be done. I just thought you should be warned so you can keep an eye out if you two are going to be on your own. I understand it's quite a remote place.'

Eva gulped. Poor Nancy. But if she'd been attacked, why would she insist it was an accident? Eva hadn't considered there could be any danger involved, but now a cold unease sat in her stomach. *The police have checked.* She wasn't reassured. *What if whoever it was comes back?* She gave an involuntary shiver and made a mental note to lock all the doors as soon as they got there. She'd see if she could get Nancy to open up about what had happened. Perhaps it *was* just an accident. Farms were dangerous places. All sorts of machinery and tools lying about. She adjusted her bucolic mental image.

The doctor carried on talking. 'Although she's a bit underweight, she seems to be recovering well, on the outside at least. Inside… well, we don't really know what damage might have been done to her brain and how well that's healing. Ideally we'd keep her in longer so we can run more tests and do observations but she's adamant that she's going home.'

'I don't think I can change her mind on that,' Eva said. 'I don't know her, you see. She's sixteen years older than me and left home when I was a baby.'

The doctor seemed a little taken aback. 'Oh… right. I was hoping you might persuade her to stay for a bit longer. With concussion, symptoms can appear a little while after the injury. As can complications if people don't rest. So you must keep her as quiet as possible.'

Eva pulled an apologetic face, completely out of her depth. 'I'll look after her as best I can.'

'I've organised an outpatient appointment with Neurology.' The doctor sighed. 'We'll just have to take it from there. But if you're concerned at all, bring her straight back.'

'Concerned in what way? What should I be looking out for?' Eva could feel her panic rising, her heart rate picking up.

'She's going to feel a bit confused at times and her memory doesn't appear to be functioning too well. She might be agitated, irritable. But those things are all to be expected. It's the physical symptoms I want you to watch out for. In particular, dizzy spells, loss of consciousness, vomiting.'

Eva nodded, the weight of responsibility heavy on her shoulders. Perhaps she should have thought this through a bit more carefully before jumping in to help. Perhaps Linda had been right. She swallowed, feeling unprepared for the task of nursing a stranger. Even if that person was her sister.

She thanked the doctor and five minutes later she was wheeling Nancy out of the ward and into the network of corridors that would eventually lead them to the outside world and a new chapter in both their lives. Nancy didn't say a word all the way through the hospital, down in the lift and across the car park. Not a single word. And neither did Eva. What did you say to a sister you hadn't known existed until a few hours ago? One who might have been attacked but was insisting it was an accident. Eva's mind was on overload, struggling to work out where to start.

CHAPTER FIVE

'You'll have to give me directions,' Eva said when they were settled in her car. It was all she could think of to say, arriving at something non-contentious and practical rather than going straight in with 'Why did you run away and pretend to be dead and not get in touch?' She'd save all that for later.

Nancy turned towards her, deep-set eyes appraising her for a moment. Then she smiled and her face lit up. She was, in fact, rather beautiful. 'Thank you so much for coming all this way to take me home. I really do appreciate it.' She shuddered. 'I'm sorry if I wasn't completely welcoming. I can't stand hospitals. The way they're always messing about with you, taking your temperature or your blood pressure, or redoing a dressing or sending you for scans and whatnot. Honestly, it's exhausting and it makes me so bloody irritable. How anyone ever gets better in those places is beyond me.' She tutted. 'And don't get me started about the food.'

Eva laughed, a little tingle of excitement as she felt the beginnings of a connection. She was sitting beside her sister. Her real live older sister. Who lived on an actual farm in a national bloody park! How could it be any better really, given Eva's passion for wildlife conservation? Now she'd get to come and spend time here, maybe on a regular basis. Little holidays. Seasonal work, maybe. Her mind raced along, developing a whole new life for herself; one that she could only dream about before today.

'Every cloud has a silver lining, though, doesn't it?' Nancy patted her shoulder, her touch like an electric current, startling

Eva from her thoughts. 'We wouldn't have met if I hadn't ended up in hospital.'

'I can't believe they didn't tell me about you,' Eva gushed, unable to help herself.

'There's nowt so strange as folk,' Nancy said, in a perfect Black-pudlian accent, making Eva laugh. But it also left her wondering why she'd left her natural accent behind and whose company she'd been keeping.

Nancy showed no sign of wanting to fill in any of the details, so Eva bit back her next question, wary of ruining their relationship before it had begun. Plenty of time to find out, she counselled herself. If she wanted proper answers, she really needed to get the measure of her sister first. *Keep it neutral. Small talk.*

Eva had mastered the art of small talk over the last three years. She'd worked with disparate groups of volunteers at the nature reserve, constantly meeting new people who joined her working parties. It was an element of her job that she'd really enjoyed. You couldn't tell by looking at someone whether you were going to get on with them or not and often it was the people she'd shied away from initially that she'd come to like the most. They were the deep thinkers, the people of substance, the ones who sat on the sidelines and watched, happy in their own company. *Is Nancy like that?* It was going to be interesting finding out.

'So you need to turn left at the roundabout,' Nancy said, her gaze on the road ahead. 'When you get to a T junction, you go left again.' She clutched the handle on the door as they sped round the mini roundabout, her face quite pale. Dizziness and nausea, the doctor had said. *No throwing this old thing round the corners.* Eva lifted her foot off the accelerator. *Nice and steady.*

Silence settled between them again, pushing their worlds apart. Eva couldn't think of anything to say that wasn't a lead-in to a big question, so she concentrated instead on the road ahead and the magnificent scenery.

Now they'd left Bangor behind, the mountains reared up in front of her, a seemingly impenetrable barrier. Wild and craggy and drawing her like a magnet. She wanted to stay here a little while, have a proper break and explore. How good would it feel to stand on top of one of those peaks and let her eyes roam the landscape for miles and miles? Now that she was here, climbing a mountain fixed itself as a goal in her head. A life experience that she desperately wanted to achieve, if only to be able to share it with her dad.

He'd be impressed if she could throw some names of mountains at him. That would surely spark some memories. He must have been all over this area when she was growing up but his adventures had been men only, way too dangerous for a child. Now, though, she could have her own adventures without waiting for his invitation. The very thought thrilled and daunted her at the same time.

When the silence was becoming awkward, she asked, 'Is it far?' She glanced towards her sister and their eyes met for a second. The exact same blue as their mother's, she thought.

Nancy pointed. 'If we go right here, that's the easiest route. Should take forty minutes or so.'

They fell back into silence, punctuated by an instruction whenever they reached a junction.

'How far now?' Eva asked after half an hour, when the road had become much narrower, threading its way between the slopes of the mountains.

'Oh, I'd say about twenty minutes, maybe a bit more if you're not confident on these sorts of roads.'

Eva laughed. 'I've been driving a post van for the last three years. I can tell you, I'm a perfectly confident driver.'

'A postie? Oh, that sounds exciting.' Nancy settled back in her seat, head on the headrest, eyes closed. 'You must hear loads of gossip. Interesting things. Come on, tell me about it.'

Eva felt ridiculously proud that her sister was interested. The rest of the journey was filled with anecdotes and an explanation of how her year was split into two very different halves, working at the nature reserve over the summer and doing postal work over the winter. As she told Nancy about her life, she realised how much she missed work: meeting new people, having a chat and a laugh with the regulars. There was none of that in her life now. Her horizons had shrunk to her parents' house and she had no idea how long for. It could be years. But she didn't want to think about it, because that was like wishing her dad's life away.

'So you must be working at the nature reserve now?' Nancy said when Eva fell silent. 'I have to say, that sounds wonderful and so fulfilling. I hope they don't mind you having some time off.'

'No. Actually, I'm not working at the moment. I can't. Not with Dad…' She glanced at her sister, realising that of course she wouldn't know. 'He's got dementia. And he had a mini stroke a few months ago.' She heaved in a breath. 'He's… well, he's not great.'

Nancy tutted. 'Oh dear.' Eva wondered if she was going to say more, but her eyes stayed fixed on the windscreen.

'Thing is, Mum… That's Linda, my stepmum. She needs me. I know she could do with help, but I also know that once I go back home, I won't be able to leave again until… well, until Dad's… gone.' Now that she'd started, she couldn't seem to stop her troubles pouring out. 'And to be honest, I'm so bloody cross with them. I always wanted a sister and they didn't tell me about you. Why would they keep that secret?'

'Turn left up here,' Nancy said, pointing at a rutted track that forked off the road. The only indication that it led to a house was the metal postbox fixed to a fence post, daubed with the name *Bryn Teg*.

Eva pulled in and stopped the car, turning to her sister.

'Aren't you bothered? Don't you feel anything for him?' Her voice rose a little higher with each question, her annoyance clear. 'Aren't you sad that your father is dying?'

Nancy stared up the track ahead of them, her face blank. 'I hardly know the man. It was all so long ago; I was practically a child when I left. I've lived away from him much longer than I lived with him. And even then, he was hardly ever home.'

Eva gave an impatient tut. 'I know he's passionate about his hobbies but I like that about him. He was always there for the important things. And he was the one who helped me with my homework.'

Nancy shrugged. 'I think we probably had different upbringings.' She fiddled with the hem of her sweatshirt, refusing to meet Eva's gaze. 'Honestly… I don't know how I feel about him now.'

Eva leant back against the car door. She bit her lip, then decided she was going to have that difficult conversation. Right now, before they went any further. She wanted some answers.

'So why did you have his contact details on you? You'll have to explain it to me, because I really don't understand. In fact, I don't understand any of it. Why you left. Why you made it look like suicide. Why nobody told me I had a sister.' She glared at Nancy. 'What the hell happened?'

The silence was so thick it was almost visible, wedging Eva against the door, her sister still refusing to look at her.

'Please, Nancy. Dad's condition is getting worse quite quickly now. I don't think he's got long.' Her throat tightened as she voiced the reality. 'I honestly don't know what to think about anyone in my family anymore. I need to know the truth.'

Nancy turned to her, an angry glint in her eye. 'The hospital had no right to ring you. No right to make arrangements without my consent. It was supposed to be my decision if and when I made contact. I was going to address the past when I was ready. But right now, I'm not.'

Eva was nonplussed by the unexpected turn in the conversation and it took a moment for her mind to change tack.

'But you did give consent. That's the thing. You signed a form.'

Nancy moved in her seat, as though she was trying to get as far away from Eva as possible. 'I didn't know what I was signing. They tricked me.'

Eva sighed, not wanting to get into a fight. 'I don't think they saw it like that. I do think they had your best interests at heart.'

'They're covering their backs, but I definitely did not give consent for you to come and look after me.' Nancy held up a hand. 'Sorry, that came out all wrong. I'm delighted you brought me home; really, it's very kind of you. But I'm not ready for this. It's come as a bit of a shock, to be honest, meeting you after all these years.' She grimaced, rubbing her forehead.

Eva's heart sank. This was getting more uncomfortable by the minute and it was clear she'd struck a nerve with her questions. *Stupid. I should have waited.* Then she remembered the doctor's words about the after-effects of head injuries and it started to make sense. The agitation. Irritation. Paranoia. Those were temporary. Nancy's feelings about everything might be completely different when she felt better.

Be patient. She's not thinking clearly.

'You don't have to stay,' Nancy said. 'In fact, just drop me off and nobody will be any the wiser.' She gave Eva a watery smile. 'I'll be fine.'

However awkward this felt, Eva's conscience wasn't going to let her just dump a woman with a head injury in a remote farmhouse and leave her to her own devices.

'I can't do that, Nancy. You're not well.' She sighed. 'I don't want to be where I'm not welcome but I would never forgive myself if I left you and…' She put a hand on her sister's shoulder, wanting to go back to the warmth she'd felt between them before she'd started asking questions. 'I'm sorry. I didn't mean to pry.' There was no reaction from the woman beside her and she wondered if she'd even heard. 'I understand that you left home for some reason and you don't want anything to do with the family. That's fine.

I promise I won't ask about any of it. I'll just stay until you feel better. Honestly, I could do with a bit of a break. Just a few days, then I'll go, if that's what you want.'

Nancy nodded, and Eva started the car again, making her way up the track at a snail's pace as she tried to avoid the jutting rocks and big dips where the rain had formed channels.

No way was she going home until she'd found out the truth, she decided, gripping the wheel with a new determination. How could she ever feel comfortable in her own skin if she didn't understand her past? The reason for the lies. Given Nancy's obvious detachment from her family, perhaps she was the only one likely to tell her what had really happened. She just had to work out how to get her to talk.

CHAPTER SIX

Eva found it took all her concentration to negotiate the lumps and bumps in the track. In a couple of places, where the wheels had started to spin, she'd wondered if they were going to make it and by the time she reached the top of the final slope her hands ached from clasping the steering wheel.

Nancy had one hand clamped round the door handle and was leaning forward, staring ahead with a fierce intensity, as if she was urging the car to get up the track with the force of her will. When they turned a bend and the terrain flattened out, she let out a sigh and settled back in her seat. 'Nearly there.'

They emerged from the tunnel of trees onto a small plateau, in the middle of which stood a sturdy stone-built farmhouse, pleasantly symmetrical in design. There was a central porch, with a window either side on the ground floor and three evenly spaced windows above. The red front door looked like it was made of four wide planks. Rugged. Ancient. A round door knocker in the middle. Next to the house, separated from it by the track, was the gable end of what must be a barn, with a yard in front of it, which presumably ran the length of the house at the back. There was no front garden. Just a cobbled area with a washing line strung between two trees.

It was half past four; a balmy May evening. The sun was shining through the trees, a gentle breeze making the leaves whisper, shadows dancing across the ground. It was the most romantic place Eva had ever seen, tucked away in a world of its own.

'Wow. This is lovely.' She glanced at Nancy. 'How the heck did you end up here? This is… Well, it's… Wow.'

Nancy pulled at the door handle, keen to get out and still in no mood to answer questions. She stood, holding the top of the door, scanning the house and the area around them.

Looking for something? Or someone?

She seemed to sway and Eva was reminded of why she was here. Quickly, she jumped out of the car and dashed round to Nancy's side, noticing that she'd gone very pale.

'Steady,' she said. 'I think maybe you stood up too fast. Just take a minute.'

Nancy's mouth pressed into a thin line, her eyes narrowed. She put a hand to her head, her breath coming in little gasps.

'Headache?'

Nancy groaned. 'It's what happens when you get whacked…' She swallowed back the rest of her sentence. Eva studied her face, curious. She glanced around, could only hear the shushing of the leaves. A wonderful medley of birdsong. The bleat of sheep in the distance.

Who'd be up here, anyway? A partner? Husband? Maybe even a child. But if she was living with someone, the hospital wouldn't have needed to contact her dad as next of kin, would they? She scanned the area but couldn't feel the presence of anyone, the house benign and urging her in.

'Come on,' she said. 'Let me help you inside.'

Nancy hesitated, then took hold of her arm.

It felt strange to have her sister's fingers curled round her bicep. The two of them were a similar height, she noticed, and although Nancy might be thin, her grip was strong. She was obviously one of those sinewy people with hidden inner strength, like a marathon runner. But then living on a farm was very physical. She was probably fit as a flea when she wasn't nursing a head injury.

Eva walked slowly, picking her way over the uneven ground until they reached the square of slate slabs that had been laid around the front door. A metal boot scraper had been cemented into the ground next to a large, flat boulder, the top of it polished from centuries of people sitting there to take off their boots. Or put them on. Or just have a cup of tea.

She could feel the history of the place gathering around her; was drawn to the stories an old building like this could tell. She'd always been fascinated by history, having so little of it in her own family. Perhaps there were old pictures and documents inside. Deeds maybe. Her mind raced on, picturing happy hours spent piecing the story of this place together. What a fun project that would be. Not to mention the bird-spotting she could do here. The farm was so pristine and untouched, it must be teeming with wildlife.

Nancy stopped by the door and passed Eva a key: an enormous metal object that looked like it would be at home in a prison. The lock turned with a satisfying thunk and the door swung open into a wide hallway with a quarry-tiled floor. The walls were fashioned from wooden boards, giving the place a rustic feel.

'Shall we get you up to bed, then I'll make a cup of tea and unload the shopping?'

Eva had picked up some basic provisions when she'd filled up at a petrol station. It was clear Nancy wasn't going to be fit enough to drive anywhere for at least a week, and she'd gathered that the house was in a location where you couldn't pop out for a loaf of bread or a pint of milk. If she was going to be staying – and she was adamant now that she was – she wanted to be sure there was enough food in the house. Anyway, Nancy looked like she could do with feeding up. It would be nice to cook for her. Maybe she could win her over with some appetising meals.

She smiled to herself as her mind galloped along, the farm a thousand times better than anything she could have imagined. The house smelled of history. It also smelled a bit damp, but that sort of went with the territory. She wrinkled her nose. What else could she smell? Onions? She sniffed. Soup, maybe. Something cooking.

'Do you live with anyone else?' she asked, turning to her sister, who was holding onto the newel post at the bottom of the stairs, looking upwards as if it was Everest she was about to climb.

'No.' Nancy spoke firmly. 'I like my own company.'

'Just smells like someone's been cooking.'

'I was cooking before I got... before I hurt myself.'

Surely that was days ago and the smell would have faded by now? Eva frowned, puzzled. 'How long were you in hospital?'

'Two days. Two very long days. I thought they'd patch me up and send me home but they wanted to do all sorts of scans and X-rays and stupid memory tests.' She was still looking up the stairs.

Eva went to her side, ready to hold her elbow, like she'd been shown to do with her dad. 'Will you let me help you?'

Nancy twitched, as if she might wrench her arm away, then relaxed and allowed Eva to help her climb the stairs. 'Which way?' Eva asked, when they'd turned at the half-landing and finally reached the top. It looked like there were two rooms to the right, two to the left and one in the middle, over the porch.

'Right,' Nancy gasped. She was clearly in pain. 'At the front.'

The room was small, just big enough for a queen-sized bed, a wardrobe and a chest of drawers. A wooden chair sat under the window, a pair of jeans flung over the back. The wardrobe door was open, the drawers of the chest not properly closed, bits of clothing poking out. Nancy was not a tidy person. Not by Eva's standards, anyway. She glanced around, considering how much better the room would look with everything put away properly, the dust cleaned off the flat surfaces, the wardrobe mirror polished.

The furniture was quite lovely. Old and made of oak, she thought, judging by the golden colour. The floor was polished boards, the widest floorboards she'd ever seen, at least a foot across and a dark reddish brown.

'Can you manage to get yourself in bed?' she asked, not relishing the thought of trying to help this prickly woman get undressed.

'Oh, it's too early to go to bed.' Nancy lowered herself onto the mattress. 'I'll lie on top for half an hour. Maybe have a little nap.' She gave a frustrated huff. 'I hadn't realised how pathetic I've become in just two days.'

'You're not being pathetic. It's a nasty head injury and the doctor said you had to rest or there could be complications.' Eva plumped the pillows, then watched as Nancy lay back with a relieved sigh, her eyes closing.

'I'll be fine now. You can go.'

'Okay, well I'll nip down and make you a cup of tea, get you a sandwich. You said the food in hospital was awful, so I'm sure you're hungry.'

'I don't want a cup of tea. And I can make my own sandwich when I'm ready. What I want is a bit of peace and quiet on my own.'

Eva ignored the sting of hurt, telling herself Nancy didn't mean it. She wasn't well. 'I can't leave you on your own, Nancy. Not when you're so wobbly on your feet. How do you think you'd manage to get down the stairs?'

Nancy's eyes flicked open. 'Honestly, you don't have to worry about me. I'll be fine once I've had a lie-down. I really don't mind if you want to get off back home to… Dad. It sounds like he needs you.'

Eva smiled at her, refusing to be sent away just yet. 'Well, *I* need a cup of tea and something to eat before I go. After driving all the way here, I'm famished and thirsty. I'll bring you a cuppa.'

She turned and left the room. In all honesty, Nancy was in no state to throw her out if she didn't want to go.

Feeling pensive, she went back downstairs. As she returned to the car, ready to bring in the shopping, something caught her eye. A flash of blue by the gable end of the barn, she thought, but when she looked again, there was nothing there, nothing blue at all. She stilled and listened. Was that a door banging? The sound of feet on cobbles? Curious, she crept to the corner of the house, her back to the wall, and peeped round the edge into the back yard – a big square bordered by the house on one side, the barn on another and a row of outbuildings on the third. On the fourth side was a fence, a gate in the middle. Beyond that, a track with a field on the left and what looked like a vegetable patch and orchard to the right.

Nobody there. But it felt like there was. The hairs stood up on the back of her neck. *Am I being watched?*

CHAPTER SEVEN

Eva hurried back to the car, grabbed the shopping and carried the bags through the hallway to the large kitchen at the back of the house. It definitely smelled of onions. She dumped the bags and surveyed the room. Large for a kitchen. You could probably fit eight people quite comfortably round the table. An ancient cooking range stood against the far wall, a rack for drying clothes suspended from the ceiling above it.

She'd never cooked on a range. Of course she'd seen them, knew roughly how they worked, but she'd never had the chance to actually use one. As she walked over to it, the smell of cooking became stronger. She reached out, an urge to stroke the black enamel, like it was an ancient beast, sleeping. It felt quite warm. *Would the heat stay for two days, almost three now?* It seemed unlikely, but what did she know?

The sink was under the window which looked out onto the back yard. As she filled the kettle, her eyes moved from building to building, looking for signs of life. There were lots of places a person could hide. And if the range was warm, that strongly suggested someone had used it since Nancy had been taken to hospital. The police checked, she reminded herself. They couldn't find anyone. But how hard would it be to hide? Not hard at all.

If there *was* someone hiding, she reasoned as she took two mugs off the drainer, the chances were it was because they'd done something wrong. Perhaps not here but somewhere else. A fugitive

Nancy had taken in, possibly? Her mind developed a new narrative, which was more like a film script than real life.

She stopped and listened. Silence.

Nobody's here except me and Nancy. Hadn't her sister insisted that she lived alone?

That doesn't mean she's telling the truth.

She opened the door next to the range and found herself in a utility room. A coat rack was hung with an assortment of outdoor clothing. Wellies and work boots lined a shelf below. Different sizes.

She was about to go outside when she heard a voice. Nancy was calling her. Quickly she made two mugs of tea, grabbed the packets of sandwiches she'd bought and took it all upstairs.

Nancy was sitting hunched over on the edge of the bed. She wore a closed-in look, like she was shrouded in pain.

'There you are. I'm so sorry to drag you back up here.' She looked up, her face pale. 'I just had a bit of a panic. It was so quiet, I was worried you might have taken me at my word and decided to go.'

'I was just... trying to find everything. Takes so much longer to do even a simple job in a kitchen you're not familiar with.' Eva put a mug on the bedside table, along with a packet of sandwiches, then went to sit on the chair by the window.

Nancy gave a sheepish smile. 'I'm like a bear with a sore head, aren't I? Growling away. So bloody ungrateful.'

Eva stopped unpeeling her sandwich wrapper and looked at her sister. 'It's okay. I'm like that when I'm not well.' She laughed. 'Must run in the family because Dad's a terrible patient too.'

Nancy sighed and picked up her sandwiches. She opened the packet and pulled one out. 'I'm feeling a bit flustered, that's all.' She took a tentative bite, cocking her head as she chewed, reminding Eva of a bird. Observing. Considering. 'To be honest, I'm a bit of a recluse.' She shrugged. 'Socially inept. That's me.'

'It's okay,' Eva said. 'I'm not expecting entertainment.'

Nancy gave a weak laugh and took another bite.

The silence felt companionable now, that edge of animosity gone, and the tension released from Eva's shoulders. Maybe she'd misunderstood, made assumptions that were just plain wrong. She supposed if she was in Nancy's shoes and lived alone, she'd feel a bit discombobulated by a surprise visitor. Especially if that visitor was a sister she'd never met. When she looked at it like that, she could see why Nancy might have been unsure about having her in the house.

Nancy picked up her tea and took a sip, smiling at Eva, her eyes crinkling at the edges. 'You must think I'm a stupid old bat.' She laughed. 'Well, you need to know that's exactly what I am. Honestly, I've no idea what's going on in my head at the moment.' Her face became serious. 'It's not that I don't want to get to know you, Eva. It's just a bit of a shock, and on top of this accident, I'm finding it… well, it's overwhelming, to be honest. You must see that?'

Eva's spirits sank like a stone thrown into a pond. Was Nancy going to tell her she wasn't up to the emotional fallout? Was that what she was leading up to? *Go home, Eva, and I'll call you when I'm ready.* She couldn't let that happen. Patience wasn't one of her virtues and she had so many questions that needed answering.

She gave Nancy a sympathetic smile while her heart hammered in her chest. 'Yes, I suppose. But we're here now and I'll only stay as long as you need me. I promise I won't ask any more questions. How's that?' She put her hands together as if in prayer.

Nancy smiled. 'Thank you, Eva. I appreciate your understanding, but…' Suddenly her face contorted and she gave a low groan, the sandwich she'd been eating falling to the floor as her hands clasped her head.

Eva jumped to her feet, going over to sit next to her sister. She ventured an arm round her shoulders, desperate to be accepted rather than rejected. 'I know you've inherited Dad's stubborn streak, but you've got an opportunity here to just have a rest and let me take care of you. Would that be so bad?'

Nancy leant forward and vomited on the floor.

Thankfully she missed Eva's shoes, but the stench shot up her nose, making her own stomach lurch. She jumped to her feet, while Nancy groaned, still bent double.

'Right, Nancy,' she said, no idea how she was going to finish the sentence, but aware that she was going to have to take charge. *Am I supposed to take her back to hospital if she's sick? Is this classed as an emergency?* She wasn't sure and she had nobody to ask, but she knew she'd never get Nancy to agree. One step at a time, she cautioned herself. Get her comfortable, clean up the mess. Take it from there.

She let out a breath, trying to stay calm, but adrenaline was whizzing round her body, making the words rush out of her mouth. 'The doctor said you need rest. Even coming home and getting upstairs has obviously been too much for you.' She saw a roll of toilet paper on the bedside table and tore off some sheets for Nancy to wipe her mouth, then handed her the mug of tea, in lieu of water. Nancy took a sip, closing her eyes as she swallowed.

'That better?'

She nodded and passed the mug back, her body swaying.

'Right, I'll... um... go and get something to clear up this mess.'

Nancy slowly keeled over so she was lying on her side. Eva put the mug on the bedside table while she gently picked up her sister's feet and lifted her legs onto the bed. She looked so vulnerable, Eva's heart went out to her; she was pleased now that she'd come to help. *Imagine if she'd discharged herself and been here on her own.* It didn't bear thinking about. She'd have keep a close eye on her, though, make sure her condition didn't deteriorate.

She went into the bathroom and found a plastic bowl, gloves and a cloth in a cupboard by the door. Ten minutes later, she'd cleaned up. It was strange, she thought, how life had a habit of forcing you out of your comfort zone. 'Character building,' said her dad's voice in her head as she tipped the foul water down the toilet and flushed it away. He was all about character building, was her dad, and she knew she had a lot to thank him for, giving her little pushes in the right direction. Making her braver than she'd ever imagined she could be.

The thought caught her unawares, a sudden rush of love for the man who had been such a positive force. She sat on the edge of the bath, tears threatening as the memories bloomed like desert flowers after rain until she could see a whole drift of colour that he'd added to her life.

'Come on, Eva. One more go. I'm sure you'll get it this time. You were so close.' Her five-year-old legs were shaking, the scrape on her knee stinging. She brushed her hands together to get rid of the gravel that stuck to her palms, then picked up her bike again. All shiny and new and a very lovely shade of blue – it was a birthday present and they were in the park. She'd already fallen off a dozen times and wasn't sure she even wanted to ride a bike anymore, but her dad beamed at her. 'That's my girl,' he said and even at that age she knew she'd do anything to bring a smile to his face. Tentatively she got back on the bike, her dad running behind her holding the saddle. Until something magical happened and she realised he'd let go and she was doing it all by herself. It felt like she was flying. Free. The most wonderful experience of her young life.

It was a moment that she'd never forgotten, an illustration of her father's belief in her, and she'd drawn on it many a time when her confidence had been knocked. Get back on the bike, she said to herself now. Of course you can do this. And if you're worried, you can ring the hospital and get an ambulance to come and pick her up.

Feeling better now that she had a contingency plan, she went back into the bedroom to check on her patient.

'I'll get you some water. You have a nap and then we'll talk later, okay?'

Nancy's eyes were closed and she didn't reply, but her chest was moving so she was definitely breathing. Asleep.

Eva picked up the empty mugs and sandwich wrappers and went back downstairs, putting everything on the drainer. The bag of medication from the hospital caught her eye, sitting on the worktop and she carefully emptied it out, reading the instructions. Nancy was due an antibiotic, so she ran a glass of water and took it upstairs. She stood in the bedroom doorway watching her sister for a moment, her gentle snores the only sound, then looked at the pills in her hand, unsure what to do for the best. Given that Nancy had just been sick maybe now wasn't the best time to be having medication anyway. Would it matter if she took it late?

Mum will know.

She tiptoed into the bedroom and left the medication on the bedside table, ready for later. On the landing, as she was about to go back downstairs and give her mum a ring, something caught her eye. A movement as she passed the door of the middle room. Her heart skipped and she hesitated, took a step back. Was it wrong to look inside? Nancy was asleep, so she'd be none the wiser. She peeped her head round the door to see a curtain flapping in the breeze, the sash window open a little, and breathed a sigh of relief. She was seeing mystery figures all over the place, just figments of her imagination. But there obviously *had* been other people in the house.

This was somebody's bedroom, a single bed pushed against the wall. There was a chest of drawers next to it, a small rug on the floor. It was clean and tidy and she could see that it was perhaps a guest room rather than a room someone was actually inhabiting.

She crept over to the drawers and slid the top one open to see that it was full of clothes. And the next one and the next. Perhaps someone was using this room after all. Or they could be Nancy's clothes. That was possible, given the small size of her room.

How on earth did someone born and brought up in Blackpool end up living in a place like this? Of course she was curious about her sister's house – who wouldn't be?

She crept out of the central bedroom and along the landing, staring at the two closed doors in front of her. Slowly, holding her breath, she turned the handle and pushed the first one open. The room at the front. It was sparsely furnished with a set of metal-framed bunk beds and a small chest of drawers. A chair by the wall. Nothing else. The mattresses were bare and it was clear the room wasn't in use.

As quietly as she could, she pulled the door shut and opened the second one. It was furnished in a similar vein to the front room but in here a sleeping bag was laid out on the bottom bunk. A pair of men's trainers were propped against the far wall, toes on the floor as if on tiptoe. A book on the floor next to them. Eva sneaked in to have a look. *Lord of the Rings*, well thumbed, as if it had been read a few times. Behind the door, clothes lay abandoned in a messy heap. A large stain coloured the floorboards, like someone had spilt a glass of red wine. It was hard to tell if the room was still in use, but if it was, there could be someone with pretty large feet around the place somewhere. The idea made her shiver.

She heard a thump from Nancy's room and shot out of the bedroom door like a bullet from a gun, closing it behind her. There would be more time to explore but she couldn't be caught snooping or Nancy would have good cause to kick her out.

'Is everything okay?' she asked, peering round Nancy's door.

Her sister was sitting on the edge of the bed.

'I need to go to the loo, but I'm so dizzy I don't think I can make it on my own.'

Eva gave a satisfied smile. 'See. You do need me to stay for a little bit, don't you?'

She helped Nancy to stand and supported her as she shuffled next door to the bathroom, then ushered her back to bed.

'While I'm still up here, you should take your antibiotics.' She picked up the box from where she'd left it next to the bed, pressed a tablet from the foil and held it out to Nancy with the glass of water.

Nancy frowned, but she swallowed the tablet and gave Eva a small smile. 'Thank you,' she murmured, leaning back on her pillows and closing her eyes. 'Thank you for everything.'

Eva sat beside her on the bed. 'Look, Nancy, I don't want to pry, but… I noticed downstairs… there's lots of outdoor clothing, some that's way too big for you. Other people's shoes.'

Nancy didn't reply.

Eva persisted. 'You don't live here on your own, do you?'

Finally Nancy's eyes blinked open and she squinted at Eva, one hand to her head. 'I've told you, there's nobody else. I'm really not sure why you don't believe me. My injury was an accident, pure and simple. My own stupid fault for not putting things away properly, and the cats were fighting and must have knocked the tools. The clothes and shoes… well, we used to have the shearing gang come to shear the sheep every year. But then I decided to sell off some land and reduce the flock, just to make it easier to manage. So I haven't needed them the last few years.' She tutted. 'Youngsters, always leaving things behind. And I never liked to throw other people's stuff away. You never know, they might be back in the area next year and come looking for it.'

Eva made herself keep eye contact, even though it was now feeling uncomfortable, like a war of the eyeballs. Who would look away first? 'You said "we",' she pointed out, her voice as calm as she could make it.

Nancy sighed, exasperated. 'Questions. So many bloody questions. You said you wouldn't do this. Promised me, didn't you?' Her voice cracked. 'Can't you see I'm in no fit state for an inquisition?' Tears welled in her eyes. 'I've told you the truth.'

Eva felt bad for pressing her and looked down at her hands. 'Sorry. I didn't mean to upset you.'

'The paramedics got all spooked out when they were up here. They started this stupid rumour. An old house like this creaks and groans; doors bang when it's windy. They're just not used to it and made a ridiculous fuss.' She was starting to get agitated. 'You're not calling the police or anyone else, understand? I don't want a bunch of incompetents crawling all over my business.'

Touched a nerve there, Eva thought, noticing the anger sparking in Nancy's eyes.

'It's bad enough you snooping around the place without them wading in.'

Eva froze.

Nancy raised an eyebrow. 'Oh, you thought I wouldn't hear you? I know every creak in this house.'

Eva cringed, a blush spreading up her neck. 'I'm sorry, I... I thought I saw something in one of the bedrooms but it was just a curtain blowing.'

Nancy gave a humph. 'I don't want you prying. Do you hear me? Have your parents taught you no manners?'

Eva gazed at her. 'Seems they didn't teach you any either.'

Nancy's eyes narrowed, then she smiled weakly. 'Touché.' She flapped a hand. 'I'm sorry, Eva. I'm being horrible again, aren't I? What a rubbish host I am.' She gave an impatient grunt. 'I just hate being ill like this. I can't remember the last time I had to stay in bed. I feel so... vulnerable. And I don't like it.'

Eva returned the smile, cheeks still burning with the shame of being caught out. Nancy was right, it was no way to behave in someone else's house.

'Look, I'm sorry if I was being nosy. Honestly, I just wanted to see what the rest of the house was like. It's such a fantastic old place.'

'It's okay. I'd be the same in your shoes.' Nancy's eyes raked the ceiling. Eva could see her chin wobbling. *Is she trying not to cry?* 'Christ, I'm a rubbish patient as well as a rubbish host.' Her fists banged the duvet. 'And I'm not doing great at being a big sister either, am I?'

'Hey, it's okay, no harm done.' Eva gave a sheepish smile. 'Are we okay?'

Nancy looked at her, eyes brimming, and nodded.

Eva felt an urge to put her arm round her spiky sister, give her a hug and reassure her that there was nothing to worry about. But was that true?

CHAPTER EIGHT

She left Nancy to snooze, deciding she'd bring her stuff in and set herself up in the middle bedroom. The other rooms were bare and functional, fitting with Nancy's description of having seasonal workers to stay, but the middle room was really quite cosy.

She ran back downstairs and out to the car and had just got herself loaded up with her bag, coat and walking boots when her phone rang. She hadn't been sure about reception up in the mountains and was delighted to find she was connected. The ringtone told her it was Linda. She dropped everything on the floor, scrabbling to answer, aware that she should have rung her sooner. *It might be about Dad. Another stroke.* Her heart fluttered.

'Hey, Mum. Is everything okay?'

Linda sighed. 'I don't know why you ask me that every time because the answer is always no. It's been a right struggle with your dad today. He keeps asking where you are and of course I can't tell him. I said you'd gone to meet up with a friend for a few days but you know what he's like. New information doesn't go in, does it?' She sounded weary. 'So the question's on repeat and with the best will in the world it's driving me mad.'

'Sorry, Mum.' Eva grimaced, feeling guilty about leaving Linda to cope on her own. 'It sounds like you've had a tough day.'

'It's okay, love. I'm just feeling a bit sorry for myself. Anyway, I rang to see how you were getting on with Nancy. Thought I might have heard from you…'

Eva looked up to the bedroom window as if she would see her sister standing there, watching. She had that sort of aura about her, keeping track of what Eva was doing. *As if she's worried I'll find something I'm not supposed to.*

'Oh, it's… um, well, it's a bit fraught, to be honest. I think she must have given the hospital permission to call you when she wasn't thinking straight. She certainly can't remember it and she was a bit cross about me picking her up. Honestly, it was like I was kidnapping her or something.' Her mum tutted. 'Anyway, I think we're okay now. Poor thing has a really nasty head injury and the doctor did say her behaviour might be a little unpredictable for a few days. I have to watch out for her symptoms getting worse, so I'm afraid I can't leave her until she's up and about and able to cope on her own.'

'Awkward and difficult – sounds about right. Not that I know her. But your dad always said…' Linda stopped herself and it was a few seconds before she carried on. 'I don't think they got on too well. But she was a teenager and teenagers don't tend to get on well with their parents, do they?'

Eva knew that she herself had had her moments as a teenager, and from their limited interactions so far, she could see that Nancy would definitely have driven her dad mad. Way too strong a personality. He liked compliance, which was why his relationship with Linda worked. The fact was, he genuinely believed he was the head of the household, even if that wasn't really the case.

'And you don't know why she left?'

'Well…' Linda started. Eva held her breath, hardly daring to believe she was actually going to get some sort of answer. 'There was a message scrawled on her bedroom mirror that just said, "I hate my life", and the suicide note that was found with her clothes said that she couldn't live without her mum and wanted to go and join her. Life wasn't fair, it was too hard. She didn't want a new family; she wanted her old one. Something like that. I can't remember the exact words.'

The sentiment behind the message struck Eva like a slap across the face. 'She didn't want a baby sister?'

Linda took a sharp intake of breath. 'Oh no, love. No, I'm sure that's not what she meant.'

Eva was pretty sure that was the only thing she *could* have meant.

'Dad must have felt terrible, losing his wife and then his daughter at the same time.'

'Mmm. It was hard for him, that's for sure. He blamed himself and it nearly broke him.' Linda went quiet.

Eva hadn't considered her father being vulnerable, his appearance giving the opposite impression. Now she had to reconsider and since Linda was in the mood to talk, she carried on probing.

'That must have put pressure on you at the time? If you had to take responsibility for looking after me?'

Linda laughed. 'Oh no, love. It wasn't like that. You know I was besotted with you from the day I met you. I've always loved babies, so for me it was a treat rather than a chore. I didn't really know your mum, so I wasn't mourning her like your dad. I kept everything going, making the meals and keeping the place clean and tidy, looking after you while he went through the grieving process.'

'And you lived next door?'

'That's right. Well, I moved into your house soon after your mum died – it was easier to look after you that way. There was a spare room that your dad used as an office, so it was simple enough to organise.'

Eva had to stop and recalibrate all her assumptions about her early years. It was Linda who'd been there for her on a full-time basis from the very beginning. She'd assumed it had been her dad, with Linda just coming to help out every now and again.

Why can't people just tell the truth from the start?

She'd learnt to live with the little smudges of dishonesty, dismissed them as being Linda's way of ensuring marital harmony. But after keeping the fact that she had a sister from her and now these new revelations, she was beginning to wonder what else Linda had not been totally honest about. She filed the thought away to study later, when she had a bit of space to think.

She changed the subject and they chatted about the journey and the house and what Nancy was like until the conversation came to a sudden halt and Eva realised her battery had run out. With a frustrated growl, she picked up her things and carried them upstairs to the bedroom. Then she found a plug and put her phone on charge. That done, she decided she'd see if she could find some clean bedding. If this was a guest room, and other people had used it, who knew when the bed had last been changed?

In the bathroom, she found an airing cupboard stacked with towels, sheets, duvet covers and pillowcases. She picked a tie-dyed blue set and ten minutes later the bed was made and she was on her way back downstairs with a bundle of bedding to go in the wash. It definitely didn't smell clean, having that mustiness about it that suggested someone else had been sleeping there.

She sang to herself as she stuffed everything in the washing machine that stood in the corner of the utility room. A large chest freezer hummed next to it. Unable to resist, she lifted the lid. Inside were great slabs of meat – whole sides of animals, she assumed – that made her stomach turn a bit. It was all right being a meat eater, but she was sort of in denial that what she ate had been part of a living animal at some point. There was no mistaking it here. Plenty to eat, though, she thought, trying to be practical, as she slammed the lid shut and hurried back into the kitchen.

She put a hand on the range as she went past. *Does it feel cooler now? Or is that just my imagination?* She sniffed the air. Either the aroma of cooking had faded, or she'd just got used to the smell.

The evidence was stacking up to suggest that Nancy's assertion that she lived alone was a lie.

Perhaps it was a worker who helped around the place and there'd been a falling-out of some sort, she reasoned. That would make sense. What if Nancy had decided to send him away and he didn't want to go? How did you rid yourself of an unwanted guest? Eva knew it was hard, because she had a friend who'd been in the same situation with a lodger. In fact, she herself could stay here at the farm, given that she was technically here by her sister's request, and Nancy would have a devil of a job getting rid of her if she didn't want to go.

The thought stuck in a loop in her mind, obliterating everything else. *She can't throw me out.* And she knew she'd be staying until she found out why Nancy had really run away and never come back.

Another question took shape in her mind. If Nancy hated her family so much, why had she made the effort to find their contact details and keep them in her handbag? Didn't that suggest an urge to find them again? And if that was the case, what had changed her mind?

CHAPTER NINE

Eva chewed on a nail as she gazed out of the kitchen window. So many unanswered questions. What a stupid family she belonged to. They wouldn't recognise the truth if they tripped over it.

The situation was intriguing, though, awakening a part of her brain that hadn't really been tasked with a complex problem since she'd finished her degree. How would it feel to discover the definitive truth about what had happened all those years ago? Would it change anything? Or would it be better not to know?

I want to find out about Mum. What she was like, who she was as a person. Whether I'm like her at all. She nodded to herself. This was the main thing, the draw to Nancy – it was her sister's knowledge of their mother. Better to focus on that rather than quizzing her sister about her own life. Perhaps that way she'd feel less threatened and the other questions could wait.

The weather had changed now, she noticed as she peered out of the window into the back yard. Instead of mellow sunshine filtering through the trees, the clouds had come down and everything was misty and opaque. She couldn't see the gate into the field anymore, and it felt like her world had shrunk. Anyone could be out there and she wouldn't be able to see them. Instead of having a quick recce outside, as she'd planned, she decided to wait until the morning, when hopefully the weather would be better. She'd lock the doors and then she could relax.

The back door was in the utility room and although there was no key, there were bolts top and bottom that she rammed home.

The front door had a key and bolts. The sash windows downstairs were already tight shut. Once everything was secured, she felt a lot better and wandered back into the kitchen wondering what to make for supper. She unloaded the shopping bags onto the table and surveyed the pile of groceries. She wasn't sure how hungry Nancy would be and decided she didn't want to faff with lighting the range, so it would have to be the pre-made quiche. Easy to eat, not much mess to clear away. Perfect. So that was that sorted.

She went to the foot of the stairs and listened. Silence. Nancy was still asleep.

As quietly as she could, she crept into the lounge. She'd just scuttled in and out to check the windows earlier but now that she felt safe she could have a proper look around, get the measure of her sister's life.

The room was a good size, with a large wood-burner in the inglenook fireplace, the glass blackened with soot, as was the stonework around it. Logs were stacked at one side of the fireplace, a basket full of twigs and small branches at the other, together with bits of cardboard and screwed-up paper to get the fire started.

A dark wooden rocking chair with a faded red cushion sat to one side, a carpet bag with knitting needles poking out next to it. In front of the fireplace, a navy rug with red patterns running through it. Dark splotches speckled the edge next to the fire, probably burns where embers had fallen. The sofa was tan leather, a tartan rug thrown over the back. It was well worn and sagged in the middle, so you'd struggle to get up again once you'd sat down. Three mismatched wooden chairs were lined up under the window. The TV was a chunky old thing and she wondered if it even worked in the digital age, or whether it was a useless relic that hadn't yet made its way to the tip.

The walls were painted render, uneven and cracked in places. They were stained cream around the fireplace but the original colour, when it was first put on many years ago, was probably white. The room smelt of woodsmoke, reminiscent of camping trips and beach barbecues. It looked very much like one of the exhibits in a country life museum Eva had once visited. Homely enough, though.

As she turned, ready to go and have a look in the other reception room, she noticed the photos on the wall behind the sofa. Three prints, faded to a pale purple with age. A wedding photo, which looked like it was taken in the 1960s, or maybe earlier judging by the design of the dress. Next to it, a family portrait – older versions of the same couple with a young boy between them. The final picture was the boy grown into a man, dressed in a green boiler suit and wellies, leaning against the huge wheel of a tractor.

What did these people have to do with Nancy? she wondered. Could the man have been a partner, a husband even? Was he still a husband? At some point, she'd have to ask.

She went back into the hallway, satisfying herself it was still quiet upstairs before creeping into the other reception room. This was a dining room and study, although from the layer of dust on the table, it didn't look like it was used very often. The furniture in here was dark oak; the bureau pushed against the wall on one side of the fireplace had ornate carving round the lid. There was a brass key in the lock. *Should I?* Her fingers twitched, but she resisted the temptation. It would be wrong to look inside. Besides, if Nancy thought she was prying into her private affairs, she'd probably clam up and not even speak to her, let alone tell her about their mum. *You've got to behave yourself.*

She moved out of temptation's way and instead studied the over-stuffed bookshelves on the other side of the fireplace, crammed with a whole mixture of fiction and non-fiction. There did seem to be an underlying filing system of sorts, with books on tractor and car maintenance, farming and bookkeeping on the bottom shelves, together with a whole stack of pamphlets: updates on farming regulations. After a cursory look, she put them away again.

The top two shelves contained paperbacks, an eclectic mix, and she scanned the titles, wondering if there was anything that might take her fancy. It was looking like she was going to have hours to herself and she did love to get lost in a book.

She picked one out and flicked through; noticed a name and address on the front cover. The owner lived in New Zealand. Probably left by the shearers, so maybe that part of Nancy's explanation was true. Which was comforting. Perhaps the sleeping bag too had been left by a careless shearer. Look at the mess people left behind at festivals or when they went to the beach. Everything was so cheap these days, it was easier to leave a sleeping bag than hump it around, if you were on your way home and no longer needed it.

A noise from upstairs startled her. She scurried out of the room to the bottom of the stairs and listened, heard the sound of feet shuffling, then the click of the bathroom door locking. She dithered, wondering whether to run upstairs, ready to assist if there were problems, but she had the feeling Nancy would hate her fussing. She had to tread carefully, try and make a friend of her rather than antagonise.

She waited, heard the toilet flush, the click of the door being unlocked.

'You okay up there, Nancy?'

No reply, so she assumed that was a yes. She went and made them both another cup of tea, took it upstairs. The door was ajar and she knocked before peeping in.

'I made us a brew.'

Nancy was sitting up on the bed, her face a healthier colour. She smiled, eyes twinkling. 'You can come in,' she said. 'I won't bite.'

Eva grinned. 'You did before. Metaphorically speaking.'

Nancy took the mug that Eva held out to her. 'I'm so sorry, Eva. I don't know what's got into me. I'm afraid we've met at a bad time.' She put a hand to her head, wincing. 'I have the most horrible headache. Every time I speak it's like my voice is too loud and is jangling my brain. I don't suppose you could get me a couple of painkillers? There's a packet in the bathroom cabinet, I think. I should have got them while I was in there, but I was concentrating on not falling over.'

Eva felt bad that she hadn't even considered painkillers, not being a fan of them herself. A headache would make anyone snappy and it made Nancy's prickly behaviour understandable. Acceptable, even. She jumped up and went to find them.

There was a cabinet over the sink, the mirror speckled with age. Inside was a ceramic jar with two toothbrushes, a couple of tubes of toothpaste and various bits and pieces including a packet of paracetamol. *Two toothbrushes?* She grabbed the tablets and decided she'd have a better look later.

They settled in silence, sipping their tea, Eva in the chair by the window again, Nancy sitting on the bed, propped up with pillows. The view outside had disappeared into a wall of mist which cocooned the farmhouse like a spider's web, bringing a chill to the air.

'How are you feeling?' Eva asked, for want of something to start a conversation.

Nancy gave a half-hearted shrug, like she wasn't sure. 'Once those painkillers kick in, I think I'll feel better.'

'Is there anything else I can get you?'

'Can we start again, do you think?' Nancy held out a hand and Eva went and sat on the bed, relishing the warm grip of her sister's fingers round her own. 'I'm so pleased you came.' She managed a weak smile. 'Thank you for looking after me.'

Eva's shoulders sagged with relief. This was better. 'Look, I'm sorry if I've been asking too many questions.' She shrugged. 'I can't help it, I'm just a nosy person. So just tell me to butt out if I go over the top, okay?'

Nancy nodded. 'Oh, I will.' Her eyes crinkled at the corners as her smile broadened. 'I'll go all big sister on you.' She shook her head. 'It feels so weird saying that. Oh dear, it's going to take a bit of getting used to, isn't it?'

She squeezed Eva's hand and Eva's heart swelled with a whole new set of possibilities.

'Do you know, I always wanted a sister when I was growing up. My best friend had a sister who was only a year older than her, and they were so close.'

Nancy laughed, clearly starting to feel better. 'It's a bit different with a sixteen-year age gap, isn't it? I think I'll be more like a mother or… a favourite auntie.'

Eva could feel bubbles of joy filling her chest. But she managed to burst them with her next thought.

'I can't believe they didn't tell me.'

Nancy pulled a face. 'I have to admit, I feel more than a bit offended. Like they wanted to forget me.' She let go of Eva's hand and picked up her tea, relaxed back on her pillows. Her face looked less pinched now. She frowned. 'Why do you think they kept my existence a secret?'

'My mum… I mean, Linda.' Eva stopped, realising that Nancy might not know who Linda was. 'She was our next-door neighbour when I was born. She hadn't lived there long, so I'm not sure if you even knew her.' Nancy's expression was blank, giving no indication either way. 'Anyway, she says they decided I didn't need to know, but you know what I think? I think it's because they didn't want me to feel guilty. My real mum died because of me, and…' She hesitated for a moment. 'Well, I think you might have left because of me too.'

Nancy's eyes widened. 'Oh no, that's not what happened at all. You've got that completely wrong. But then Linda will always put her own spin on things.'

Eva blinked. So Nancy did know Linda. Not just that, but she seemed to have an opinion about her.

Nancy adjusted her pillows. 'Let me tell you what really happened.'

CHAPTER TEN

Eva's heart was thumping so hard she felt it might jump out of her chest. This was what she'd been waiting for. At last someone was going to give her the honest truth about a missing piece of her personal history. Would she feel better then? Less guilty? She knew that if her mum had never been pregnant with her, she'd still be alive today. And it was quite a burden to carry round – the fact that your birth caused your mum's death. Her mind jumped on the merry-go-round of thoughts that sat in the back of her head, twirling her in a never-ending circle.

Stop it! Just listen. For once in your life, just bloody listen.

'The first thing you need to know is…' Nancy looked down at her hands, fingers entwined in her lap. Her lips pressed together like she wasn't sure how to phrase whatever it was she had to say.

Eva swallowed, waiting. 'Come on, Nancy, don't do this to me.'

At last her sister glanced up, her teeth nipping at her bottom lip. 'Honestly, Eva, I shouldn't have said anything. It's the past, over and done with. I think it's… well, it's probably better to leave well alone.'

Eva shook her head. 'No, no, no. I need to know. Surely you can understand that?' She stood, pacing the floor, trying to explain how she felt. 'Imagine if you were the one who had just found out after twenty-four years that they had a sister. How would you feel if that information had been kept from you all your life? It's making me question everything I know about myself and my family.' She put her hands together. 'Please, Nancy. Whatever you know, please tell me.'

Nancy sighed before she spoke. 'Okay. But remember, you wanted this.'

Eva nodded, eager for her to carry on.

Nancy took a deep breath. 'Your mother didn't actually want you. She was forty-two when she fell pregnant and she didn't want to start again with a new baby. She had plans, you see.'

Eva could hardly breathe, let alone speak. *That can't be right.* Of course her mum had wanted her. Of course she had. And what was with the 'your mother'? Surely she was *their* mother? Why was her sister disowning her?

Nancy nodded. 'Sad but true. She thought she'd started the menopause early and was just putting on a bit of weight. She only found out she was pregnant when it was too late to have a termination, or you, my dear, would not be here.'

Tears sprang to Eva's eyes. 'That's not true.' Her fist smacked on her thigh. 'She made me a lovely bedroom. Painted it herself. That's what Dad told me. If she didn't want me, why would she bother?'

Nancy didn't reply, her fingers plucking at the duvet cover. It was only then that Eva realised her sister had lost her mother too.

She pulled an apologetic face, fighting to control her emotions. 'Sorry. I wasn't calling you a liar. Honestly, it's just… to be told something like that…' Her hands clasped her cheeks as Nancy's words rattled round her brain. 'It's a bit of a shock.'

Nancy frowned. 'I'm so sorry, Eva, but the whole story is shocking. Are you sure you want to hear the rest of it?'

Eva's heart skipped a beat, the word *no* echoing in her head. But she gritted her teeth and nodded. She had to be able to view her life as it really was, not how she'd romanticised it. Wasn't this why she'd come?

'Yes,' she whispered. Then, more firmly, 'Yes, I do. Please… carry on.'

Nancy sighed. 'The thing is, your mother was not a happy woman. She no longer loved your father and she wanted to leave.

Then she found out she was pregnant and that threw everything into turmoil.'

Eva's mouth dropped open. 'Mum was leaving Dad?'

'That's right. She'd had enough of him and his selfish ways. He'd had an affair with someone not much older than I was, you see.'

'But…' Eva was really confused now, unable to see how her father would be in contact with a girl that age, let alone have an affair with one. 'He's an insurance salesman. Was. He was an insurance salesman before he fell ill. Are you sure you've got this right?'

Nancy stared at her for a moment, a flash of bewilderment in her eyes. 'He taught at Baines School, Poulton-le-Fylde. That's where he worked before… I left.' Then a glimmer of understanding. 'He must have changed jobs when you moved to Nottingham.' She gave a derisive laugh. 'Not surprising given the circumstances.'

Eva gazed out at the wall of mist, not seeing anything outside, only the scenes from her life playing out in her mind. Snippets of overheard conversations began to make sense now, her mind pulling things together to make a picture that tallied with Nancy's story. So that was why her dad was so familiar with school systems, knowing what he'd had to do to get some extra support when she was struggling in maths. That was why he'd been so insistent on homework routines and had known how best to help her when she was practising exam questions for GCSEs and A levels. That was what those cryptic comments to Linda about 'a past life' were all about.

Nancy's voice cut into her thoughts. 'She didn't study at the school where he taught – they met on a joint school skiing trip to France, but still…' Eva could see her sister's reflection in the window, noted her disapproving expression. 'Ellie, she was called. Something like that. It went on for years after she'd left school and then your mum found out. He said it was over but your mum was fuming. Hurt. Betrayed.' Nancy threw up her hands. 'All of that. Anyway, she had a job by that point, had some money saved. The florist shop where she worked had a flat above it. We were going to move in there once it was refurbished. Everything was planned.'

Her mum was coming to life as a real person in Eva's mind now, but not in the way she'd imagined.

She opened her mouth to speak, then closed it again, cautioning patience. *Let Nancy finish the story.* In her imaginings, her parents' marriage had been torn apart by tragedy – complications during her birth. She'd never imagined them as anything but happy. From the way her dad had spoken about her mum, in the few conversations she could remember, she'd been sure he loved her. Well, he probably did at some point, or they wouldn't have got married. And once someone was dead, she'd come to understand, they did tend to become more like saints than the flawed people they actually were. *Especially if there's guilt involved.*

Her mind was spinning now. Her whole life had been a mismatch of facts and wrong assumptions, like a badly made patchwork quilt. She needed to unpick what she knew, throw away the falsehoods, find the bits that were true and sew it all together again.

She stared through the mist at the ghostly shapes of trees as she tried to understand what Nancy was telling her. *Dad, a cheat?* Never would she have thought that. Never. He might like his own hobbies but he loved Linda. Of that she was sure. He'd always bought her surprise presents. Taken her out for little treats. Then a thought hit her – *what if they were apologies?* Was he a serial cheater? The very idea brought a chill to her skin and she wrapped her arms around her chest, hugging herself tight.

'Anyway,' Nancy continued. Eva turned to listen. She needed to be fully engaged in this – no misheard facts, no jumping to conclusions. After all the lies she'd been told, this was the truth and she wanted to embed it in her brain. 'Once they knew there was a baby on the way, they started trying a bit harder to keep the marriage going. I think she got used to the idea eventually but being in her forties the pregnancy really took it out of her. When she wasn't working, she was asleep.'

'You felt neglected.' Eva cursed her stupid comment. *Talk about stating the bleeding obvious.*

Nancy nodded. 'To be honest...' She pulled a face, sadness in her eyes. 'It pains me to say this, but I've had a lot of time to think about it.' Her words came out in a rush. 'Truth is, they weren't the world's greatest parents. They were two selfish people who should never have had kids in the first place.'

Eva was shaking now, the revelation that her ghostly mother was not the perfect person she'd fantasised about knocking the strength from her body. She wondered if she wanted to know any more. But she'd got this far and Nancy seemed in the mood to talk – she had to seize the opportunity while it was there for the taking.

What she really needed to know was the truth about her birth, the thing that had riddled her with guilt all her life.

'So tell me... what actually happened to Mum?'

Nancy gazed at the ceiling for a moment, and Eva remembered again how traumatic this must be for her sister. It was what she'd run away from all those years ago, what had kept her hidden. Eva had been so wrapped up in her own need for information, she hadn't considered Nancy's feelings at all. That was what all the 'your' mother and father stuff was about, she realised. Nancy had taken herself out of the whole situation, made it impersonal, so it was like it hadn't happened to her, one step removed.

'Oh God, I'm sorry,' Eva said. 'All these questions. It must have been... Mum dying must have been terrible for you.'

Nancy blinked a few times, a tear rolling down her cheek. She wiped it away and tore some toilet paper from the roll by her bed, blew her nose.

'I was told she had an "accident".' She curved her fingers to put imaginary speech marks round the word. 'She had a fall at home, ended up in intensive care and never came back out. You were born by Caesarean. Then she died.'

A fall? Eva's head felt it might burst with all this new information, things she had never known or even imagined.

She frowned. 'What happened exactly?'

Nancy's mouth twisted to the side, her jaw hardening. 'You'd have to ask Linda for specifics.' She raised her eyebrows as she spoke, a flash of venom in her voice.

Eva tried to remember what she'd been told, what she knew to be true. 'Linda lived next door.'

'Handy,' Nancy said with a huff.

Her eyes dropped to her hands, which were smoothing the duvet cover over and over again, like she was trying to rub out a stain.

CHAPTER ELEVEN

Eva stared at her sister in stunned silence. Nancy winced and closed her eyes, her hands covering her face. 'I'm so sorry, Eva.' Her voice was weary. 'I don't think I can do this anymore.'

Eva stood and left the room, closing the door behind her as if it might hide her sister's revelations. The story so different from the one she'd lived with all these years. Her parents so different from the people she'd thought they were.

She was shaking, a trembling coming from her very core, making her feel nauseous and unsteady. She decided to go and have a lie-down herself, needing space on her own to allow these new facts to settle. A low ache throbbed at the base of her skull. All those lies and misunderstandings – the past was a landscape she didn't even recognise anymore. *What's real?* That was the question. Was it Nancy's version, or that of her parents? Could she trust any of them? She stumbled into her bedroom, shutting the door behind her.

She'd hardly had a chance to sit down before she heard the shuffle of feet on the floorboards and the door swung open. Nancy was standing there, clutching the door handle so tight her knuckles were white.

'I'm sorry, Eva, I should have told you about sleeping arrangements. You can't use this room.'

Eva jumped to her feet like she'd sat on an ants' nest, looking around her to see if she'd missed something that would have told her she couldn't be in here. She frowned, confused. 'But it seemed like the guest bedroom. The others have bunks, so I thought they were for your shearers.' Heat spread through her body. She felt wrong-footed again, caught in the act of doing something that wasn't permissible by Nancy's unwritten rules. She fumbled for her things, slinging her handbag over her shoulder, the holdall in her hand.

Nancy leant her head against the door, clearly struggling to stay upright. 'This room belonged to a very dear friend of mine. That's all.'

So she hasn't always lived alone. And when did this dear friend leave?

Eva scowled, her cheeks glowing. 'I'm sorry. But how was I to know?' She glanced at the bed, as if someone might have magically materialised there.

'You can use the room next door. I think you'll be comfortable enough in there. I see you've already found where the bedding is kept.'

She noticed the sweat gathering on Nancy's top lip. Her sister swayed as though she might fall over and Eva's annoyance fizzled away. This woman was seriously unwell. *Head injury, remember? Erratic behaviour.*

She blew out a breath. 'You need to get back to bed. Honestly, you look rough.'

Nancy's lips twitched. 'Funny, that's exactly how I feel. I don't suppose… Could you help me back to my room?'

'I'll just dump these next door.' Eva had a quick scan round the room to make sure she'd picked everything up. Noticing her phone on the chest of drawers, she dropped the bags and reached down to unplug it.

'I'm afraid you won't get much reception for that thing,' Nancy said, eyeing the phone.

'I managed before.' Eva picked up her bags again. 'Mum rang when I was outside.'

'Ah yes, well it's okay outside, and sometimes in the kitchen, because that's an extension and the walls are thinner. Everywhere else is solid granite.' She put a hand on Eva's arm as she moved past her in the doorway. 'Promise me you won't tell Linda any of my business? Now you know what happened, you can see why I'm not a fan.' Her expression had a new intensity that made Eva stop. 'It's my decision if I want her to know anything about me. Okay?'

Eva could sense the animosity towards her stepmum flowing through Nancy's fingers and into her skin. Her heart started to race, as though she was under threat. Not physically – her sister was leaning on the door for support and was so thin you'd think a strong breeze would blow her over. It was the words she was scared of. What else might be lurking under the surface; what new revelations might rock her world?

She had a sudden urge to run downstairs and leave. Get out of there before she learnt any more secrets. Instead of the truth making her feel complete, it had undermined her very existence. Made her question what sort of people her parents really were. And she didn't want that. What she really wanted was to have listened to Linda in the first place, let her tell the hospital it wasn't possible to come and keep an eye on Nancy. Then she'd still be living in a world she knew and loved.

'Look, I'll go,' she said, glancing at the stairs. 'I'll call the hospital and see if they can organise some home care or something. They'll understand that I'm here on sufferance and Mum really needs my support and—'

'What? No.' Nancy looked horrified. 'You can't go now.' She squeezed Eva's arm. 'Not when I've only just met you.' Her face puckered, tears welling in her eyes. 'Talking about the past… it's made me realise… I don't think I've really dealt with what happened. Mum dying.'

She started sobbing and Eva dropped her bags and wrapped her in a hug. She could feel her own emotions stirring and worried that she might join in.

Nancy held on tight and the two of them stayed there for a long moment. Finally she pushed away, wiping her face with her hands. 'What a stupid woman I've become,' she muttered. 'I don't blame you for wanting to leave. And I can't keep you here. But I would be very grateful if you would stay. Just for a couple more days.' She blinked back tears. 'I hate being this pathetic but there's nothing I can do. I've just got to wait for the healing process to run its course.' She heaved in a breath and swiped at her wet cheeks. 'It's bloody annoying,' she muttered, banging the door with her fist.

Eva held out her arm for support and they made their way back to Nancy's bedroom. She sat next to her on the bed and held her hand, feeling a little closer to her sister after their embrace. 'Everyone has accidents and gets ill sometimes. If you would only stop fighting it, I'm sure you'd heal quicker.'

'You're right.' She sounded resigned, defeated. 'But I don't… I don't want to be on my own. Not yet.' Was that a tremble in her voice?

Eva gave her a reassuring smile and released her grip on Nancy's hand before standing.

'It's okay, I'm not going anywhere. You get some rest while I sort out my bed. Then I'll get supper ready.'

Nancy settled back on her pillows, eyes fluttering closed. Eva left the room, keeping the door ajar so she could hear her if she was needed.

What a confusing day it had been, so many mixed emotions, and it must have been the same for Nancy. Stirring up the past had muddied Eva's feelings about her mum. Both her mums. It was going to take a bit of time to sort out how she felt about everything, and she was glad of the excuse of poor reception to delay checking in with Linda. There was a difficult conversation to be had but she was too exhausted to think about that now.

She took her bags to her new bedroom. The metal-framed bunk bed looked cold and unwelcoming, the metal springs squeaking when she sat down. But the mattress didn't feel too bad and she thought it would do for a couple of days. She went to check the chest of drawers, pushed against the opposite wall, and found it was empty. A wooden chair sat by the window. Hands on hips, she turned in a circle, surveying the spartan space. Functional was the best description she could come up with.

At least it was clean and she had somewhere to put her clothes, unlike in the other room. Hmm. That had been strange, the way Nancy had reacted when she'd found Eva in there. Who was the dear friend, and where were they now?

She found more bedding in the bathroom cupboard, including a duvet and pillows. They smelt a little musty but once the covers were on, she hoped they'd be okay.

As she worked, she thought about Nancy's last comments, a distraction from thinking about her parents and what had happened in the past. If Nancy was frightened to be on her own, did that mean someone *had* attacked her? Or was it just that she knew she couldn't manage to look after herself just yet? Aware that her imagination was prone to overactivity, Eva decided it was the latter.

Once she'd finished getting her bed ready, she sat by the window, gazing into the swirling mist. It teased her with glimpses of a view before closing again, pressing against the window like it wanted to come inside. She could hear the steady dripping of moisture falling onto the roof from the huge tree that guarded the house. She shivered, chilly now, and unzipped her bag, looking for her fleece jacket.

She needed to keep moving to stay warm, so she busied herself with unpacking her clothes, just as something to do, letting her mind float free. In recent weeks, her life had become untethered, with no job to get her out and about, but now she felt like she was in a different stratosphere, floating about with no gravity to bring her back down to earth. She wasn't sure how to go forward with her life when her past was built on lies. Could she really return home and behave like everything was the same?

And what would happen… afterwards?

Afterwards. She swallowed, the word unpalatable. It implied a finality that she didn't want to consider. Her dad was dying. That was the reality, his deterioration happening at a frightening speed.

To say she was conflicted about her feelings for her father would be an understatement. On one level – a distant, unemotional level – she could see what Nancy was saying about him being too selfish to be a great parent. His outdoor activities had always taken up a lot of his time. Linda, thankfully, was the opposite, so that made up for it. Sort of. But what child didn't want their father's approval?

He was a competitive man, though, saw success in winning, in being the best. Eva had always felt he wanted her to be like that too. Except she wasn't. There was no straight path to the winning line for her. She was the sort who'd stop and admire a flower, wander off to study the shape of a tree, or the architecture of a house, while daydreaming about who'd lived there over the years. She ambled through life, letting her curiosity lead the way. Success was therefore hard to measure, and although she'd allowed herself to be pushed to go to university, she'd always felt that she'd fallen short of her father's expectations.

One of his regular pep talks played in her mind. 'You need to step up a gear, Eva. If you're going to get the best out of life, you've got to put your best in.' When she was younger, she sometimes found it hard to focus on one thing, when life was full of so many interesting diversions. *Jack of all trades, master of none.* That was another of his regular comments and she knew he had a point. How many times had she taken up a new sport at school, only to drop it a few months later?

Linda, on the other hand, would say, 'I just want you to be happy, love. I want you to enjoy being young. Experiment, discover new things. Don't tie yourself down before you're ready.' She wondered now if that was her stepmum's way of having a little dig at her dad, telling her to do the opposite of his advice. Had they been playing power games through her? She gave herself a mental shake, appalled at the direction of her thoughts. *Mum and Dad aren't like that.* They'd always been two halves of a whole; together their parenting had pretty much worked.

She studied the water droplets caught in a spider's web on the outside of the window, glittering like jewels, and thought of all the good times, determined to find a positive spin on things.

Going through the photo albums with her dad had made her appreciate that her memories and what had actually happened were often two quite different things. Yes, her dad had hobbies, but surely everyone was allowed that. It had made him interesting, knowledgeable and more relaxed when he did spend time at home. *Just think about all those hours playing cards.* Or watching films together. Working on creating a wildlife garden. Taking her birdwatching when she'd asked. And he was never too busy to help with homework, or come to school plays or parents' evenings. He'd been there for the things that mattered and her love for him burned bright in her heart.

Could she trust her sister's version of what had happened?

Eva chewed at her lip as she thought. One thing she did know for sure was that Linda was a lovely mum, born for the role of parent. Maybe she fussed too much, but that was only because she cared. *Is she too good to be true? Am I seeing the real person, or is she someone who'd steal another woman's husband?*

An urgent desire to know fired up her limbs. She stood, grabbed her phone. The kitchen had reception, she remembered, and she hurried downstairs. If she could just talk it through with Linda, perhaps she'd be able to work out the truth for herself.

After walking round the kitchen holding the phone high and low, she managed to find a place by the sink where she got enough of a signal to make a call. It went straight to voicemail, though, which suggested Linda's phone was off. Or the battery was flat. Gritting her teeth, she tapped out a message, asking after her dad and saying she needed a chat, would she please call.

She filled the kettle and stared out of the window, the buildings surrounding the yard invisible in the opaque mist. A sudden rattling drew her eye to the door that led to the utility room. She thought maybe she'd imagined it, but no, there it was again. The hairs on the back of her neck stood up as she imagined a face looming out of the mist, pressing against the kitchen window.

With a scream stuck in her throat, she turned and ran upstairs, into her bedroom, slamming the door behind her.

CHAPTER TWELVE

Eva paced the floor, heart beating nineteen to the dozen, as if she'd seen a ghost. But that was no ghost at the door. It wasn't the wind rattling the door either because there was no bloody wind. Someone had been trying to get in. Thank God she'd thought to lock everything earlier. *What about the windows?* Her hand went to her chest, her brain frozen for a moment. She'd checked those, hadn't she? Made sure all the latches were tight. She puffed out a breath, her hands buried in her hair. *What to do? What to do?*

'Eva… Eva.' Nancy was calling her. Eva went to the door, then hesitated a second. *What if someone's outside on the landing?* Her skin prickled, pulse racing even faster. 'Eva, are you there?'

Nancy needed her. If there was someone upstairs, it was Nancy they would have been looking for, and she was fine, wasn't she? She tightened her jaw and threw open the door, her fist ready to punch any intruder in the face, the hope being that an element of surprise would give her an advantage. Her heart skipped with relief when the landing was empty. *Of course there's nobody there.* Hysterical woman, she chided, feeling breathless and a little light-headed as she hurried to Nancy's room.

Her sister was sitting on the end of the bed. 'I was just wondering about something to eat. I was going to go down and get it myself, but I honestly don't think I can. Every time I stand up, I feel dizzy.'

'Don't be daft,' Eva said sternly. 'You're not going anywhere. You go back to bed. I bought some quiche if you're okay with that. I've never used a range for cooking so I don't think we'll be having a hot meal tonight, but I promise I'll try and get it working tomorrow.'

'Quiche is fine.' Nancy winced as if speaking was causing her pain, her voice weak. 'Anything. I don't care.'

'Right, I'll go and get it. And you're probably due some tablets. Another painkiller, would that help?'

She nodded.

'I'll bring the medication upstairs and we can see what you have to take and when.'

Eva left the room, walked down the landing, stopped at the top of the stairs. A feeling of foreboding like she'd never had before lurked at the back of her neck. The light was dimming now, the mist dulling the day and the evening drawing in. It looked pretty dark down there. What she really wanted was a weapon of some sort, something that might help her to feel a little braver. She knew there was nothing in her bedroom or the one at the back, but the middle room…? She went to have a look, pushed the door, but it wouldn't open. Locked.

'What are you doing?' Nancy's voice from the bedroom. *Ears like a bat.* She must have recognised the sound of the door handle being turned.

'It's okay. I was looking for something and thought I'd left it in the bedroom but it's actually in my pocket.'

Eva hurried along the landing and down the stairs. In the gloom of the hallway, she stopped and listened. A muffled thump. Her heart leapt, ears straining, adrenaline firing round her body. Her eyes swept the hallway in front of her and she could have cried with joy when she saw the umbrella standing in a tall pot by the door. Next to it was a walking stick, the end shaped like an eagle's head. She grabbed them both, one in each hand, feeling much braver now, and crept along the hallway towards the kitchen, stopping in the doorway. A draught blew on her face, making her frown, puzzled as to where it might be coming from. *I closed everything.*

But it only took a little crack for air to get in. She inched into the room, fumbled for the light switch next to the door, blinking in the glare of the strip light as it flared into life. The room was empty.

She felt a little stupid, melodramatic, until her eyes were drawn to the utility room door. *Did I leave that open?* She didn't think so, and as she went over to push it closed, she felt another waft of air on her face. She swallowed, tightening her grip on her weapons before peering into the room. Through the gloom she could see that the back door was still bolted. Everything else was as it had been.

The waft of air again.

It was coming from the corner by the washing machine. Her hand felt up and down the wall until she found the light switch and clicked it on. A bare light bulb lit the room with a dim glow. Following the cool stream of air, she found a small window hidden behind the mound of outdoor clothing hanging on the pegs. The catch was open and the window flapped in the breeze as if it was breathing.

With a relieved tut, she secured it as best she could, although it was a bit of a struggle; the frame had obviously swollen and she wasn't convinced the catch would hold. She stared at it, waiting for the latch to ping off the fastening again, but it stayed put. Satisfied, she went back to the kitchen, clicking off the utility room light before shutting the door behind her. No wonder she hadn't spotted the window earlier; it wasn't visible unless you were right beside it. But then she remembered she *had* been beside it. When she'd put the bedding in the washing machine. Had it been open then? *Would I have noticed?* It was the sort of window that would always be left open, though, to let the room air with all the wet outdoor clothes and washing.

Her mental chatter went on at full speed while she looked through the pile of groceries for the quiche. She was sure she'd left everything on the table, but maybe she'd put it in the fridge, on autopilot. She checked but the only thing in there was a tub of margarine. Puzzled, she looked at the groceries again. Nope, there was no sign of it.

Did I even buy a quiche? Maybe it was wishful thinking. Her brain was scrambled and anything was possible. She studied the receipt on the table; there was definitely a quiche listed.

Her breath whistled between her teeth as a new possibility came to her. *Has somebody been in the house and stolen it?* No, that was a stupid idea, more melodrama born of her vivid imagination; she'd just left it at the shop. Forgot to pack it. *Wouldn't be the first time I've done that.*

Hands on hips, she glared at the pile of groceries before putting the chilled foods in the fridge and leaving the tins and packets and bread on the table. It looked like toast and pâté was the only option for their evening meal. But she'd bought bananas and a couple of vanilla slices. That would have to do. In all honesty, after the emotional storm she'd been through, she wasn't that hungry.

Ten minutes later, she had everything ready on a big wooden tray she'd found in a cupboard. With a last look round to check that she'd remembered everything, she made her way into the hall, making sure she left all the lights on. No way was she coming down into the dark again. That had been properly scary.

'Sorry,' she said as she walked into Nancy's room. 'I could have sworn I'd seen the quiche when I unloaded everything but it seems to have gone missing. Anyway, we've got pâté on toast and a cake for pudding. If you're still hungry, I bought some bananas.'

She put the tray on the bed, sitting next to it so they could both reach the plates of food and mugs of tea.

'I'm not a fussy eater,' Nancy said, eagerly picking up a slice of toast and biting into it. 'I used to be, before I came here. But you learn to eat what's available, even things you don't like, when that's all there is.'

'If you don't mind me saying, you look like you could do with feeding up. It must be a hard life living in a place like this.'

Nancy chewed and took another big bite, obviously ravenous. 'This year's been more of a struggle. Every year is different, depending on the weather, but we usually manage.'

They ate in silence for a while, Nancy devouring the toast at a speed Eva couldn't keep up with.

'Good to see you've got an appetite,' she said with a hint of sarcasm as she watched her sister take the last two pieces of toast, squash them together and take a massive bite. Nancy stopped chewing for a second, then carried on, not speaking until she'd finished, delicately wiping the crumbs from the corners of her mouth.

Eva's stomach rumbled.

Only then did Nancy seem to realise what she'd done. 'Oh Eva, was that your toast? I'm so sorry. You can always go and make some more, I suppose. Or have my cake instead.'

Eva glanced at the doorway, very aware of the darkness of the landing, where there was no working light bulb. 'No, I'm fine.'

'Marj used to make her own pâté,' Nancy said as she picked up her tea and took a sip. 'It was fabulous. I wish I'd asked her for the recipe.'

'Who was Marj?' Eva asked. Was she the 'dear friend' her sister had talked about?

Nancy gave a wistful smile. 'She was my surrogate mother. Marj and Bill owned this place. I came here when I was about… well, I'd have been nearly nineteen, I suppose. I'd been travelling with this trustafarian.'

Eva frowned. 'What's a trustafarian?'

Nancy laughed. 'Oh, they're rich kids with trust funds who have dropped out. Usually been to boarding school, hated their parents and rebelled. A lot of them have dreadlocks for some reason. Hence the name.' She took another sip of tea, a hint of mischief in her eyes. 'Anyway, I was invited to tag along. In the summer we travelled between music festivals, and in the winter we generally ended up on council sites, where there were at least some facilities.' She pulled a face. 'It was pretty grim, to be honest, but when you're young and homeless, you don't tend to mind so much. Until she overdosed and then that was me out of there.'

Eva's eyes widened, hardly believing what she'd just heard. 'As in…'

Nancy nodded, sadness twisting at her mouth. 'Poor girl died. Some sort of tablet she'd got from a guy at the festival we'd been to. I scarpered in case I was blamed.'

'You just left her?' Eva stared at her sister. 'She was dead and you—'

'What would *you* have done?' Nancy snapped, defensive all of a sudden, clasping her mug to her chest. 'It wasn't my fault she died. There was nothing I could do. Anyway, I was nineteen and scared out of my wits.'

Silence descended like a barrier between them, the rasp of Nancy's indignant breath the only sound.

Eva frowned. 'And you never thought about coming home?'

Nancy gazed at her. 'No,' she said. 'I let chance take me somewhere new. I was hitching, Marj and Bill picked me up, and I ended up here.'

Eva popped the last of her cake into her mouth, not understanding Nancy's logic but deciding not to press the point further. She hadn't lived Nancy's life, didn't know the finer details, so who was she to judge? She steered the conversation down a different track. 'Are they the people in the pictures downstairs?'

Nancy's gaze hardened, a slight edge to her voice. 'You've been having a good look round, haven't you?'

Eva could feel the blush travelling up her neck. She shrugged. 'I went to find something to read while you were asleep. That's all.'

Nancy gave her a sudden smile. 'I'm sorry, that came out wrong. I honestly don't know what's got into my brain. I think one thing and say another. Very confusing!'

Eva returned the smile, relieved. 'It's that head injury again. No need to apologise.'

Nancy's eyes travelled round the room. 'It's a lovely house, isn't it? I thought I'd landed in paradise when I ended up here. The farm had been in their family for at least a hundred years, probably more. A few generations. Bill was a bit vague about things like that.'

'So the young man in the pictures was their son?'

Nancy nodded. 'That's right. Caradog. I never met him, though. He died quite young, in an accident. He was mad about tractors, four-wheel-drive vehicles, all that stuff, and it ended up being the death of him. I think that's why they took me in. Or at least that was Marj's thinking. She missed him and needed someone to mother.'

'Oh that's sad,' Eva said, sipping at her tea.

'Poor Marj never got over it. She liked to sit and tell me all about him. Bill was one of those strong, silent types and thought she should put it behind her. He didn't understand her need to process her grief, how it was helpful to remember the good times.'

Eva looked down at her mug, swilled the remains in the bottom. Nancy's words had struck a chord with her. Dad's like Bill, she thought. That was why there'd been no mention of Nancy, no pictures in the house. He'd put that episode behind him and moved on. She wondered what Linda had made of that, how she'd felt about it. It was wrong to make assumptions; she shouldn't judge Linda's actions until she'd had a chance to talk it through with her. *Perhaps I've been a bit hasty.*

She decided she'd try giving her mum a ring again once she'd tidied up their supper plates, feeling bad that she'd stormed off, leaving Linda to cope on her own.

'It was good for a while,' Nancy said, breaking into Eva's thoughts. 'Then Marj died quite suddenly. Ovarian cancer. After that, Bill decided he wasn't up to farming anymore. So he went to live down in the south of England and left me to look after the place.'

Eva nodded; another of her questions answered. 'You don't own it, then?'

Nancy flapped a hand. 'As good as. He's not interested and without me it would be derelict by now. I think of myself as a caretaker until he dies. He said he'd leave it to me in his will. He's no other relatives, you see.'

'It's a lot to do on your own.'

'We've sold off bits over the years to make it more manageable and cover running costs. It's more of a smallholding than a farm now. But we try to be self-sufficient. A few pigs in the woods. A couple of cows, a small flock of sheep and some chickens. That's it for livestock these days. And anyway, I'm not on my—' Nancy stopped, looked a little flustered. 'I manage fine.' Her eyes dropped to the tray and she picked up her cake, taking a big bite. Eva sensed the conversation was over. That part of it, anyway. But it left a question hanging in the air. Who was the 'we' she kept referring to?

CHAPTER THIRTEEN

The conversation turned to Nancy's medication. Eva emptied the bag that the hospital had given her. Antibiotics because the wound had been infected and anti-inflammatories. Easy enough, she decided, and gave Nancy the rest of her tablets for the day, putting everything else back in the bag and leaving it next to the bed ready for morning.

Once she'd got Nancy settled, she went to take the tray back downstairs. It was dark now, the landing in shadow. She thought she might move a light bulb from another fitting, maybe take the one from the back bedroom, because there was no way she was going downstairs unless the place was properly lit.

What a scaredy-cat, she chided as she sat on her bed, putting the tray beside her. The doors and windows were locked. Everything was secure. But then a loud screech sent her heart racing and she caught a flash of white outside the window, making her knock a mug off the tray, sending it spinning across the floor.

The wind had got up now, whooshing through the leaves, sweeping the mist away. Out of the window she could see the outline of a mountain ridge on the other side of the valley, clouds hovering above it. A splatter of rain against the window made her jump, and she got up and pulled the curtains tight, feeling better now she couldn't see what was out there.

The screech came again, right above her now. She looked up at the ceiling as if some phantom creature had flown into the room, but all she could see were wisps of cobwebs, and the bodies of dead flies, wrapped in their cocoons. Then she realised what she'd heard. *It's a bloody barn owl! Nothing to be scared of.*

She shook her head and tutted with impatience. She was so jumpy, so on edge, and it wasn't helped by this stupid imagination of hers. She thumped the pillows into shape and checked her phone, groaning when she realised she hadn't switched the socket on. She'd have to leave it for ten minutes or so to have enough charge for a conversation with Linda. In the meantime, she'd find a light bulb.

The light from her bedroom cast a glow onto the landing, her shadow flitting across the wall, causing her to snap her head round and check if there was anything behind her; she was starting to annoy herself now. She pressed her lips together as she went to open the door of the bedroom next to hers. It rattled but wouldn't open. She twisted the handle, put her weight against it, but still no movement. It too was locked.

Frustrated, she went back to her own room and sat on the bed. Nancy was certainly keen that she didn't go into the other bedrooms. Not that there'd been much to see in the back room. Just the sleeping bag, the book and the trainers. Her brain made a sudden connection. *Maybe that person didn't actually leave. Maybe he's still around and it was him trying to get in, to reclaim his possessions. Maybe they argued and she threw him out. Perhaps he attacked her and she fought him off? Maybe…*

Her brain galloped off on a meandering path of maybes until she reined herself in. *All theories, no substance to any of it.* And hadn't Nancy said nobody had come to help this year? Those things could have been in that room for a while. Years, even. Her mind focused on the stain she'd seen on the floor. *Was it wine?*

A longing for her mum swept through her. She was so out of her comfort zone, in this weird countryside setting, with a stranger of a sister who had given her a completely contradictory version of her family history. *Perhaps it's all lies.* That was something she needed to consider. If she could hear Linda's voice, get back in touch with something familiar, she thought she'd feel reassured. Her mum would put things in context and that might calm her down.

You're being selfish again, she scolded. Life isn't just about you. She should find out how her dad was this evening, if he'd settled down. Ask her mum how she was getting on. Listen to whatever she needed to get off her chest. Tell her that she loved her. Because she did.

Before she could talk herself out of it, she unplugged her phone, retrieved the mug from the floor and picked up the supper tray. Carefully she made her way downstairs, her eyes scanning the hallway, the glow from the kitchen door. *Thank God I left the lights on.*

The expanse of blackness presented by the kitchen window felt threatening, exposing, but there were no curtains or blinds. Unfortunately, it was the only place in the room she could get reception, so she had no choice but to stand there. She turned away from the darkness, but that felt worse, imaginary eyes burning into the back of her neck.

Linda answered after the first ring. 'Eva! I've been waiting for you to call.'

'I tried earlier, but it went to voicemail.'

She sighed. 'Oh yes, I turned it off when the physio came. Didn't want to be disturbed.'

'How's… how's Dad?'

'Struggling, love. We both are, to be honest.' Another long sigh rattled down the phone. 'I never imagined I'd be a carer at my age. Your dad was so fit until this horrible disease got him.' Her voice was shaky, emotional. 'When you were little, I used to imagine him and me travelling all over the world once you'd left home, visiting all those places I've only seen on TV.' She sniffed, cleared her throat. 'Anyway, how are you getting on, love? We got cut off before, just as it was getting interesting.'

'Yeah, my battery went flat. I was telling you about the house, wasn't I?'

Eva updated Linda on everything Nancy had told her about how she'd come to be at the farm, a little voice in her head whining at her to stop, reminding her that Nancy had asked her not to tell Linda anything. She didn't mean it, she tried to convince herself. It was the head injury talking.

'So she's got a farmhouse?' Linda sounded impressed.

'That's right. It's not hers as such but it seems like she can live in it as long as she wants and will inherit it when the owner dies.'

'Well, well.' Linda laughed. 'If you'd seen Nancy as a teenager, all her make-up and fashionable clothes, you'd never have guessed she'd end up on a farm.'

Eva tried to imagine her sister in high heels and a dress but she honestly couldn't make it work. 'I think it was just chance that led her here but she obviously liked it or why would she stay?'

'Hmm.' They were both silent for a moment. Eventually Linda spoke. 'Do you know why she never got in touch? Or why she had our contact details?'

'No. She hasn't answered that one yet. But I think she's warming to me. I'm hoping she'll tell me a bit more tomorrow.'

'I still can't believe she's alive. I had this really strong feeling she was dead, and you know me and my feelings. I'm generally right, aren't I?'

'Well, not this time.' Eva took a deep breath, preparing herself for the difficult questions she was revving up to ask.

'No. Apparently not.'

'Um… Mum, I've got to ask you…' She stopped and picked at a blob of paint dried on the worktop next to the sink, not really sure how to broach the subject. 'Nancy said that you and Dad… well, she suggested you were… having an affair before my real mum died.'

Silence.

'She said that?' Linda's voice was a shocked whisper.

'Yes, she did.' Eva hesitated, but pushed on. 'Is it true?'

'She probably just thinks that because your dad asked me to move in when he brought you home from the hospital. Said it would be more practical. I remember he said Nancy had kicked up a right fuss about it.' Her voice was higher and faster than usual, a telltale sign that Eva knew well. 'And there wasn't just you to look after, there was your dad as well, and…' She ground to a halt, her explanation lacking conviction. A simple 'no' was all Eva had wanted to hear.

'I didn't ask about you moving in. I asked whether you were having an affair.'

Linda's breath crackled down the phone. 'It's not as straightforward as that, love.'

Eva's shoulders tensed. 'It's a yes-or-no answer.'

It was a moment before Linda spoke again. 'The truth is, your dad and your… your mother had drifted apart. He only stayed with her because she was pregnant with you.'

'Really?'

'Yes, really. You'll have to take my word for it.'

'Hmm, well…' She sighed, disappointed that Nancy had been telling the truth. She wasn't the longed-for baby of her imaginings but rather a problem to be solved. An inconvenience her parents had had to address, the result being an attempt at gluing a marriage together. Her heart sank, her shoulders hunched as she leant against the sink. 'Nancy said as much.'

'There you are, then.'

Linda's words had a finality about them, as though she'd won. Eva realised she'd not actually given her a proper answer. Her avoidance, however, made it sound very much like a yes.

'Nancy said something else that puzzled me.'

'And what was that?' Linda sounded nervous.

'She said my mum didn't die in childbirth. Why did I always think that's what happened?'

'Well, technically, she didn't. Technically, it was just after.'

Eva gritted her teeth. 'You're missing the point, Mum. The point is, childbirth was not what caused her to die. She had an accident, didn't she?'

'Yes, that's right. She was decorating the nursery. Mike said he'd do it, but she was too impatient to wait. She fell off a ladder, hit her head on the windowsill and broke her neck.'

The starkness of her account was like a physical blow, the emotional disconnect quite shocking. For a moment Eva couldn't respond.

A noise made her eyes flick up to the dark expanse of window in front of her. In the reflection she could see a shape looming behind her. She screamed, dropping her phone, which landed with a clatter on the floor, breaking apart, pieces skittering in all directions. She spun round, ready to run or kick and fight, only to see it was Nancy.

Her hands went to her chest as if to steady the erratic beating of her heart.

'Christ,' she gasped. 'You scared the living daylights out of me.'

Nancy swayed and grabbed at the table, then lowered herself into a chair. She looked like she might be sick again. Eva frowned, hands gravitating to her hips, chin jutting, annoyed at the shock Nancy had given her and the fact that she'd made her drop her phone.

'What are you doing down here?' she snapped. 'You should be in bed. You know you just have to call me if you want something.'

'I was feeling a bit better.' Nancy put a hand to her head, wincing as she spoke. 'I thought I heard you talking to someone and it sounded like you were arguing. I… was worried about you.'

'I was on the phone to Mum, that's all. I was just…' Eva stopped herself, remembering her sister's request that she shouldn't tell Linda anything about her life. *Did she overhear?* She had no way of knowing how long Nancy might have been lurking in the hallway. 'Dad's not doing great,' she said, looking at the floor and the scattered innards of her phone.

She could feel Nancy's eyes on her as she crouched down, trying to collect the pieces in the hope that there might be a way to fix the thing. After a few minutes, she knew it was hopeless. The screen was shattered and she had no idea how the bits and pieces were supposed to fit back together.

'That cost me a bloody fortune,' she muttered as she gazed at the electronic paraphernalia in her hand. She definitely didn't have the money to replace it and now she had no way to contact home. No way to talk to her mum or keep track of how her dad was doing. Presumably Nancy had a mobile. But would she let her use it to ring a woman she so obviously despised?

'I'm so sorry,' Nancy said, apology in her eyes. 'I didn't mean to scare you.'

Eva sighed and put the pieces in a small heap on the table. 'Not your fault. I'm a bit jumpy, I suppose. I've never stayed in a place as remote as this; there's all sorts of weird noises.' She gave a nervous laugh and looked at the black window, reflecting the two of them in the kitchen. 'I thought someone was trying to get in before.'

Nancy didn't reply, her face pale, eyes unfocused as her lashes fluttered and she slid off her chair onto the kitchen floor.

CHAPTER FOURTEEN

Ten minutes later, Eva stared at her sister, thankful that her prayers had been answered when her eyes flickered open. Nancy's head was propped on a cushion, her body tipped on its side in the recovery position. In both her jobs, Eva had attended regular first-aid courses, because dealing with emergencies came with the territory, and now she was grateful for the training.

Nancy moaned.

Eva tutted as she knelt beside her, relief swelling in her chest. She'd been worried for a few minutes, no idea how to call for help now her phone was broken. 'You do know you're a lousy patient, don't you?' she scolded.

Nancy's eyes settled on Eva's face. 'I'm not making this easy for you, am I?'

Eva laughed. 'Talk about understatements.' Nancy was the opposite of easy, but in a strange way, she liked that about her. There was no denying she was determined. 'You gave me quite a fright.' That was an understatement too.

Nancy gave a poor attempt at a smile, reaching out for Eva's hand. 'What an idiot I am. If there was an intruder, I'm in no fit state to help fight them off, am I?'

Eva smiled back, but her pulse raced. *An intruder.* Her sister had obviously thought someone had got into the house. That was why she'd come down. She glanced over her shoulder at the black expanse of glass, the feeling that they were being watched creeping up the back of her neck.

She gave a little shiver before turning her attention back to Nancy.

'When you're feeling strong enough, I'll help you up the stairs but you've got to promise me you'll stay there.' It struck Eva that she sounded just like her mum did when she was telling her off. She softened her voice. 'You'd get better a lot faster if you'd just rest.'

'Okay, okay. No need for a lecture,' Nancy mumbled but there was warmth in her eyes and her hand grasped Eva's a little tighter. 'I promise I'll behave myself.'

'Yeah, well…' Eva had made a decision while she was wrestling an unresponsive Nancy into the recovery position. She wasn't qualified to cope with the situation she now found herself in. In a way, she felt it was all her fault. Nancy had asked her not to talk to Linda, but Eva had gone ahead anyway. If she hadn't heard her talking on the phone, she would have stayed in bed. So Eva being in the house was creating anxiety and was in no way helping her to rest and recover.

She looked at their hands clasped together and wasn't sure what to do for the best. 'Look, I've been thinking. If you're not feeling any better tomorrow, I think I should take you back to hospital.' She sighed. 'To be honest, I feel a bit overwhelmed by the responsibility. If anything happened to you because I didn't know what to do…' she grimaced, 'well, I'd never forgive myself and I'd have to live with it for the rest of my life.'

Nancy's eyes widened, a look of horror on her face. 'No, Eva. Don't even think that. I can't go back there.' She sounded panicky. 'I'm sorry. I'm just not myself.' She frowned. 'I'm all jittery. It's hard to describe… And I'm so restless stuck in bed. I should be outside doing things.'

There was a tremble of fear in her voice and Eva softened, the compassionate side of her nature overriding the need to get herself out of this uncomfortable situation.

'What sort of things? Maybe I can do some of it for you. Then you can stop worrying and just relax and allow yourself to get better.'

Nancy nodded. 'The sheep and cows are out in the fields, so they'll be fine. But there's the chickens. In the barn. They haven't been fed for days now, though they've got water, so they should be okay.' She caught Eva's eye. 'If you could feed them tomorrow, that would help. There'll be eggs to collect as well.'

Eva smiled. She'd always fancied keeping chickens, but Linda had been dead against it. Said they had parasites and they got sick and carried diseases and it would be more trouble than it was worth. Now she'd get to tick a little something off her bucket list, however trivial it might sound. There was something very wholesome about collecting eggs and then eating them for breakfast.

'I can definitely do that.' She gave Nancy a reassuring smile. 'Right, are you feeling ready to get back upstairs? Then I think we should call it a day, reset and start afresh tomorrow. Take it from there, okay?' She helped her to her feet and they slowly made their way upstairs.

'Thank you,' Nancy said as she flopped back on her pillows, and with a sigh of relief, Eva closed the door.

The next morning, she was woken by a loud rumble of thunder, a flash of lightning and then the sudden pounding of rain on the roof. She had no way of checking the time now that her phone was in pieces, but she could see the light seeping underneath the curtains. Another monstrous crack of thunder, right overhead, so loud it made her jerk upright, the air fizzing with static. She went to the window and opened the curtains, the view obscured by the sudden torrent of rain that battered the window pane.

They certainly get a lot of weather in these parts, she thought, wide awake now. She sorted out some clean clothes for the day, grabbed her towel and went to the bathroom. Thankfully, the water was hot and she massaged her aching shoulders, working out the knots of tension as she showered.

There was no doubting that the previous day had given her an emotional pounding; even though she'd just got up, she felt weary and conflicted. There'd been so many revelations, which had screwed up her picture of the past and thrown it in the bin. She'd have to start again, rebuild the mental foundations of her life and decide for herself which version she chose to believe.

It was clear there was animosity between Nancy and Linda, each of them denouncing the other, although Linda was more subtle in her approach. What it did mean, though, was that she couldn't trust either of them to give her the honest truth. She had the impression there was still a lot more to learn about the circumstances surrounding her mother's death and Nancy's decision to disappear. Today, she promised herself, she'd make sure she got Nancy talking about it, try to wheedle the information out of her.

She felt a bit better now she had a plan – and she'd already signalled her intention to take Nancy back to hospital if she wasn't any better, so she had an escape all sorted should she need it. Once she was dressed, she popped her head round the door of Nancy's room to find her still fast asleep. She decided to leave her and quietly closed the door. Another rumble of thunder and flash of lightning had her running downstairs, feeling far too close to the raw power of the storm up on the first floor.

Through the kitchen window she watched torrents of rain lash down into the yard, falling so hard it was bouncing off the concrete surface, pouring out of downspouts, gurgling down drains. It was quite hypnotic. She watched it for a while, sipping a cup of coffee, startled every time another thunderbolt cracked through the heavy air.

The kitchen clock said it was coming up to seven o'clock, early for her to be up since she'd stopped work, but she liked that time of day, when it was quiet and still, with nobody else around. Liked to have a moment to herself to let her mind float on the freshness of a new day.

Relax, she told herself, seeing her reflection in the window, her shoulders scrunched around her ears like a protective shell. There's nothing to worry about. So why did she feel so anxious and on edge?

She decided a bit of reading might help her to unwind. There was bound to be something on the bookshelves she could get lost in for a little while. Aware of Nancy's aversion to her looking around the house, she crept like a ninja along the hall and into the dining room, which was directly below her sister's bedroom. She'd have to be quiet, given the sharpness of Nancy's hearing, although the storm would do a good job of masking any sound she might make.

She scanned the shelves, and after a few minutes she found a Lee Child thriller. That would do, she decided, not wanting to take too long in case she was accused of snooping again. She'd enjoyed a few of his books and was sure this was one she hadn't read.

Her ears strained for signs that Nancy was awake, but all was quiet upstairs, the storm still rumbling away outside. Her eyes travelled round the room and landed on the bureau on the other side of the chimney breast, the key in the lock. She bit her lip, telling herself she shouldn't look inside, but the need to know more about her mysterious sister was fighting her better instincts. It might be the only chance you get, the devil in her pointed out.

Her fingers twitched as she weighed up the risks. There might be something in there that would give her some clues about her sister's life, things she wouldn't volunteer to tell Eva herself. She stood in front of the bureau, noticing the initials *W & M* carved on the front, stretched her hand out and turned the key.

Carefully she lowered the drop-leaf top. There was an inset leather writing surface, dark green and blotched with ink. In front of her were a number of compartments, all stuffed with papers and envelopes. In the centre was a set of three drawers. She pulled the top one open to find chequebooks and paying-in books. She had a quick look. Mr W. Wyn Jones was the name of the account. That must be the Bill Nancy had talked about. She flicked through the stubs, saw that the last cheque written was dated only a couple of weeks previously. That was odd, given that Bill lived down south. But maybe he'd left her some signed cheques to pay for house maintenance or something. *Does it matter?* She stopped her train of thought, conscious that precious seconds were ticking away.

Quickly she put the chequebook back and opened the next drawer. It contained a wad of banknotes. Not British, but a mixture of currencies, all bundled together in an elastic band. There was also a wallet. Nancy's, she assumed, but when she looked, she found it belonged to Ryan Wilson, from New Zealand. His bank cards were in there along with his driver's licence. *How strange.* She wondered if Ryan had been one of the shearers and he'd left the wallet behind along with his sleeping bag and clothes. It seemed like a logical assumption. But who would leave their wallet? Each drawer seemed to present another mystery rather than answering questions.

She put everything back and opened the bottom drawer which was full of photos. They seemed to go back years, some of them black and white. Eva's heart leapt with joy. Old photos were her favourite sort of history. You could learn so much from one image when you studied the details – what people were wearing, things going on in the background, vehicles and buildings. Most of these had been taken round the farm, by the looks of things.

She stopped and listened, satisfying herself that Nancy was still asleep before she had a quick shuffle through the pile, flicking them over to see if anything was written on the back – something to give a clue as to the date they were taken and the people in the shots. One in particular caught her eye: a woman sitting on a pile of hay bales with a couple of young men. The woman had turned when the picture was taken, looking over her shoulder, so only the side of her face was visible. On the back it said: *Nancy, Ryan and Levi.*

'Eva! Eva, are you there?' Nancy called from upstairs.

Her heart leapt. She couldn't be caught in here. She slipped the photo in her back pocket to study later, putting everything else in the drawer and closing it as quietly as she could.

'Eva?' The sound of feet on the floorboards above.

Panic made her clumsy, and the bureau lid banged shut. *Christ! You idiot.* There was nothing she could do but hope Nancy hadn't heard it over the sound of the storm. She crept out of the room as quietly as she could, not answering until she was at the foot of the stairs.

'I'm here,' she called. And froze when she looked up to see Nancy staring down at her. *Did she see me come out of the front room?*

CHAPTER FIFTEEN

Sweat gathered under Eva's arms, her blush a telltale sign that she'd been up to no good. She cleared her throat, forced a smile. 'I was just going to check if you were awake.'

Nancy said nothing.

'Shall I bring you breakfast in bed? I've got some cereal if you fancy. And there's toast and jam. I can do a pot of tea. Or coffee, whichever you prefer.' She was gabbling and knew it, but couldn't stop herself. 'I'm afraid I can't cook anything yet, I haven't got the range working, but I'm going to have a go once we've eaten. Then I'll go and get the eggs and feed the—'

'Stop. Eva, please, just stop, will you?' Nancy's hand was clasped to her forehead. 'I need some painkillers, but my eyes won't focus. I don't know where I've put my glasses and I can't work out which packet of pills is which.'

'Oh, okay.' Eva felt limp with relief. She grabbed the banister and started up the stairs, eyes focused on each step lest Nancy should detect the guilt in her face. 'Let me sort that out for you first, then.'

She made herself smile when she got up to the landing and followed Nancy into the bedroom. Adrenaline was firing through her veins, making her hands clumsy as she fumbled the tablets out of the packet.

'What's wrong with you?' Nancy asked. 'You're shaking like a leaf.'

'Oh, it's… um… it's this storm. I've never been good with thunder and lightning. But this feels so… I don't know…' Eva pulled a face. 'Dangerous?' She jumped at another crack of thunder. 'It just feels like it's going to come through the roof.'

Nancy laughed, despite her headache. 'You are a funny little thing. How did you grow up to be such a wuss?' She held up a hand to stop Eva's reply. 'No, don't tell me. I already know. Being brought up by Linda, it seems like it was inevitable.'

Eva bristled. It wasn't fair, all this negativity about her mum. 'Linda's lovely, actually,' she said, all snippy. 'She's really kind and thoughtful and has always made time to do things with me. I don't know why you have to be so horrible about her.'

Nancy sighed then and lay back on the pillows, staring at the ceiling. 'I wish I'd had that from my mum,' she murmured. 'She just couldn't be arsed. Her career was way more important. She shipped me off to…' She stopped mid sentence. Blinked.

'Shipped you off to where?'

Nancy frowned and turned towards her. 'Sorry?'

'You were saying about Mum shipping you off. I just wondered where to.'

Nancy shrugged. 'Do you know, I haven't a clue what I was going to say.' She gave a feeble smile. 'I keep losing track of what I was thinking about. Most peculiar.' Her eyes met Eva's. 'Anyway, did you mention breakfast?'

Back downstairs, Eva filled the kettle and started to get their meal ready. Toast with some cheese, that was Nancy's request. She'd said there was a big block of Cheddar in the fridge, but Eva was damned if she could see it. The bread was another puzzle. She was sure she'd bought two loaves. They'd eaten most of one the night before but she couldn't find the second one, unable to remember where she might have put it.

Hands on hips, she gazed around the kitchen, as if the loaf might magically appear. A sudden thought made her heart flip. *Was I right about somebody stealing food?* It was the only conclusion that made any sense. She frowned, confused. *But how did they get in?*

Deep in thought, she poured two bowls of cereal – the only remaining option – and made the tea while her mind processed the latest puzzle. Then picked up the tray and hurried upstairs.

'I'm sorry, Nancy, but this is all there is. The cheese has disappeared. And the bread. It's like the quiche last night.' She stared at her sister, looking for signs that she might know what was going on.

Nancy's eyes widened, just for a second, before she frowned. 'What on earth are you talking about?'

'Food has disappeared from the kitchen. How do you think that's happened?'

While she waited for Nancy to answer, Eva put the tray on the bed and sat down. She picked up her bowl and began to shovel cereal into her mouth, hunger gnawing at her insides. But her sister didn't reply; just sat looking at her breakfast, making no effort to eat it.

When Eva had finished, she decided she needed to push Nancy a little harder to get answers. 'Somebody has been in the house and stolen the food and I think you know who it is, don't you? That's why you came down last night.'

Nancy started eating, indicating that she couldn't answer because her mouth was full.

Eva's jaw tightened. 'Okay, well, I'm not going to play games. This is what I think. I think you did have shearers here. And I think you had a falling-out and that's how you got injured. Now one of them is out there, probably sleeping in the barn or something, waiting to get his belongings back and sneaking inside to steal food.'

'You have a very vivid imagination,' Nancy said, between mouthfuls.

'I've seen—' Eva stopped herself just before she said 'the wallet'.

Nancy frowned, a curious glint in her eye. 'You've seen what?'

'Well, there's the sleeping bag in the back room. The room you've now locked. Just like the middle bedroom.' Eva gazed at her, determined not to be intimidated. 'Why be so secretive? What are you hiding?'

'You have a very suspicious mind, Eva. Why would I be hiding anything? I'm just used to having privacy.' Nancy's expression had grown as thunderous as the weather. 'And guests respecting it.'

Eva picked up her tea, knowing she'd reached stalemate again. 'Well, I've no idea where the food's going,' she snapped. 'Maybe you have some giant rodents who can open the fridge and help themselves?'

'Now you're being childish.'

'And you're being bloody awkward.'

Nancy glared at her, then her shoulders started to shake and she burst out laughing. 'I always wondered what it would be like to have a sister.' Her whole body was shaking now. 'It's bloody awful, isn't it? So much bickering.'

Eva couldn't stop herself from laughing too, recognising the behaviour she'd witnessed in her friends and their siblings. Somehow that made her feel better.

Nancy picked up her tea and took a sip.

Eva watched her, suddenly serious. 'Why did you never think of coming home?'

Her sister sighed. 'I didn't go home because my parents didn't love or care about me. That was the truth of it. I decided I was better off on my own.' She shrugged a shoulder. 'And I have been.'

It was hard for Eva to hear such detachment. Her love for her father was without question. How could Nancy ever imagine that he didn't care?

'Why did you have Dad's contact details then? Mum said they moved when I was a baby. You would have had to do quite a bit of research to find out their new address and phone number.'

Nancy gazed out of the window. Eva thought she was going to refuse to answer yet another question when she started to speak. 'When you get to forty, I suppose it's a time to stop and pause and consider your life. Decide whether you want to go back and pick up some of the pieces you dropped along the way.'

Was that all her family were to her? 'And did you decide you wanted to pick up some pieces?'

Nancy finished her tea and put her mug back on the tray. 'I decided not to but the hospital got confused about what I wanted and decided to make me pick them up anyway.'

Her stare was so intense, Eva had to look away. That was her told, wasn't it? She'd thought they might be bonding but every time she felt she was getting closer to her sister Nancy shut her out again.

CHAPTER SIXTEEN

Eva cleared up their breakfast things, sorted out Nancy's medication and left her to have a rest. She put the tray on the drainer, her feet crunching on bits of glass from the screen of her phone. The loss of her only means of communication with her mum left her feeling bereft and very alone. She was also worrying about her dad. It had obviously upset his routine now that she wasn't at home, and he could be very hard to handle when he got upset. She felt torn. Where should she be? At home helping her mum look after her dad, or here looking after a sister she barely knew?

In truth, the adventure she'd embarked upon had lost its appeal. The house was beginning to feel hostile rather than welcoming. She no longer cared about its history, or Nancy's secrets. *Haven't I learnt more than enough?* Her sister had made it clear she didn't want anything to do with her family and Eva had an inkling she was only letting her stay because she needed her. Once she was well enough to cope on her own, she'd want her gone. Did she want to experience the humiliation of being told she had to leave?

As she washed the breakfast dishes, she made a decision.

I'm going. Mum needs me. I'm sure that by tomorrow Nancy will be able to cope on her own. And if she wasn't, then she'd ring the hospital and give the problem back to them.

She felt better for having a definite timescale and wanted to let Linda know that she wouldn't have to cope on her own much longer. If she couldn't be there in person, she really wanted to give her mum that crumb of comfort.

Nancy must have a phone. She thought for a moment. *In her handbag?* Which was still in the car. She hadn't brought it in; she was sure of it, could visualise it tucked under the passenger seat out of the way. *I could use that to make a call.* Hopefully it would be an old model and wouldn't have a PIN number or need unlocking. It was worth a try.

The storm had passed now, the rain still falling but no longer torrential.

She unlocked the front door and ran to the car, sliding into the driver's seat and slamming the door behind her. Her hand fumbled under the passenger seat and she pulled out Nancy's bag. She hesitated for a moment, knowing it was wrong to rummage in someone else's personal things. But this was an emergency. Exceptional circumstances.

She delved in and her heart skipped with joy when her hand settled on an oblong of cold metal. She pulled it out, tried to turn it on, but nothing happened. *Dammit.* It needed charging. She pulled in a deep breath. No matter. Her charger had loads of different attachments and she was sure that one of them would fit. She'd just have to sneak the phone up to her bedroom without Nancy noticing. She tucked it in her back pocket.

Now that Nancy's bag was open on her lap, she had a terrible urge to see what else was in there, to give her some clues about her sister. She hesitated, knowing she really shouldn't invade her sister's privacy, but there was a lot Nancy wasn't telling her. Things that Eva had a right to know.

The bag was well worn, made of leather and quite small. She looked inside. A packet of tissues, a purse containing some coins, a compact umbrella and a notebook. She pulled out the notebook and opened it up. On the first page was Nancy's name and underneath was her father's name, address and phone number. So that was how the hospital had found their contact details. It made sense now. They had the same surname, so there was an obvious connection.

As she flicked through the pages, she realised this was Nancy's research – the names and numbers of organisations that helped people to track their families, scribbled notes from conversations. A loose piece of paper dropped onto her lap and slid to the floor. She bent to pick it up and realised it was a photograph. She recognised her dad and her birth mother, an older version than she was used to looking at, but definitely the same people. Standing between them was a child of about ten. She had ginger hair and looked just like their mum… and nothing like the woman upstairs.

She dipped into her back pocket and pulled out the photo she'd found in the bureau. The one with Nancy's name written on the back. She hadn't had time to look at it before but from the profile she could see that the young woman in the picture was an older version of the child. There really was no doubting it.

She glanced up at the house and saw a face at the bedroom window. The woman was looking at her. The woman who wasn't her sister.

CHAPTER SEVENTEEN

She can't see me, Eva reassured herself, even though the woman appeared to be looking directly at her. She doesn't know that I know she's a fraud. Her heart was racing and her thoughts with it. *Where's the real Nancy?* The photos showed that her sister had definitely been here. But when? Was it recent, or were these pictures taken years ago?

She studied the picture again, flipped it over, something niggling in her brain. *Ryan.* That was it. The wallet in the bureau belonged to Ryan Wilson. She studied his face and thought it could be the same as the one on the driver's licence. She took another look but couldn't decide how old her sister might be to any degree of accuracy. Could that back room, with the sleeping bag and possessions, have lain untouched for years?

All the unanswered questions were making her head hurt.

'It's not my problem,' she muttered to herself. 'None of it. It really isn't.'

Her car keys were in her lap. *Shall I just go?* Her hand closed round the cold metal, and before she knew what she was doing, the key was in the ignition and she was reaching for her seat belt. Her instinct was to run away, return to the normality of home – yes, it would be difficult to face up to her father's illness, but it would be better than being here with this strange woman, however much she might need looking after.

Before she could start the engine, though, she remembered that her clothes were still in the bedroom, along with her handbag, money, ID – everything was up there. There was no way she could leave without it, as the car wouldn't get home on the fuel she had left in the tank. She gritted her teeth and thumped the steering wheel in frustration. She'd have to go back and get everything.

It won't take long. In and out. No need to speak to her.

Nervously she glanced at the window again but the figure had disappeared. Hopefully she'd gone back to bed and Eva could grab her stuff and get away without having to face her.

Come on, time to be brave. She stuffed everything into the handbag and put it back under the front seat, then grabbed a raincoat from the floor behind her. She'd pretend that was why she was out in the car if the woman challenged her.

When she climbed out and shrugged on her coat, she noticed that the rain had finally stopped. The trees dripped, the air still but fresh, washed clean by the storm. A gap in the trees at the front of the house gave her a wonderful vista over the valley and the mountain ridge beyond. It was a very picturesque setting, but so isolated you could probably do whatever you wanted here and nobody would be any the wiser. She'd noticed that even the postman didn't come up to the house, instead leaving mail in a box at the entrance to the track.

She turned and studied the house, marvelling at the way her thinking had changed, from being excited about the setting and the history of the place to being scared of what might have happened here. And what might yet happen. However much she told herself to stop letting her imagination twist reality, that sense of foreboding still weighed heavy on the back of her neck. She'd had it when she was a postie: certain houses she didn't like to go near, something about them that made her pulse quicken.

Running away again? her inner critic chided as she walked towards the door. What about your sister? Don't you want to know what happened to her? Of course she did. She was desperate to know. In fact, she was worried for her, but she also didn't want to stay here a minute longer than she had to.

A raucous squawking startled her out of her thoughts; she remembered the chickens in the barn. They hadn't been fed for days, the woman had said. She bit her lip, wondering what to do. *They'll be fine.* But she couldn't think of leaving them to starve. *Like you're going to leave that woman to starve? She can't look after herself yet, can she?*

She stopped and closed her eyes. 'Bloody hell,' she muttered to herself as she clenched her fists and stomped round the side of the house towards the barn. 'Nothing's simple, is it?' She'd feed the chickens. Then she'd call the hospital and get them to come and fetch the woman. Yes. That was exactly what she'd do. Then she could go home with a clear conscience.

Or would she? Surely she had to find out where Nancy was before she left. Make sure she was safe and well.

More than anything, she wanted to talk to her mum. But Eva's phone was broken and the woman's phone was dead. Should she wait here long enough for it to charge, then tell Linda what was going on?

Mum's got enough on her plate, said the voice of reason. It wouldn't be fair to drag her into this. Linda was the sort of person who absorbed other people's problems, always putting herself out to help, often at her own expense. Looking after her husband was worry enough without burdening her with whatever was going on here.

You're a big girl now. Eva gave an emphatic nod. *That woman's not well, she's no threat.* Her pep talk didn't make her feel any less nervous as she rounded the corner and strode across the yard to the barn.

It was as big as the house, built of stone, with a corrugated-metal roof. Inside she could see an ancient red tractor and a number of implements used for goodness knew what. The walls were hung with more tools that obviously had a specific purpose. Many were rusted and looked as though they hadn't been used for a long time.

Her eyes tracked up the walls to a mezzanine floor, which stretched across half the length of the barn, with a broad wooden ladder for access. *A good place to hide.* Her skin prickled and she wondered whether it was wise to go any further.

Just leave. Ring the RSPCA about the chickens. Come on, get out of here.

A fresh burst of angry squawking broke out, leading her to a dark corner under the loft which had been fenced to provide a secure run for the chickens. A black plastic bin stood by the access door; she lifted the lid and found it was full of grain. When they saw her, the birds crowded by the door, anticipating a meal. Not wanting to let them out by mistake, she got a scoop full of grain and flung it through the wire mesh, watching as it scattered over the floor, the hens darting this way and that in a chorus of clucking as they hurried around pecking it up.

She observed them for a moment, relieved that she'd been able to at least stop them from starving to death and wouldn't have that on her conscience.

The feeling that she was being watched sent a sudden chill down her spine. She spun round, squinting in the gloom. 'Who's there?' she called. Then realised that might not have been the wisest thing to do. Not if the person hiding was the one who'd attacked the woman in the house. If she *had* been attacked. Nothing was certain anymore now that Eva knew she was a fraud.

She looked around for a weapon, something that would make her feel brave. A shovel was propped against the wall next to her, probably used for cleaning out the chickens. With her heart pounding, she picked it up, satisfied with the heft of it in her hands, the wooden handle polished from years of use.

Nervously she scanned the massive interior of the barn. So many dark nooks and crannies, someone could be in here and she wouldn't know. A noise above her head made her look up. She willed the chickens to be quiet so she could hear properly but they carried on with their excited clucking, scraping and scratching at the floor. Was that a patter of feet up there? She froze, listening.

An animal, not a person, you idiot.

Adrenaline was firing round her body, all her senses on high alert. Her eyes travelled up the ladder. There was no way she was going to look up there. A sudden noise made her head flick round: something clattering on the floor. She swallowed a squeak of fear.

Despite all her instincts telling her to run, she stalked round the tractor to the farthest corner of the building, where the sound had come from. Another clank, and two cats came dashing out, one chasing the other, brushing past her legs and startling her so much she screamed and dropped the shovel. It landed with an almighty clang, leaving her ears ringing, while her eyes scanned the barn for movement, signs that someone else was there. All she could hear was the mewling of the cats, who were now having a stand-off out in the yard and looked like they were squaring up for a fight.

Her heart was racing so fast she felt light-headed, her eyes skimming the jumble of farm equipment in front of her trying to detect movement. *Stop being such a wimp! You're getting this way out of proportion.*

She ran her hands over her face as if washing away her fears, while going over everything she knew. Nancy must have spoken to the woman about her past because she'd told Eva things that only her sister would know. Had they been friends? She felt they must have been for her to know so much detail about their family.

She sighed, conflicted about what to do next. Really, she was in a position of power, with the woman still being weak and dependent on her. *Surely I can make her tell the truth about Nancy in exchange for me staying to look after her. Unless the truth is so ugly...*

Deep in thought, she bent to pick up the shovel, and noticed for the first time a dark stain on the blade. A dark red stain, the colour of dried blood. And was that hair stuck to it? Her hands drew back to her body as though the shovel had a magnetic force field round it, repelling her. She turned and ran. Out of the barn, away from the house and her car, where the woman might see her, unable to think about retrieving her possessions until she'd had time to process what she'd just seen.

Whose blood was it? Was it the woman's? Was that what she was attacked with? Or did it belong to somebody else?

CHAPTER EIGHTEEN

There was a kissing gate next to the track leading out of the yard. She pushed through it and into a kitchen garden that ran away from the side of the house along the hillside. It was lined with vegetable plots to her right, then fruit bushes in neat rows in the middle and an orchard beyond. Here she was hidden from prying eyes, as there were no windows on the gable end of the house. She saw a wooden bench in the middle of the garden, at the end of the fruit bushes, and headed over to it, her legs shaky with the shock of her latest discovery.

Rain had pooled on the wooden slats. She brushed it away with her hand, then took off her raincoat and spread it over the seat to sit on. Her elbows rested on her knees, her head hung between her shoulders, chest heaving while she tried to calm herself down.

Gradually her heart rate slowed to something approaching normal. It was peaceful here in the garden, and she straightened up, looked around. It appeared to be well tended, the fruit bushes hung with blossom and the trees dotted with newly formed apples. Behind her, a thick hawthorn hedge had been planted to protect the area from the wind funnelling up from the valley below. She noticed a patch of earth near the bench that had obviously been recently disturbed. Maybe a new bed was being dug, or more trees were about to be planted.

She leant back, forgetting that the bench was still wet, her coat only big enough to cover the seat. The dampness leached through her shirt, cold fingers touching her back. She jumped up, pulling the cloth away from her body. *Can't I get anything right today?*

She stomped off round the garden while she mulled over her choices, noticing a bed of courgettes and butternut squash. There was spinach too, a patch of herbs, and tripods holding up runner beans. It was a productive area and she supposed, with the right menu plan, you could probably be self-sufficient for much of the time. Not that the woman looked like she thrived on whatever she was eating; in fact it was more the opposite.

Maybe she's ill. Perhaps that was the problem. Maybe she hadn't been attacked at all and that was just an assumption made by the paramedics. Eva had seen how bad her balance was, how weak she appeared. Perhaps she'd fallen while she was dealing with the chickens and hit her head on the shovel? That could have happened.

Now that she'd found a new line of thought, it all seemed very plausible. Perhaps the cats had been to blame, getting under the woman's feet. There were numerous possibilities when it came to accidents on a farm, especially if you weren't functioning properly and feeling fragile. Hadn't the woman always insisted it was an accident?

Eva thought she'd reached a logical conclusion.

The only thing spoiling it was the fact that the woman had things that belonged to Nancy in her handbag and had pretended to be Eva's sister. Or was that another assumption, this time on Eva's part? Had she just gone along with the mistake the hospital had made because at the end of the day she really did need someone to look after her for a little while and Eva would do? Perhaps she had no formal ID of her own. Not everyone had a bank account or credit cards, did they? Because now that Eva considered it, there'd been no ID in the handbag at all. Just the notebook.

Maybe the woman was planning on telling her the truth when she was feeling better and able to look after herself. Then she'd say it was all a big mistake and send Eva on her way.

If that was the case, perhaps she was catastrophising and things weren't as bad as her panicked mind was making her believe.

What about Ryan Wilson, the shearer, and his wallet, though? You wouldn't leave that behind, would you?

Potentially two missing people. That can't be coincidence.

She wandered past the fruit bushes and through the orchard. Could she really leave without knowing where her sister was? The answer to that was no, because there were things the woman had said that'd made her view her parents, and her past, in a different light. She needed to speak to Nancy – the real Nancy – to find out what was true, and the only person who might be able to help with that was the woman inside the house. Perhaps Nancy did live here but was away for a few days. Perhaps she and Ryan weren't missing at all but off on a bit of a holiday together. That was a definite possibility.

The more she thought about it, the more she was able to rationalise the woman's actions and make herself believe the situation was perfectly benign.

After she'd weighed everything up, she decided on a new plan. First thing was to charge the phone, then she could call for help should the need arise. Then she would confront the woman about her lie and see how she responded. If she got a sensible explanation as to where her sister was – and why the woman had allowed the hospital to assume that she was Nancy – all well and good. If she didn't, Eva would grab her things and leave, and when she was a safe distance away, she'd call the police and leave the problem with them. Whichever way it panned out she would have done her bit.

Satisfied that she'd be able to go with a clear conscience, whatever the outcome, she headed back to the bench to pick up her coat. On the way, something in the patch of disturbed earth caught her eye. She bent to have a look. A piece of clothing. She pulled at it, but it wouldn't come out of the soil, as if there was a heavy weight on the end of it. She scanned the bed, looking for clues as to what she might have hold of. Poking out of the soil further down was something she recognised as the tip of a boot. And attached to it was something pale and long. A bone?

Oh my God, it's a body!

She let go of the cloth, backing away, her hands to her mouth as she gulped down the bile that shot up her throat. *Is that Nancy?*

Now she knew she had to leave. *Grab your stuff and go.*

CHAPTER NINETEEN

Eva snatched up her coat from the bench and ran back to the house. As she burst through the front door, the woman appeared in the entrance to the dining room, the mere sight of her making Eva's heart miss a beat. But she didn't stop, just swerved around her and dashed up the stairs to her bedroom, closing the door behind her. No time to charge the phone, she decided, abandoning her plan. *Just get the hell out of here.*

She flung open the drawers and stuffed her clothes into her bag, then collected up the bits and pieces from around the room and squashed them in on top.

'Eva?' The woman's voice drifted up the stairs. The steady thump of footsteps drew closer. 'Eva, what are you doing?'

'I won't be a minute,' Eva called, her heart feeling like it might burst out of her chest. 'I just got wet out there and need to change my shirt.'

The plod of footsteps continued up the stairs.

'Where've you been? I saw you in the car and for a moment I thought you might be leaving me here on my own.' Her voice had a tremble to it; Eva could feel herself being swayed, her compassion voicing concerns about abandoning this frail woman. *Perhaps you've jumped to the wrong conclusion?* Could she really leave her to fend for herself?

She stopped what she was doing for a moment, wondered if she was being rash, then told herself not to be so bloody ridiculous.

Something was buried in the garden! That was not normal. That was freaking wrong on so many levels.

'I remembered you said the chickens needed feeding,' she called, feeling quite breathless as she struggled to zip up her bag. 'So I went to do that. But I had to go and get my coat out of the car first.'

'You've been in the study, haven't you? In the bureau. Meddling with my things again.' Her voice was sharp, getting closer.

'No, no, you've got that wrong. I only went in there to get a book to read.' Eva managed to zip up her bag and glanced round the room to make sure she'd got everything.

'The bureau was unlocked.' The woman was right outside the door now. 'It's never unlocked.'

Dammit. How did I forget to lock it again? Then she remembered she'd been disturbed and had been in a rush to put everything back as she'd found it.

The door swung open and Eva spun round, her cheeks burning, heart thundering in her chest. The woman clutched the door frame, her jaw set, eyes sparking with anger. Her hand was still clasping the door handle, her body blocking Eva's exit.

'Look, I'm really sorry,' Eva gabbled, looking past her to the landing and her escape route, 'but I'm going to have to leave. Dad's taken a turn for the worse and I've got to get back.' She tried to look apologetic, but her face was not cooperating, fear baring her teeth in a rictus grin.

'And how would you know that?' the woman said, her words coated with a thick layer of disbelief. 'You broke your phone. There's still bits of it on the kitchen floor.'

Eva cursed. She'd never been great at lying and under pressure she was lousy at it. Now she'd been completely caught out.

Be brave. Look, she's frail as anything. Tough it out.

Hooking her handbag over her shoulder, she picked up her bag. 'I really need to go. It was wrong of me to leave my mum with Dad so poorly.' She gave the woman another attempt at a smile, trying to keep her voice calm, as if everything was normal. 'You seem a lot better today. I'm sure you'll manage, and you'll be happier here on your own, won't you?' The woman just stared at her. Eva took a step forward to make her intention clear. 'Please, I'd just like to get past.'

'I'm sure you would,' the woman said, still blocking the doorway.

Eva's pulse whooshed in her ears. She didn't want to hurt the woman but it looked like she'd have to push her out of the way. *She's a murderer.* The thought broke into her mind, waking her up to reality. *She could have killed my sister.*

'I know you're not Nancy.' Her breath hitched in her throat. *No, no, no, no! Why the hell did I say that?* For a moment she was paralysed by her own stupidity.

The woman's eyes widened and before Eva could think to take her chance and push past her, the door slammed shut. She heard an ominous click. A key turning in the lock.

'No! You can't lock me in.' She tugged at the handle, but the door rattled in its frame, staying firmly shut.

'I just did,' the woman said, a note of satisfaction in her voice.

Eva banged on the wood, desperate to keep the woman's attention, so she could at least try and negotiate a way out. 'Look, I'm sorry if you think I've been prying, but I wanted to know about my sister.'

'It didn't have to be like this,' the woman hissed. 'You're just too nosy for your own good. If you'd kept out of my business, we could have managed fine for a few days. Then you could have been on your way.' She tutted. 'Obviously that can't happen now.'

Eva listened to her footsteps walk away, wondering how she was ever going to get back home.

PART TWO

Then: Nancy

CHAPTER TWENTY

Nancy dried her tears. She'd done so much crying in the three days since her mum had died, she wondered how there were any tears left. She was alone in the house; her dad and their neighbour, Linda, had gone up to the hospital to collect the baby and bring her back home.

She hated her squalling sister and the way her dad had cooed over her at the hospital. And it was all they'd talked about when they'd arrived home the previous evening. Her mum had died, for God's sake. Was nobody going to talk about that? It was like Nancy had become invisible and her mum had never existed. All that seemed to matter was the bloody baby and how they'd look after her. Didn't they understand that Nancy needed a bit of love and affection too? Some comfort? Her mum hadn't been the cuddliest and most demonstrative of people, but Nancy knew she'd loved her. Now she didn't feel loved at all and she hated how, in an instant, her life had changed.

She also hated Linda.

It was despicable how fast they'd decided she should move in. Did they really think she wasn't aware that they slept together? Of course she knew. Well, they were welcome to each other.

She took her reddest lipstick and wrote 'I hate my life' on her mirror. Then she wriggled the bag out from behind the wardrobe. The one with a couple of changes of clothes in it that she'd packed earlier. Not much, but enough to get her started. She'd hoped to leave in the middle of the night, when nobody would see her, but now that the baby was coming home and Linda would be up doing night feeds, that wasn't going to work. Anyway, she'd come up with a plan.

It was twilight now. Soon it would be dark and she'd be able to hide more easily. The beginning of March was not a great time to be sleeping rough, but she had thermals and a thick jacket, gloves and scarf, so she was prepared. She couldn't stay in the house any longer, feeling like a spare part, like it was wrong somehow to grieve for her mother.

Her dad had been pretty useless as parents went. He'd not said a word about her mum's death. Not a word except, 'We've got to think about the future.' How could she think about the future when there was so much she didn't understand about the past? Like what the hell had happened to her mum anyway.

The day it happened, Nancy had left for school as usual, her mum in her dressing gown, her huge belly poking out. It was actually quite gross to have a mum who was pregnant at her age. Some of her friends had grandmas who were younger, for God's sake. It made her cringe and had made life at school too embarrassing to endure. So she'd been bunking off. Nobody had really cared.

They'd been planning a new life, her and Mum. Once her dad had been found out and he'd finally come clean about his relationship with that schoolgirl, her mum had decided she'd had enough. Well, she'd been a schoolgirl when he'd first met her, but it seems the affair had been going on for years. This baby was a glue baby. It would never work but her parents were pretending it was exactly what was needed to mend their broken marriage. Yeah, good luck with that, Nancy had thought at the time. Honestly, adults were so deluded sometimes.

Anyway, later that day, Linda had come and picked her up from her friend's house, saying her mum was in hospital and her dad had gone with her. She needed to come straight away. At first she hadn't understood, said she'd see the baby when they came home. But of course that wasn't the problem. Her mum had a broken neck and internal injuries. She was in ICU.

Nancy had been there when she died, holding her hand, her dad holding the other one. The machine started beeping, all hell broke loose and Nancy was ushered out of the room while they whipped the baby out. It had been horrendous, shocking, and she was still struggling to believe it was real.

The anger had built inside her until it was an impossible rage, robbing her of sleep as she replayed those last moments with her mum. It wasn't fair that she was gone and her baby lived and now ruled her dad's heart. It wasn't fair that Linda was about to move in and was trying to take her mum's place. She hated them all with a ferocity that scoured her thoughts until all she could think of was how to get away from them.

Faking her own death was her best bet, she'd decided. She could turn her back on this life and start again. Reinvent herself.

It was time to go. She let herself out of the back door, climbed over the fence and made her way down the alleyway. She was wearing a commando outfit with a baseball cap – something she would normally not be seen dead in, except at the fancy-dress party it had been bought for. In her hand was a plastic bag containing the outfit she'd been wearing when her dad and Linda left for the hospital. The promenade was quiet this time on a Tuesday evening, and she managed to cross without anyone seeing her. She laid out her clothes under the pier and slipped a suicide note on top, weighed down with a large stone. Then, checking there was nobody around, she made her escape.

The only problem was money – she didn't have any – but she hitched rides, pretending she was in the Territorial Army and had been on manoeuvres and was trying to get home.

'Where's home?' asked a woman who'd picked her up at the service station on the M6 where she'd spent a restless night.

'North Wales,' she replied, because it was where they'd last been on holiday and been happy as a family.

'How funny, I'm heading for Caernarfon. Will that do?'

'Perfect,' she said, with a smile, hoping the woman wouldn't notice that her purse was missing until after she'd dropped her off.

She bought herself some food with the cash from the purse and there was enough to buy a new outfit too. Clothes her dad didn't know she possessed so wouldn't come up in any description of her if anyone was looking. Then she went into the public toilets and got changed, putting her commando outfit in the shopping bag her clothes had been in and stuffing it in her backpack. Now she felt more relaxed, sure she wouldn't be recognised. With her long hair hidden in a woolly hat, and dressed in skinny jeans, trainers and a red jacket, she looked completely different.

Fortunately she didn't have to wait long for a lift out of town. Not more than fifteen minutes after she'd decided on where she'd stand to hitch, a battered Land Rover pulled over. The driver was a young woman with bouncy brown hair and laughter in her eyes. She was wearing a colourful knitted sweater, which was bright enough on its own to make you want to smile. Nancy had promised herself she'd only get in vehicles with women drivers and she'd been sure this would turn out to be a man. What a relief to discover she'd been wrong.

'Where are you heading?' the woman asked. 'I'm going through Beddgelert if that's any good to you?'

'Perfect,' Nancy replied. She didn't have a clue where Beddgelert was but didn't care; she just wanted to get out of Caernarfon before the woman whose purse she'd stolen called the police on her. She'd sleep in an outbuilding, a barn, even the public toilets if she had to. It'll be fine for one night, she told herself, sure she could find somewhere dry.

'I'm Judy,' the woman said as Nancy climbed in. 'Everyone calls me Jude.'

'Nancy,' she said, immediately regretting giving her real name. Would it have been on the news that she was missing, or would they have gone with the suicide? She really had no idea. Nerves tugged at her stomach. Perhaps this hadn't been such a great idea after all.

'That's a lovely jacket,' the woman said. 'It really suits you.'

'Thank you,' Nancy said, caught unawares by the compliment, a blush warming her cheeks.

'Have you come far?'

'Um… yeah. Just having a bit of time out.' She rubbed her nose, thinking she needed to work on her backstory, get the lies lined up so she wouldn't be caught out like this again.

'Oh, we all need that, don't we?' Judy laughed, a lovely carefree sound that made Nancy smile and lightened her mood a little. 'You can't beat a bit of an adventure.' She glanced at Nancy, caught her eye. 'And I really admire a girl who's willing to strike out on her own. Good on ya.'

She swung the car round a roundabout and the mountains loomed up in front of them, majestic in the chill spring air, snow still dusting the tops. Nancy's chest tightened, a pinch of panic catching her breath. It looked cold out there. Too cold to be sleeping outside.

A song came on the radio and Judy turned it up, started to sing along. 'I love this one,' she said. Her voice was clear and true, and after a minute Nancy joined in. When the song finished, they both started laughing. After that, the conversation flowed, just chatter about pop songs and bands they liked. Judy had lots of snappy one-liners and Nancy found she was enjoying herself, her troubles lost in the conversation. How wonderful it felt to be able to forget for a little while.

'Nearly there,' Judy said, and Nancy fell silent, looking out of the window at the cold greyness of the sky, the bare trees, the starkness of the scenery. Beautiful, yes, but definitely inhospitable.

'I could do with someone like you to give me a hand,' Judy said. 'I know this is a long shot, but I don't suppose you fancy a few days helping me get ready for lambing, do you? My assistant got appendicitis and had to go back home and now I haven't anyone lined up, so I'll have to cope on my own.'

Nancy almost wept with relief as she nodded, managing a strangled 'yes'. Obviously she knew nothing about sheep, or lambing, or what she might have to do, but she didn't care. At this moment in time, she'd be happy to clean toilets all day if it meant she had food and somewhere to stay. Lambing sounded exciting, wonderful even, and she instinctively liked Judy. A few days of work would give her some breathing space to decide on a longer-term plan.

As they travelled along increasingly narrow roads and the scenery grew more dramatic, Nancy knew, because everything had fallen into place so easily, that leaving home had been the right thing to do. She couldn't rely on her dad to look after her, not with Linda and the baby on the scene. But she was more or less an adult now and it was time to make her own way in the world. Good on ya, she thought to herself.

She had a strong sense that her mum was guiding her, making sure she was safe until she found somewhere new to call home. Mum didn't want to stay with Dad, she kept reminding herself. And neither did Nancy. She'd loved him once, but his cheating had shaken her confidence in him, and since her mum had died, she hated him with a fury that she hadn't known existed. If her mum hadn't been pregnant, she wouldn't have been decorating the nursery, wouldn't have had the accident and wouldn't have died.

It's all Dad's fault.

Now he was completely absorbed with the guilt child he'd created, and the awful Linda was there all the time. Yeah, well here's another dollop of guilt, she thought as she watched the magnificent scenery of Snowdonia unfold around her. If he won't take responsibility for his wife's death, let him take some for his daughter's.

CHAPTER TWENTY-ONE

The journey to the farm was exciting, the surroundings so different from the flat suburbs of Blackpool where she'd grown up. Nancy was enthralled. How wonderful to be able to stay here and work for a bit while the fuss about her suicide died down. It would feel like a holiday. As they drove up the winding track into the woods, it was like being in a fairy tale. She'd never imagined it would be so easy to escape her old life and find a safe place to stay. *Who's going to find me here?*

'How come you're not at school?' Judy asked with a smile when she'd made them hot chocolate. They were sitting in the warmth of the kitchen, in two chairs drawn up on either side of the old range. 'Or are you one of those twenty-five-year-olds who looks sixteen?'

Nancy tensed. 'I've left school,' she said, before blowing on her drink, her eyes focused on the ripples that her breath had made rather than the woman sitting opposite.

Judy studied her for a moment. 'You know, I ran away from home when I was your age.' She pulled a face. 'Honestly, it was so scary but it turned out to be the best thing I ever did.' She laughed. 'I was picked up when I was hitching, just like you. And I ended up here. Such a lovely old couple.' Her smile wavered and she blinked a couple of times. 'They were like the parents I should have had.' She flicked some specks of fluff from her jeans. 'More like family than my own useless parents ever were.'

Nancy's eyes widened, Judy's words resonating deep inside. Here was someone like her, someone who might understand. *Could I tell her the truth?*

'My parents didn't have time for me,' Judy continued. She gave a dismissive huff. 'To be honest, I was like a pet rather than a daughter.'

Nancy felt the pull of a kindred spirit, her tension easing, words tumbling out of her. 'Oh, I know exactly what you mean. My dad prefers his climbing mates to me. And our neighbour. And my mum just died and it's like I'm invisible.' She swallowed a rush of emotion. 'They've got a new pet to play with now they've got my baby sister.'

'Oh my God, Nancy. I'm so sorry to hear about your mum.' Judy's face filled with concern. 'No wonder you need some time out. But I understand what you're going through. My parents died not long after I left home.' She caught Nancy's eye. 'I like to think it was karma.'

In that moment, a connection was made. It was okay to hate your parents. Never had Nancy been able to voice her real feelings to anyone, but here was a stranger who'd been through the exact same thing. She felt an exquisite release that made her a little breathless. She'd thought she was a bad person, having all these negative emotions swirling inside her. But maybe she wasn't. Maybe it was her father who was bad.

Karma. That's what brought me here.

It was the universe helping her to make the right decisions. *With a bit of help from Mum.* There was no need to feel guilty about running away and making them think she was dead. And didn't her dad deserve to suffer for the way he'd behaved? Appearing to forget that his elder daughter even existed at a time when she'd never needed him more in her life.

Karma.

For the first time since she'd left home, Nancy felt safe.

The few days became a couple of weeks, and Nancy found herself settling in to life on the farm. She'd had to abandon her new clothes in favour of the jeans, baggy sweatshirts and fleece jackets that Judy lent her. The clothes she'd brought with her weren't robust enough for farm work, and she wanted to keep her new jeans and trainers clean for when she had to move on. Unlikely as it seemed, she was happy to reinvent herself as a farmhand. Why not? It wasn't for ever, just a bit of an adventure until she'd worked out what she really wanted to do.

She discovered that she enjoyed looking after the animals. Her parents hadn't wanted pets, neither of them being dog or cat people. Even a guinea pig or a hamster had been deemed too much trouble. But Judy had two dogs, Sky and Bella, and there were three farm cats who lived outside to keep vermin at bay. Not to mention the flock of sheep, a herd of black cattle, a handful of pigs and a dozen chickens. To Nancy, it seemed like she'd been beamed into a different world, so far from the life she knew. She was kept busy, her mind engaged in learning new skills, desperate to please and prove her worth.

For a time, while her anger and resentment still burned strong, it was easy to forget what she'd left behind. Why would she miss being unloved and ignored? Anyway, the person she'd loved most, her mum, was still with her in her heart. She could feel it. And she had a new friend in Judy who was fun to be around, always singing and making Nancy laugh.

'You're such a fast learner,' she said to her when she'd taught her how to spot which sheep were about to go into labour. 'You'll be a fantastic shepherdess.' She had hugged her then. 'We're the dream team, Nan. You and me. I'm so glad I picked you up that day. Honestly, it was fate, wasn't it?'

Nancy grinned and hugged her back, delighted to receive such glowing praise. At last she'd found not only something she was good at, but a friend who thought she was the bee's knees. That had never happened before. At school, she'd always been the one tagging along, rather than being sought after. A surge of happiness filled her heart, chasing away her anger and grief.

Perhaps I'll stay a bit longer, she decided. After all, where on earth would she be rushing off to? She had no money and knew it would be hard to get a job. Here, she didn't need money; she was fed and clothed and had a lovely cosy room. Plus she got to hang out with Judy, who treated her like an equal. A grown-up. Being around Judy was like having an older sister, someone to guide her and help her through the hard times. Someone who always had her back.

It wasn't long before Nancy had been handed tasks that were hers alone to complete. She liked being trusted to do her part, a proper worker. At twenty-six, Judy was young to be running a place like this and after a couple of weeks Nancy felt confident enough to ask the question that had been puzzling her.

'How come you're here on your own? What happened to the couple who took you in?'

They were in the field closest to the house, checking the boundary fences, ready for lambing. Judy stopped what she was doing and straightened up, wiping her hands on her jeans before she answered.

'Marj died. She had ovarian cancer. I nursed her at home for a bit, but it took her so quickly. She wasn't the sort to complain, you see. Took pain in her stride, but that's not always a good thing. Not if it's a warning that something is seriously wrong.' She looked into the distance, her lips pressed together, a sheen of tears in her eyes. 'It wasn't the same after that. Bill went into a decline. They'd been together over forty years, can you imagine? Anyway, he decided to move to the south of England, where it was warmer, and he left me to look after the place.' She shrugged and carried on with her task. 'Said he'd be leaving it to me when he died anyway, as he had nobody else.'

'So he's still alive?'

'Yep,' she said. 'Can you pass me the wire cutters?'

And that was the end of the conversation. Nancy felt reassured after that. Nobody was going to come along and throw her out or send her back to her father. It was just her and Judy.

It turned out they had a lot in common. Everything that had happened in Nancy's life was mirrored in Judy's, so she understood what Nancy was going through. It now seemed even more like fate that they had met; she liked to imagine it was her mum's doing, sending her someone who was happy to listen as she finally talked through her problems.

One lunchtime, while they were sitting in the yard, Nancy admitted to something that had been weighing on her mind.

'So you stole the woman's purse?' Judy looked horrified and Nancy instantly regretted telling her.

'I didn't want to, but it was the only way I could get money to buy food. At home, I was always getting advances on my allowance to buy clothes and make-up, so I had no money of my own. Just a jar of coins, but I could hardly lug that around with me. So I nicked ten pounds from my dad's pocket. That was it, all I could find, and I had to spend that on food at the service station.'

She knew she sounded defensive, and it did come across as bad: stealing from someone who had given her a lift, done nothing but show her kindness. Her stomach churned. Would Judy tell her to go now she knew she was a thief? Would she think she couldn't trust her?

Judy blew out her cheeks. 'So what did you do with it? Have you still got it?'

'I took the money then threw the purse away.' She bit her lip but there was a gleam in Judy's eye.

'You are such a badass!' She laughed and gave Nancy's knee a playful slap. 'Needs must and all that.'

Nancy let out a relieved breath, hardly able to believe she had taken it so well.

'I hadn't realised you were so naughty,' Judy said, mock stern, wagging a finger at her. 'But we're going to have to be careful, just in case the police are looking for you. Better that you stay here if I have to go out.'

Nancy nodded her agreement, relieved that she wasn't going to be thrown out. And the idea that the police might be looking for her meant she was happy to stay behind when Judy went on errands.

When Nancy had been on the farm for six weeks and was feeling quite exhausted during the throes of lambing, her resolve started to waver. Instead of focusing on all the negatives up to and after her mum's death, she yearned for the hugs her dad would give her when she was upset. His silly jokes. The way he smiled at her and ruffled her hair. The smell of him. She found herself waking up with her face wet with tears.

She was desperate to speak to him and was pretty sure there was a phone in Judy's room, but she kept the door locked so there was no way Nancy could sneak in and call him without first asking permission. Now she thought about it, she'd never heard the phone ring, so wasn't certain it was even connected.

If the phone wasn't working she'd have to find a phone box, and God knows where the nearest one of those would be. She hadn't ventured outside the farm in the weeks she'd been there and hadn't a clue about the geography of the place. It would be so easy to get lost in these winding lanes; her sense of direction wasn't great at the best of times. Wherever she was going to ring her dad from, she'd need Judy's help.

At breakfast, she worked up the courage to admit she was homesick.

'I think I should ring Dad and tell him I'm okay.' The tightness in her throat made it hard to speak, her voice thick with emotion at the thought of hearing his voice. 'Look, Judy, I think it's time I went home. I've made him suffer enough and I feel bad now and just want to get back to how we were. I'm sure he'd come and get me.'

Judy froze, her knife hovering over the margarine tub for a second before she carried on with rapid movements, scraping the spread onto her toast. Tension filled the air, the silence punctuated by the rasping of the knife.

Nancy bit her lip, afraid that she'd caused offence. Judy could be a little scary when she went quiet like this, then her temper would flare like a lit match. But she fizzled out just as quickly and was always apologetic afterwards. Anyway, on the few occasions it had happened, Nancy didn't blame her, knowing she'd deserved a telling-off for being stupid, not understanding instructions and causing unnecessary work.

'Thank you so much for giving me somewhere to stay,' she gushed, eager to defuse the situation. 'Honestly, I really am grateful.'

Judy gazed at her then, blinking, her chin trembling. 'You want to leave me in the middle of lambing? The busiest time of the year?' Her voice cracked. 'Is that what you're saying?'

Nancy was appalled. She'd expected a burst of anger but not tears. Her heart clenched. She wanted to say yes. With all her heart, she wanted that word to come out of her mouth. 'No, no, that's not what I meant,' she said instead. 'I… um…' She sighed, and looked at her toast, wishing it was something else. Every morning, two slices of toast and a bit of butter. She longed for Coco Pops or Cheerios in a big bowl. Eggy bread just for a change. Maybe an omelette. Even porridge with a bit of syrup. Anything but toast.

The appeal of their limited diet was starting to wear thin. No takeaways, no sugary treats apart from the occasional hot chocolate, no bags of snacks. Everything was made from scratch. Even the bread. In fact, the appeal of farming and the noisy messiness of lambing was wearing thin too. The incessant bleating. Afterbirth all over her hands, her face, in her hair. Death – a part of the process she hadn't considered, which brought her full circle back to her mum and her aching sense of loss.

Judy rapped on the table with the handle of her knife. 'Speak to me, Nancy. What's going on? I thought you were happy here.' Tears trickled down her face. Nancy had to force herself to keep eye contact, because to look away would suggest she didn't care. 'I thought I'd found a proper friend in you. A sort of sister. Family.' She looked down at her plate, her voice a disappointed murmur. 'And I thought you felt the same. But if you don't want to be here… if it's not good enough…' She sniffed and buried her head in her hands, shoulders heaving as she sobbed.

Nancy swallowed. To be honest, she hadn't considered the effect her leaving would have on Judy, how she might find it hard to cope on her own. Now she was mortified that she'd made Judy cry. A bead of panic lodged in her chest as her mind searched for a way out of the awkward situation she'd created.

'I think… I'm just a bit tired.' She focused on her poor excuse for a breakfast. 'I thought I could have a break.' Surely she was due a holiday? She'd been working seven days a week since she'd arrived. For someone who wasn't used to physical labour, it had been exhausting.

'You'd seriously consider leaving me?' Judy's voice was plaintive, like one of the lambs separated from its mother. 'Just when I need you most? I know we don't live in luxury but I've shared everything I have with you. I thought…' There was a tremor in her voice. 'I thought we were a team.'

Nancy's resolve was now wafer thin. *Am I being selfish?* A flush of guilt burned through her.

'We *are* a team.' She picked up a slice of toast and bit into it, unsure what else to say.

Judy gave herself a shake and brushed her wet cheeks with the back of her hand. 'You do what you think is best, Nancy.' She managed a feeble smile. 'It's not like I can keep you here, is it? You're a free agent. Go if you want to. But honestly… I think your dad deserves the pain of guilt for a little longer.' Her words were infused with a sudden flash of rage. 'As penance for the neglect he made you suffer. He doesn't deserve you.' She jabbed the air with her finger as she made her point. 'And I've found that people don't change.' She fumbled in her pocket for a tissue, blowing her nose. 'We hope they will, but if they've let you down once, they'll do it again. And again.' She gave an emphatic nod. 'And that's me speaking from experience.' More tears rolled down her cheeks. 'Let me tell you about my parents.'

Nancy sat up a little straighter.

Judy's finger traced a pattern on the table as she spoke. 'My parents ran a business. They sent me away to school so I wouldn't be in the way, even though I hated it. I didn't fit in with the other girls. I didn't have pots of money like them. Didn't have ponies, had never been to ballet classes and had no idea what or who they were talking about half the time.' She squeezed her eyes shut. 'I can tell you it was the loneliest time of my life. My parents didn't even want to be with me during the holidays. They left me to entertain myself while they worked.'

Nancy's heart went out to her friend. They'd talked a few times about not fitting in and now she could understand why it had been a problem for Judy.

'Honestly, I tried my best to be good. Did what they asked to gain their approval but it was never enough. I felt like I was this weight holding them back. Something they'd thought was a good idea at the time then lived to regret.'

'Oh, I'm sure they didn't think that.' Nancy put a reassuring hand on Judy's arm and Judy clasped it, holding tight. *Poor Judy, what a horrible upbringing.* How amazing that she'd turned into such a lovely person with that going on in the background.

'Anyway,' she continued, her eyes meeting Nancy's, 'you're not going to believe this, but when I was sixteen and away at college trying to get some of those stupid qualifications they wanted me to have, my parents moved abroad.'

Nancy was not sure why this was so bad. 'But that's nice, isn't it? Exciting to live abroad.' She frowned, puzzled. 'Didn't you like it?'

Judy's jaw hardened and she leant across the table. 'I didn't get a chance to like it. They didn't tell me where they'd gone. They sent me a letter saying I was old enough to look after myself. And that was it. Never seen them again and haven't a clue where they went.'

Nancy's mouth dropped open. 'Oh my God, Judy. I can't believe anyone would do that.'

Judy nodded and sat back in her chair. 'I know. Harsh. But it illustrates my point. People don't change. They'd never been loving. I don't know why I expected any different. And it's the same with your dad. He's always neglected you and that's the way it will carry on. If you go back, you're doing it for the wrong reasons. You're doing it because you feel guilty that he might feel bad about your disappearance.'

Nancy felt a jolt of recognition in Judy's words. *Is she right?* It was true that guilt gnawed away at her, making her doubt her choice to run away. Now she'd have to reconsider her motives, have a proper think about why she wanted to leave. What she thought she was going back to.

She took another bite of her toast and knew she'd have to wait until everything was clear in her mind. When lambing was over. She owed Judy that, didn't she? And maybe Judy was right after all. *Dad did neglect me, didn't he?*

CHAPTER TWENTY-TWO

As time marched on, Nancy found the urge to go home being extinguished by the idea that she'd been neglected. The more she talked to Judy about it, the more she realised it was true. How lucky she'd been to find a new home here. And as Judy would say during these conversations, 'We're family now. Why do we need anyone else?'

A gang of shearers from New Zealand came in late May and stayed for a couple of days to clip their flock. Having four men in the house brought a buzz of excitement to the place and the banter was a lot of fun. They came every year, the personnel changing slightly depending on which members of the family were available. The gang master stayed the same, though – a grizzled little man with a complexion the colour of polished oak and wrinkles on his face so deep they looked like a relief map.

One of his sons was with him this year, along with two cousins. A family affair, the bonds between them, the mutual affection, touching Nancy's heart. It stirred a longing in her. She had a sister, a real sister she'd barely met, a family she'd deserted, and she longed to be like the shearers, together again with her clan.

'Blood is thicker than water,' the older man said. 'So thick they're stuck to me and I can't shake the bastards off!' His comment was met with laughter, followed by a raucous bout of play fighting.

She spoke about it to Judy the evening the gang left, the place feeling empty and quiet without the sound of their voices.

'You don't know what's going on under the surface in families,' Judy replied. 'You can't choose your family, but you can choose your friends.'

Nancy fell quiet then, and soon afterwards went up to bed, unsettled by her conflicted feelings – loyalty to Judy, who needed her, and love for her dad. However much he might have neglected her, her feelings for him burned bright in her heart.

When August faded into autumn and a chill crept into the morning air, Nancy's mind turned to the future. Whatever she was going to do for a career, she'd need qualifications. She began to think about furthering her education.

There'd been a rough patch at home, before her dad's infidelity had come to light. Emotionally her mum had not really been there for Nancy, and she'd had to navigate the flood of hormones and her social awkwardness on her own.

Then her mum had dropped the bombshell. She'd taken her out for a McDonald's, so Nancy knew there was news coming, though she'd had no idea what it would be.

'I've got something to tell you,' her mum had said, nibbling on a fry. She took a sip of her coffee. 'Me and your dad…' She grimaced. 'You must have noticed there's been a bit of tension?'

Nancy nodded and bit into her Big Mac. Had he lost his job? That had happened to her friend's dad and it had caused a lot of trouble between her parents.

'The thing is… he's been having an affair.'

Nancy's jaw dropped. That was the last thing she'd expected. Her dad was way too goofy to be a cheater.

Her mum nodded. 'Yes, it's been going on for quite some time. So I'm leaving.'

In her panic, a piece of burger got stuck in her throat and Nancy started to choke. Her mum jumped up and thumped her on the back until the meat dislodged and she could breathe again, coughing and spluttering as she leant over the table.

'I'm sorry, love,' her mum said, rubbing her shoulder before she sat back down. 'Really I am, but I can't live with him after this.'

'Don't go, Mum.' Nancy stretched across the table and grabbed her mum's hand, tears spilling down her cheeks. 'Don't leave me.'

'No, no, silly. Of course I'm not leaving you.' She took Nancy's hand in both of her own, the warmth of her skin offering some comfort. 'You're coming with me. We're going to live in a lovely little flat above the florist's. We just have to wait a few weeks for my boss to get it tidied up and decorated, then it's all ours.' She gave a quick smile and squeezed Nancy's hand. 'Don't say a word to your dad, though. It's our secret. I just wanted you to know what's happening.'

Nancy couldn't think of a single thing to say, her food forgotten as her life disintegrated around her.

Keeping the secret had been a dreadful burden, her loyalties split between her parents. A couple of months later, her mum's pregnancy had prompted a U-turn, and when she'd decided they were staying after all, things became harder still. What a mess. Nancy was stuck in the middle of it, resentful of the emotional toll her parents' relationship was taking on her. It was exhausting, upsetting and unsettling. No surprise that her school work had suffered.

Now, as she gathered the eggs, she wondered if she'd been rash to leave before she'd taken her exams. It had definitely narrowed her options in terms of future careers.

She decided to tell Judy what she was thinking. That she needed to go home until she'd finished school and had some basic qualifications. Then she'd promise to come back. At least this way she was giving her some notice, enough time to find a replacement to help out. She hoped she would understand. And let her use the phone to ring her dad.

Judy was making sandwiches for lunch when she went into the kitchen.

'I haven't a single GCSE to my name.' She laughed as though it was funny when Nancy told her what she was planning. 'It's never held me back. I have a job, a house, a great way of life. What more do you need?' She slapped a couple of slices of bread on the worktop and started buttering them.

It wasn't the response Nancy had anticipated, and she had no ready answer. Every adult she'd ever spoken to had stressed the importance of good exam results. She'd never thought about a future without them.

Judy glanced at her, stopped what she was doing.

'Look around you,' she said. 'We live in paradise. And you can stay here as long as you like. You know that. We can run this place together. Aren't we the dream team?' She gave Nancy a playful nudge with her elbow. 'Why would you need qualifications when you can learn on the job?' She beamed. 'We have the school of life right here, my friend.' She arranged some slices of cheese on the bread, made the sandwich and cut it in half, handing it to Nancy.

'Because… well, I might decide I want a… different job.'

Judy stopped halfway through cutting the next slice of bread, the smile falling from her face. 'Wow. Why do you want a different job? Isn't this good enough for you?' She blinked, and it looked like she was getting a bit teary at the thought.

Nancy forced a smile, feeling guilty that she'd upset her friend. 'Of course it's good enough. I just…' She flapped a hand, decided that plan B might be a better option – staying here and going to college. She wouldn't mention returning home, not with Judy in this sort of mood. 'I thought if I went to college and got my GCSEs I could get a part-time job and bring in some extra money.' Surely that was a good thing? And it would give her a little bit of freedom.

Judy swiped a tear from her cheek, slicing the air with the breadknife. It came down with a loud thunk onto the worktop, making Nancy jump. 'I thought we were sisters, you and me. Haven't we said that?' She turned to face her, disappointment in her eyes. 'Honestly, I've invested all this time in you, teaching you things because I thought you shared my values, my love of a simple, honest life.' Her voice rose as she grew visibly more upset. 'It seems I was wrong. You don't want what I can offer. Is that what you're saying? There's something better out there?'

Nancy swallowed, her heart racing. Plan B was obviously a non-starter as well. Judy was getting herself all worked up. She couldn't deal with emotional people, hated the tension. It reminded her of her mum and dad. That awful time before… The sting of tears brought her thoughts to a sudden halt.

She studied her sandwich.

'I'm sorry, forget I mentioned it.' Her mind scrabbled for some excuse, something to smooth the awkwardness. 'I suppose I've just been conditioned to think that's what I should do.'

'Damn right you've been conditioned,' Judy snapped, turning back to the loaf, sawing at it like she was cutting off a limb. 'Can't you see you can be a free spirit here? No need for all that unnecessary pressure of exams. And who needs to know about Pythagoras or bloody calculus or any of that bollocks?' She was getting increasingly irate now, stabbing the knife into the butter like she was trying to kill it, before spreading it on the bread.

Nancy couldn't possibly voice her real thoughts with Judy in this sort of state. Couldn't admit that she missed her family, having friends to hang out with, going shopping, buying the odd treat, new clothes. Everything she wore was chosen and supplied by Judy, usually picked up from charity shops. Obviously she was grateful to be clothed and housed and fed. But she did work hard, and at the end of the day, she missed her independence. She'd rather earn money and choose for herself how to spend it.

As they ate their lunch in silence, she debated the merits of Judy's argument. Why put herself through the struggle of exams if she didn't have to? The reality, though, was that without Judy's blessing, she wouldn't even be able to get to college. Public transport links were practically non-existent up here in the mountains; she'd have to walk miles to get to a bus stop. It didn't take long to convince herself that her desire for qualifications was a hangover from a previous life which was no longer relevant. As Judy had said, she had freedom here, everything she needed.

'Look, it's your life and it's not for me to tell you how to live it,' Judy said as she cleared the plates into the sink. She turned and gave a shaky smile. 'We have something pretty special here. Who gets to run a farm at our age?' She flung her hands in the air. 'It's a blessing. You said yourself that you thought your mum led you here.' She leant forward, stressing each word. 'Maybe this is what she wants for you. A clean, wholesome existence, away from the crap life she left behind.'

Her words struck a chord with Nancy, setting off a new line of thought that she hadn't considered before. Her mum had been a florist, a lover of nature. She would have adored this place. Even her dad might approve, given that he was an outdoors kind of guy. In fact, he'd like it better than her original plan to be a beautician or a hairdresser, which according to him lacked ambition. Perhaps Judy had a point.

'Come on, Nancy, think about it. We have a farm business to develop. What an opportunity. Why not focus your energies on that?' Judy put her hands on Nancy's shoulders and looked into her eyes. 'We could really make this place something special, you and me. Exams don't come into it, do they? As long as you can do simple sums and learn to understand the growing seasons, qualifications are pretty much irrelevant.'

Nancy couldn't fault her argument and let herself be persuaded. Even became excited by the idea of running a business with her friend. Judy was right – what an opportunity. And she was thinking long-term, not just a few months ahead. No school. No exams.

How lucky was Nancy? And how lovely that Judy thought of her as a business partner. For a sixteen-year-old, that was something quite special, wasn't it?

Having reshaped her situation into an amazing life prospect, the sun came out on her world again and she settled into the farming routines with a new sense of purpose. Her mum had led her here. This was her destiny, and it was up to her to make the most of the fabulous chance she'd been given.

CHAPTER TWENTY-THREE

Together they worked hard, Judy sorting out a division of labour that suited their respective skills. She went out to fetch supplies and run errands, sorted out all the paperwork, did most of the cooking and looked after the house. Nancy found herself doing the outside labouring activities. There were some jobs, though, that needed both of them, like checking the boundary fences, because Judy didn't want Nancy being out on the hillside on her own in case she had an accident and died of hypothermia.

'I'll be fine,' she insisted, liking the idea of a bit of time on her own, being trusted to do the job.

But Judy wasn't having any of it. 'Oh no, I'm not taking the risk. Let me tell you a story. Honest to God, this is true. It happened to a farmer across the valley. He went out to round up the sheep, slipped on a wet rock, hit his head and ended up drowning in a stream.'

Nancy's heart flipped. She hadn't really thought about the dangers of being out on her own like that.

Judy put an arm round her and gave her a hug. 'I can't allow anything like that to happen to my best mate, can I? My little treasure.' She ruffled Nancy's hair like she was her kid sister. 'So checking the boundaries we do together. Bringing the sheep down we do together. I don't mind you being out and about near the farm, where you can call if something happens. But it doesn't take long for hypothermia to kick in at this time of year if you're lying out there injured. Understand?'

Nancy nodded, remembering her dad telling her a story about a fell runner friend who'd died out on a run. He'd fallen and twisted his ankle and couldn't get himself back down to safety. 'You've got to respect the mountains,' her dad would tell her. 'It's not a playground.' Which was why she wasn't allowed to go along on his adventures with him. 'It's no place for a child.' How often had he said that? She'd thought he was using it as an excuse, so he didn't have to be bothered with her tagging along, but maybe he'd had a point.

She hugged Judy back, glad to be working with someone who treasured her.

Nancy didn't know exactly how big the farm was in terms of acres, but on the days they walked the boundaries, checking walls and fences to make sure they were intact, it was a very long way and involved a lot of steep climbing.

The land didn't go to the top of the mountain, so she never saw what was on the other side, but in their valley, she could only see wilderness. Sometimes she'd make out the silhouettes of people on top of the ridge on the opposite side of the valley, tiny ant-like specks, and it would remind her of her dad. She wondered if one of them might be him. It was possible, after all, as he and his friends often came to Wales. Her heart ached with memories, the good things about the past she'd left behind. Had it really been so bad? Then she'd remember the neglect and the fact that her dad had cheated and all the other things that, as Judy kept reminding her, had made her want to stage her suicide in the first place.

One evening, they were sitting in front of the fire, Judy teaching her how to knit. They'd been chatting about grandmas, because it was Judy's gran who'd taught her to knit when she'd been a child. Nancy's gran had taught her how to bake. Just talking about it brought a wave of homesickness crashing down on her.

'Don't you ever miss your family?' she asked.

Judy smiled at her and gave her shoulder a rub. 'My family is right here. Why would I need anyone else when I've got the best sister I could ever have wished for?'

Nancy blushed, a swell of warmth in her heart. It was lovely that Judy felt that way. *Home is where the heart is.* She remembered her mum saying that when they were talking about moving into the flat and Nancy had been worried about living in a different part of town. Is my heart here? she asked herself now.

'I miss my dad sometimes,' she said. 'And I wonder if maybe I've misunderstood. You know… judged too quickly. Or made assumptions about things that might not be right.'

Judy put her knitting down and gave Nancy her full attention. 'The problem is this,' she said carefully. 'Memories aren't real. Our minds change them all the time depending on how we're feeling. That's why people talk about wearing rose-tinted glasses when they think about certain events from the past. Because they didn't happen the way they remember them. Their minds rearrange things, make them look better, different than they actually were.' Her voice was melodious, hypnotic; Nancy hung on every word. 'Our minds want to get rid of the horrible things, so they change them, make everything more palatable.'

She pulled Nancy to her and kissed the top of her head before releasing her and picking up her knitting again.

'I've never thought about it like that,' Nancy said, checking for dropped stitches in the scarf she was knitting. Could Judy be right? Was her mind playing tricks on her, trying to draw her back to a family who never wanted her in the first place?

'Marj explained all this to me when I arrived here. She was so lovely, you know, listening to me going on about my family. She was a real mother, not like the one who gave birth to me. Bill and Marj… they were proper parents.' She gazed at the pictures on the wall. 'They taught me that the family you find can be more important than the one you were given by birth. Their son was adopted, you see. But boy, did they love him. And I genuinely felt that Marj loved me.' She blinked. 'For those few years, she taught me what it felt like to…' She beamed at Nancy, eyes glistening. 'I was missing her so much until you came along. And now I've got you to love instead.'

Nancy could feel herself welling up. 'What a lovely thing to say,' she murmured, glowing with pride.

A few days later, Judy returned home from a trip out to pick up some groceries. She looked unusually flustered when she came into the kitchen, where Nancy was at the sink, washing up.

'You'll never believe what just happened,' she said, flopping into a chair at the table, a hand clasping her forehead.

Obviously it was a rhetorical question. Nancy waited patiently, concerned by the state Judy was in. She'd never seen her like this before, all worked up and breathless.

'Let me find it for you,' Judy said. She started rummaging in the carrier bags she'd brought in, then tutted when she couldn't find whatever it was she was looking for. She went back out to the Land Rover but returned empty-handed. 'I don't believe it. I put it to one side, especially to show you.'

'Judy, what's the matter? Just calm down and maybe I can help you look for whatever it is.' Nancy leant against the worktop, drying her hands.

Judy slapped her cheeks with both hands, annoyance in her eyes. 'Oh, I know what I've done. I left the stupid thing in the shop.' She shook her head. 'The thing is… Oh, Nan… they're looking for you.'

Nancy's heart leapt. 'What? Who is?'

'The police.'

Her mind started to race. 'Is it about the purse? Surely they would have forgotten that by now. It's almost a year ago and—'

Judy raised a hand to stop her flow. 'No, that's not it. Apparently your mum's death is being investigated as murder, not an accident, and your dad and Linda have pointed the finger at you. They say that's why you committed suicide.' She grimaced. 'Although there is a question mark over that, because someone saw a person matching your description at a service station on the M6. Anyway, they would have expected your body to have been washed up on the beach by now.'

Nancy's knees went weak, a sickening feeling in the pit of her stomach.

'That's a lie. I didn't… I wouldn't… Oh my God, what am I going to do?' She burst into tears, her world turned upside down. *Wanted for murder? No, no, no. It was an accident. An accident.*

Judy came and wrapped her in a hug, shushing her as she stroked her hair. 'Hey, it's okay. Who's going to find you here? The only people who've seen you are the shearers, and they won't say anything. I think you just need to lie low for a while. I know we don't really get anyone coming up here, but if anyone does happen to come to the house, don't open the door, okay? Make yourself scarce, then nobody will even know you're here, will they?'

'You won't tell anyone, will you?' Nancy hiccuped, her tears refusing to stop.

'Come on, remember what we were saying? We're family.' Judy's voice was emphatic. 'I've always got your back. Always.'

Trembling with relief, Nancy sank into the embrace, knowing that she'd trust Judy with her life. Only a true friend wouldn't ask the question: was it true that she'd played a part in her mother's death?

CHAPTER TWENTY-FOUR

Nancy kept a low profile after that, too frightened to venture out. Judy, ever protective, alerted her to any new developments in the case. Now she even had to hide when the shearers arrived, lest they mention to other farmers that she was there. Shortly before they were due at the farm, the women fixed up a little nook for her in the loft in the barn, and for two nights at the beginning of June, when the weather was mild, she managed just fine.

Days turned into weeks, then months and years. The farm became Nancy's world and her mental horizons shrank to fit. But as Judy said, who wouldn't want to live in such a paradise?

Shortly after her eighteenth birthday, on the second anniversary of her mum's death, she suffered a crippling bout of homesickness and decided she had to speak to her dad, explain what had really happened. The phone was locked in Judy's bedroom, and she knew she couldn't ask to use it without causing upset. She just had to be patient.

Her chance came when Judy's sheepdog was seriously ill one morning. Nancy had to wake her, and she rushed out of the house to the vet's, forgetting to lock her bedroom door. With her heart in her mouth, Nancy sneaked into the room and dialled the familiar number. At last she was going to speak to her dad. Would he forgive her?

A continuous tone filled her ear. She frowned and dialled again. Still she got the continuous tone. Her third attempt produced the same result. She rang directory enquiries to see if perhaps the number had changed.

'I'm terribly sorry,' the operator said. 'I have nothing for that name at that address.'

'What? I don't understand. It's my dad. That's where he lives.'

'I think his contact details must have changed. He's no longer the account holder at the address you've given me.' There was silence for a moment. 'Is there anything else I can help you with?'

Dumbstruck, Nancy put the phone down. Her dad had moved and she had no way of contacting him. Why would he do that if there was a chance of her coming home? Unless… he didn't want her to come home. Or he genuinely thought she was dead. Judy's story about her own parents moving without telling her where they'd gone echoed in her mind along with her words. *People don't change. He neglected you.*

She sat with her head in her hands, trying to sort through her feelings now her past was out of reach.

A couple of weeks later, she came into the kitchen at lunchtime to find Judy sitting at the table, studying sheaves of paper. She picked up the kettle and went to fill it for a cup of tea.

Judy glanced at her, frowning. 'Can you come here a minute and have a look at this with me.' Her tone was crisp. Nancy tensed.

She peered over Judy's shoulder and her heart clenched when she saw a printout of the phone bill. *Oh God, she knows.* She wiped her clammy palms on her jeans, frantically trying to work out an excuse, but her mind was blank, rubbed clean by panic.

'I noticed this call here, to directory enquiries.' Judy gazed at her. 'That was you, wasn't it? Who were you calling?'

Nancy wished she was in *Star Trek* and could ask Scotty to beam her up. Her cheeks glowed, and she sank into a chair, words flowing out of her mouth before she could check the wisdom of what she was saying. 'I'm sorry, Judy. I know it was wrong to go behind your back, but it was the anniversary of Mum's death and I just wanted to talk to Dad. I was feeling so homesick. And not knowing how he felt and what was happening with the investigation and I just—'

Judy slapped the papers onto the table, fury burning in her eyes. Nancy had never seen her so angry before. Upset, yes, snappy, maybe, but this was something quite new. 'I can't believe you did that. Not only sneaking into my room behind my back, which is a gross invasion of my privacy, but…' She was struggling to speak. 'I can't believe you'd try to ring your dad after all the effort I've gone to, keeping you safe from the police. I've protected you for two bloody years, and then you do this?' Spittle flew from her mouth as she spoke, her voice getting louder and louder. 'Not to mention the fact that I'm knowingly harbouring someone who is wanted for questioning in a bloody murder inquiry. Can you imagine how much trouble I'll be in? That's a criminal offence on its own.' Her face was going a darker shade of red, eyes popping out of her head as she smacked the papers on the table to emphasise her point. The look she gave Nancy brought a chill to her bones.

'I'm really sorry,' Nancy whimpered, shrinking away from this wild woman who'd taken over Judy's body. 'Honestly, I didn't think—'

'And that's the problem, isn't it? You don't bloody think! It's all about you, you selfish…' Judy gave a furious growl. 'You've betrayed me. Betrayed my trust.' Her eyes bored into Nancy, making her shrivel inside. 'You want to go running back to Daddy, get arrested and thrown into jail? Hmm?' She sprang to her feet. Nancy shrank back in her chair, sure she was going to get a slap.

Judy's face was inches from her own. 'If you want to go home, you do that.' She pointed to the hallway. 'Go on. Pack your things and go.'

'No, no. Please, Judy.' Nancy's heart was racing, panic making her gabble. 'It won't happen again. He's moved house. Can you believe that? I don't even know where he lives now.'

'Ha! Well, that's your problem, isn't it? If you don't want to be here, if this is second best, how can I trust you?'

'You know you can trust me. Honestly, Judy, I was feeling sad about Mum and… I had this urge to be with my family.'

'Oh, so this was a "please come and pick me up, Dad" sort of a call, was it?' Judy was incandescent with rage now, her hands flying through the air as she spoke. Nancy bit her lip, unable to admit that was exactly what had been on her mind. She wanted to meet her little sister, have a proper conversation with her dad and straighten out what had happened two years ago.

'Don't you understand that you're wanted for *murder*?' Judy leaned in, her finger tapping the side of her head like a woodpecker. 'Hasn't that fact reached your brain?'

Nancy blinked back tears, wondering how long this tirade was going to last. She'd never before been in a situation like this, on the receiving end of such anger. *You've only yourself to blame.* Would it be like this if she went home? Would her dad be this angry? There was a possibility he might be.

'Your father set you up. That's how much he loves you. He was willing to point the finger at his own daughter.'

'I'm sure it's just a misunderstanding. If I could talk to him—'

'Don't be ridiculous,' Judy yelled, stamping a foot in frustration. 'You're in denial, do you know that? You *were* to blame. Your mum's death is on you.'

A tear rolled down Nancy's cheek.

'I remember when you told me. Clear as day. You know it was your fault.'

'It wasn't me, it wasn't. I never said that.'

Judy gave a derisive snort. 'Yeah, you keep telling yourself that.' She paced up and down, her chest heaving. 'Right, I want you out of here.'

Nancy's jaw dropped. 'But… but I've nowhere to go. No money.'

'That's not my problem.' Judy jabbed a finger at her. 'I feel so betrayed, I can't bear to have you in the house.'

Nancy didn't move, her hands clinging to the chair seat.

'After everything I've done for you, this is a kick in the teeth. Go and pack your bags. Give me my clothes back and you can leave with what you came with.'

It was the end of March and bitterly cold, the mountains covered in a thick blanket of snow. Nancy could see flakes drifting into the yard and knew the weather was due to stay cold for the next week. The clothes she'd arrived in would be no protection – she'd be hypothermic in no time. Not to mention the fact that she'd nowhere to go and didn't even know where the nearest house was.

'Go on!' Judy shouted, pulling her from the chair and throwing her to the ground. Get out of my bloody house and stay out.' She was crying now. 'I thought we were family, you and me. I trusted you.' She drew in a breath between sobs. 'GET OUT!'

Nancy cowered on the floor, unable to move. Hoping that this rage would blow over and she'd be able to apologise, makes things right.

She heard Judy stomp into the utility room and her heart flipped when she saw her come back into the kitchen with the air rifle, which she used for shooting pheasants and rabbits.

Adrenaline fired round her body as she clambered to her feet, Judy prodding her with the gun to make her walk into the hallway and up the stairs to her bedroom. She wasn't messing about; this was no idle threat. She really wanted Nancy to leave. The snow was coming down more heavily now, thick flakes sticking to the window pane as Nancy pulled her bag from under the bed. She opened the bottom drawer where her old clothes were stored. They looked so pitiful. Childish. She was no longer that girl who'd arrived here two years ago. She'd grown a couple of inches, filled out round the chest and shoulders and wasn't sure the clothes would still fit.

'Judy, please, I don't want to go.' She swallowed her tears. 'I'm really sorry. Honestly, I won't do it again.'

'I don't want you here. Not if you're not committed.' Judy prodded her with the gun again. 'I can't trust you anymore, can I? Any time I go out I'll be wondering if you'll still be here when I come back. I can't run a farm like that.' Her chin quivered. 'More to the point, I can't let you hurt me again.' She sniffed. 'I feel like you just ripped out my heart and trampled it in the dirt. Clearly I mean nothing to you… I got it all wrong.'

'No, you didn't get it wrong. You didn't.' Nancy's voice caught on a sob. 'We are family, you and me.' Her eyes pleaded with Judy, her heart racing at the thought of being banished from a place she had thought of as home for the last two years.

'But you prefer your cheating father and a screaming baby to me. That's what you said. Well, off you go.' Judy poked the barrel of the gun into Nancy's ribs, making her zip up her bag. 'Go on. Hurry up.'

It was too late, Nancy thought, to plead for forgiveness. She'd never seen Judy this upset and had no idea how to reason with her. But maybe in the morning, when she'd calmed down, she'd be prepared to listen. Reluctantly she put on the camouflage outfit, the trouser legs flapping round her ankles, the buttons only just fastening. She slunk past Judy and down the stairs, squeezing herself into the red jacket she hadn't worn since she'd arrived, then left the house, aware of Judy's eyes on her back.

She trudged down the track until she was out of sight, then doubled back, round the rear of the barn, and sneaked inside, glad that the fresh snow would cover her tracks. At least she had her little refuge in the loft, with a sleeping bag to keep her warm and a camping stove to make a hot drink. She even had a few tins of food left over from the previous year. It could have been worse, she thought as she filled her camping kettle from the tap by the chicken pen and settled herself in for the night.

Her mind wouldn't let her sleep and the cold settled in her bones as she lay awake listening to the sounds of the animals of the night. Mice scurrying, the soft whisper of wings as the barn owl left its nest in the eaves. The subdued clucking of the hens settling to roost.

Judy's words went round in her mind, scraping and scratching at her view of her world. She'd really messed up this time, and if she didn't make things right, she'd be a homeless fugitive wanted for murder. She wished her recollection of the day her mum died wasn't so muddled.

Nancy vaguely remembered a night when they'd shared a couple of beers and confided in each other. Judy had told her about her friend Zara, how she wished she'd stopped her from taking the tablets at the festival. Her heartbreak when Zara had died. Which had led Nancy to talk about her mum's accident. But the memories of that night were elusive, blurred by alcohol, and she couldn't remember what she'd said.

Fat tears rolled down her cheeks as she wondered if she'd fatally damaged their friendship. More than the idea of never seeing her family again, the idea of being separated from Judy felt unbearable. She was someone she could always rely on. Whereas her family… they'd moved house, knowing that if she wasn't dead she'd struggle to find them. You didn't do that to someone you loved, did you?

Judy was right, as usual. Better to forget the past. Think only of the present and the future. She was safe here, and always would be.

The following morning, she trudged to the kitchen door, expecting to find it locked, but it was open. The welcome heat drew her in. She found Judy sitting huddled in a blanket in front of the range, dark rings round her eyes suggesting she'd had a bad night's sleep as well. As soon as she saw Nancy, she jumped up and threw her arms around her.

'Oh, thank God. I thought I'd lost you.'

Nancy clung on tight, promising herself she'd learnt her lesson and would never be so stupid again.

CHAPTER TWENTY-FIVE

After that, life settled into a familiar routine and Nancy's world was the farm and the farm alone. Initially it was the fear of being recognised and arrested that stopped her from wanting to go out, but over time, the thought of venturing further afield was in itself too scary to contemplate. Besides, the situation she found herself in was the best she could ever have hoped for after the terrible things she'd done. She had love and laughter, didn't she? And as Judy would often say, who needed men complicating things? They had a challenge to keep them focused: making the farm sustainable.

Of course it wasn't all wonderful. There were times when she was struck with bouts of homesickness. Times when she'd challenge Judy for giving her all the horrible jobs. Then they'd have a big argument, Judy would tell her to leave, and Nancy would get halfway down the track before she reminded herself she had nowhere to go. Her family didn't want her. The police thought she'd killed her mother. And she had no money and no means of looking after herself. At that point she'd understand that living at the farm was her only option. Then she'd retrace her steps, sneak back into the barn for the night and they'd make up in the morning.

As each year passed, the arguments were less frequent, and in the end they stopped altogether. Nancy found that her inertia became a way of life and she really didn't mind it too much. Most of the time she was so busy, there was no space to consider what she'd like to be different. Loneliness wasn't an issue, as she had a constant companion in Judy, who was also the business brains, making sure they stayed clothed and fed. The work was hard but wholesome, and Judy was right when she said they should count their blessings. She'd bring back news of local people who'd lost their jobs, rising levels of unemployment, people being evicted from their houses and left homeless. It was a heartless world out there and Nancy was happy to be away from it. Her mind switched from sometimes wanting to get away, resenting Judy's controlling tendencies, to wondering why she'd ever wanted to leave their little oasis.

Her happiness rested on her mindset and with Judy's guidance she came to a point where she understood that she was in control of how she felt. It was all a case of rephrasing her wayward thoughts.

On days when she was feeling inexplicably down, or when her hormones were leading her thoughts astray, she would go through her 'gratitude' list, something Judy encouraged her to do. On balance, she supposed there were a lot of things that were great. The peace and quiet, the physical work keeping them fit, organic food keeping them healthy. Their friendship – although that could feel a little one-sided at times. Yes, many blessings.

The memories of her past faded like a photograph left in the sun, the details blurred, the faces hard to make out. She knew she couldn't rely on her memory, Judy had proved that to her many a time, when she'd misremembered events or conversations. It was something they often laughed about. Or argued about, if it was something important.

They had a couple of scares, the worst one just after the anniversary of her mother's death, when Judy heard that Nancy's case was being reviewed and the authorities were looking for her again. That made her jittery for a while, scurrying off to hide if anyone came to the farm.

When Nancy had been there almost nine years, an unfortunate incident with the shearers brought a major change. She was hiding

in the barn, as usual when they came to stay, when she was woken
by Judy calling her name, shaking her shoulder. It was dark, Judy's
face lit by the torch she was carrying.

'What's the matter?' Nancy asked, confused at being woken up
in the middle of the night and at the sight of Judy's tear-stained face.

'It's Ryan. There was a fight. Him and Levi.' Judy sank to the
floor, her face in her hands, shoulders heaving.

Nancy had never seen her friend so distraught. From the way
Judy talked about Ryan, she had an inkling she quite fancied him,
but wasn't sure if anything had come of it.

'Is he okay?' She sat up and put an arm round Judy's shoulder,
unsure what to do for the best.

'They've taken him to hospital,' Judy sobbed. 'Oh Nancy. You
should have seen the blood. So much of it.'

'Well, he's in the best place,' Nancy murmured. She was aware
that it was a meaningless platitude but it was better than nothing.
She hadn't heard an ambulance, or any sort of disturbance, but
then she did sleep very soundly when the shearers were at the
farm, for some reason.

She rubbed Judy's back as her sobs stuttered to a halt. 'Men,'
Judy said with venom in her voice. 'They're just too much trouble.
That's the last time we're having shearers here.' She gave a frustrated
grunt. 'The very last time.'

'I suppose we could have a different team,' Nancy suggested,
panicking that she'd be left to shear the whole flock on her own.

Judy pulled away from her then. 'Don't you see how dangerous
it is allowing people to come here? What if the police had been
called and they'd found you?' She shook her head, lips a determined
line. 'We can't risk that. No, we'll just have to do things differently.'

The decision was made to sell off most of the flock so they could
manage the remaining sheep by themselves. Judy also managed to
convince Bill, who still owned the farm, to let her sell off a chunk
of the land to raise some cash to keep them going and make the

place more manageable. After that, it was much easier in terms of physical effort, but harder to make the economics work.

Sometimes Nancy would find Judy curled up in Ryan's sleeping bag, which he'd left behind when she'd banned the family from returning. It convinced her there'd been something between them, a blossoming love affair, but she didn't like to ask.

It was weird how the years flew by, their focus on the seasons and planning what needed to be done to keep a steady supply of food and firewood. Some years were lean, when the weather was bad and things didn't grow so well, but they pickled and preserved, bought a big chest freezer and butchered their own animals.

Sometimes Nancy would gaze at the night sky and feel an emptiness in her heart. She'd wonder about her dad and how her life could have been. Then she'd catch hold of her thoughts and do a reality check. Her dad had disowned her. The police were looking for her. And Judy was the most loyal friend she could ever have wished for.

One day, Nancy was sitting up in the top meadow, chewing on a piece of grass, trying to keep her hunger at bay. Judy was being quite stingy with rations these days and Nancy was worried that the money had run out. Judy had developed a habit of talking to herself, which Nancy took as a sign of stress and this had increased recently. These past couple of months the older woman was out a lot and definitely preoccupied, always snapping and tetchy, keeping Nancy at a distance. Something was wrong.

'I'm trying to find new markets for our produce,' she'd said when Nancy had asked her about it. 'It takes work. You have to go and speak to people, show them what you have. Or discuss what you could have. It's very time-consuming.'

She'd gone out then, saying that she'd no idea when she'd be back. Nancy noticed she was wearing new clothes, smarter than usual. She even had a bit of make-up on. And perfume, judging by the scent that was left behind.

Over the years, there had been a few occasions when Judy had done a similar thing. It was good that she could do the selling, Nancy thought, as she herself would be useless at it. She wasn't even sure she could hold a sensible conversation these days, her vocabulary limited to words that related to farming and tractor maintenance.

Now she scanned the mountainside in front of her, the vast emptiness that was her home, and felt it echoing inside her. She'd be forty soon, and what did she have to show for it, apart from hands covered in calluses?

How would her life have turned out if her mum hadn't died, Eva hadn't been born and Linda hadn't moved next door? If she could turn the clock back and have her time again, would she still run away? Her memories of that period were so conflicted and blurred, she had no real answer. But there was no doubt that she was full to the brim with regrets. A deep sadness rested in her heart.

She remembered what a spoilt brat she'd been. An only child who'd been given everything she wanted to keep her quiet and let her parents get on with their own interests. At least here, Judy actually wanted her company. Most of the time. Sometimes it felt a bit uneven, but then it was Judy's farm and older sisters were usually bossy, weren't they?

It was funny what you got used to, what became the norm. So much so that you ceased to question anything about it. She'd learnt to tread the path of least resistance, expecting little and being grateful for everything, accepting that she'd chosen to run away, chosen to come here with Judy, chosen to stay. Then she could experience an element of contentment. As long as she didn't dwell on what could have been, it was fine.

Still the echoes of the past haunted her, the melancholy mood refusing to shift. Was her dad still alive? Did he think about her? Had he forgiven her? It was a constant ache, and troubling to think that she'd never know.

'Hello!'

The shout broke into her reverie. She looked round, wondering if she'd imagined it. But no, there were two people walking up the hill towards her, waving. She jumped to her feet, a shot of adrenaline flooding her body as her eyes scanned the field for her best getaway. She mustn't be seen. Hadn't Judy told her a thousand times how important it was to lie low?

Her head told her to run, but they were young, these people. Surely they would never have heard of her, let alone recognise her. After all, she looked nothing like the sixteen-year-old who had arrived here almost twenty-four years ago. Now she was a scraggly thirty-nine-year-old, with home-cut hair and scars on her arms where she'd got her comeuppance over the years when she and Judy had argued and Judy had whacked with whatever came to hand.

The youngsters looked like a couple, with big backpacks weighing them down, sweat glistening on their brows. Her legs wouldn't move, and she realised she was desperate for a conversation with someone other than Judy.

She watched them getting closer, listened to their excited chatter as they approached.

'I'm so glad we've seen you,' the young man said. 'We're looking for somewhere to camp for the night. We haven't much money, so we can't afford a campsite, and anyway, we prefer wild camping. But the forecast is shite for later, so we wanted somewhere sheltered.' He looked behind him, pointing. 'There's a lovely flat spot next to the stream by the wall. Would it be okay if we put our tent up there?'

Nancy didn't know what to say, her mind whirling as she weighed up the question. She wasn't really in a position to say yes, but then, she reasoned, it wasn't her place to say no either.

'Please,' the young woman begged, hands together. 'We've been all over the place looking for somewhere, got ourselves completely lost. Honestly, I'm not sure I can walk any further.'

'Just for a day or two,' the young man said, with an engaging smile.

'No problem,' Nancy said, surprising herself. 'But you have to stay up here. Don't come any closer to the farm. The woman who owns it has a gun, and she's a bit... hasty sometimes.'

The couple looked down the hill, the chimneys of the farm just visible through the trees.

'She won't come up here, will she?' the woman asked, her voice tinged with fear.

Nancy smiled, realising that these people wouldn't think of a gun as normal. *Judy won't come up here, will she?* She didn't think so. Nancy had been given full responsibility for all the outside activities these days, Judy complaining that her feet hurt, and her hands hurt, and she thought she was starting with arthritis.

Nancy suspected she was making it up. In fact, lately she'd begun to suspect a lot of things. It was like she'd been living in a mist that had suddenly cleared, revealing the true nature of her friend and her life as she knew it. It was too late to change anything, but she clasped that understanding to her like a shield, protecting her from further harm.

She broadened her smile. The last thing she wanted was to frighten them away. 'I probably shouldn't have mentioned the gun. But don't worry, it's just for shooting rabbits, and there are plenty of those in the bottom fields, so she won't be coming up here.'

She started down the hill, beckoned them to follow. 'Come on, let's find you the best spot.'

They set about clearing the space of stones and she chatted to them while they put up the tent, marvelling at the construction of the thing. So very different to the old tent her family had used when they used to go camping. This one had three bendy poles that slid into sleeves and crossed over each other at the top, then there were half a dozen pegs, a few guy lines and it was up. Ten minutes at the most. Thankfully, it was dark green, and she'd made sure it was positioned just over a little rise, not visible from the house at all. It'll be fine, she reassured herself, revelling in her covert rebellion.

'I can't believe how quick that was,' she laughed as the woman crawled inside the tent and started to unpack her rucksack.

'We've been camping all summer, so we've got it down to a fine art.' The woman popped her head out. 'Can we make you a cup of tea of something? Ooh, I've got a packet of biscuits here somewhere, if you fancy one?' Her hand came out, waggling a packet of jammy dodgers. Nancy hesitated, then took them from her. How long since she'd had one of these? They'd been a childhood favourite, and each bite took her back home to her mum and dad and the good times that increasingly dominated her thoughts.

The man wiggled a stove out of his rucksack, along with a little kettle and a couple of tin mugs. He caught Nancy watching him as he filled the kettle from the stream. 'It's okay, we'll share a mug; you can have the other one if you like?'

She nodded, a surge of emotion filling her chest at the idea they wanted her to stay a little while.

'Have another biscuit.' He nodded towards the packet clasped in her hand. 'Then you can pass them over here. I'm bloody starving.'

Nancy did as she was told, nibbling at the edge of her biscuit, trying to make it last. The man popped one in his mouth whole, then took another three and proceeded to wolf them down.

'I'm Tyler,' he said. 'Ty.'

'And I'm Jade,' the woman added.

'Nan…' Nancy stopped herself, realising that was a really stupid thing to have done.

The woman smiled. 'So you've got grandkids then?'

Nancy stared at her for a moment before she realised that Jade had misunderstood. Relieved, she just nodded and finished her biscuit.

Ty made the tea, but before they could drink it, Jade took a flat metal oblong out of her pocket and pointed it at the mugs, tapping the thing a couple of times. Nancy frowned, unsure what she was doing.

'I'm posting an Insta diary of our trip,' Jade said, noticing her expression. 'Want to see?'

Without waiting for a reply she came and sat next to Nancy. That was when she realised the object was a camera.

'Gosh, those are lovely photos,' she said, amazed at the clarity and the depth of colour in the spread of pictures she was being shown. Jade talked her though them while they drank their tea, adding anecdotes about things that had happened on the way, people they'd met, places they'd been. The two of them were easy company and Nancy felt a lovely glow. Oh, she'd missed this. Just chatting, no hidden agenda, no need to be careful about what she said. No apologies required.

'Hey, I should get one of you,' Jade said, turning the camera to face her.

'What? No!' Instinctively Nancy shielded her face with her hands.

Jade laughed. 'No, don't be shy, you've got a lovely face and I can use filters if you like.'

'No photos,' Nancy snapped, horrified at the thought. 'Promise me. I don't want you taking my picture.' Her voice shook with panic, and she caught the warning glance Ty shot his girlfriend.

'Come on, J, leave the poor woman alone. Not everyone wants their face spread all over Instagram.'

'What's Instagram?'

The couple burst out laughing. 'You've got to be kidding me,' Ty said. 'You're joking, right?'

Nancy laughed, pretending it *had* been a joke, hoping that it would all become clear. Things had obviously moved on technology-wise in the twenty-four years she'd been at the farm.

The chatter resumed while they finished their tea, Nancy moving the talk on to the weather forecast and more neutral ground.

'I'm just going to call Mum,' Jade said. 'I've got a signal here.' She walked away a few yards and started talking into the camera. Nancy was intrigued. That thing was a phone as well? Wow, things really *had* come on. She could hardly get her head round it; couldn't even begin to wonder how it worked.

Her brain ticked over faster and faster, thoughts that she hadn't allowed herself to consider making themselves heard. She had an opportunity she'd believed would never come. *I can ask to borrow the phone, can't I?* With all her heart she wanted to speak to her dad, make that connection back to her family.

If only I had his number.

CHAPTER TWENTY-SIX

'Nancy! Nancy! Where the bloody hell are you?'

The faint sound of Judy calling made her scramble to her feet. She'd been up here too long and couldn't risk Judy finding her new friends. Not now she understood the potential of their presence.

'Got to go. Remember, keep on this side of the field, stay hidden and don't go anywhere near the farm. Okay?'

Ty looked up from his screen and gave her a nod. 'Yep, got it. Don't you worry. I'll tell J when she's finished her call.'

'I'll see you tomorrow, shall I?' Nancy asked, hopeful.

'It'd be great if we could stay put for a couple of days, actually. Then we're on our way home. Would that be okay?'

'Nancy? Get here now!' Judy sounded irate, and Nancy knew better than to keep her waiting.

She gave Ty a quick thumbs-up and ran, aware that she was already in trouble. She hurtled down the field, across the next one and over the gate, stopping herself before she got to the orchard to pull in a few deep breaths. She glanced back over her shoulder, glad to see that the tent wasn't visible from down here. Her heart skipped with relief and she jogged into the yard to find Judy coming out of the barn.

'There you are. Didn't you hear me?'

'I heard one of the pigs squealing. She'd got stuck in the fence.' She pointed down the hill towards the oak woodlands, hoping to divert Judy's attention from where she'd really been. 'Made a bit of a mess, so I had to go and fix it.' Her chest heaved from all the running. 'I came as soon as I heard you.'

Judy stared at her. One of those long, cold stares of hers that made Nancy squirm inside. She'd been doing more of that lately, or was Nancy just becoming more aware of her behaviour?

'I need you to unload the trailer.'

Judy turned and went inside. Nancy waited a minute to catch her breath before she began the task of humping the bags of feed into the barn. It wasn't such a regular task these days, now they'd cut down on the number of animals they kept, but Judy did a monthly trip for supplies and it was still a lot of weight to shift. It had been worse when they'd still had the dogs, but when the last one had died a few months ago, Judy had decided they were more trouble than they were worth, and he'd not been replaced.

Nancy knew it was a punishment. That dog had been hers from a pup; she'd trained him, and he was her constant companion, her best friend, who'd added an element of joy to her life. It still wasn't clear how he'd died. Judy had found him and buried him before Nancy had known anything about it. She had her suspicions, but of course she couldn't ask outright if Judy had killed him. That would be seen as a challenge, and Nancy knew better these days than to bother even trying, not unless she wanted to spend a night or two in the barn.

She'd kept her thoughts to herself, but that act had unleashed something in her. Awoken a defiance that she didn't know what to do with. It unsettled her, made her view her life in a different light. Instead of being grateful for her peaceful existence, with no worries except how to maintain the status quo, she started to question things. It turned everything upside down and back to front in her mind. There were always two sides to every story and she'd started to seriously consider the other side of hers.

Now, as she unloaded the chicken feed, her thoughts zoomed in on the young couple. How free and fun their life was. How she'd never had any of that. How she wanted the sort of life they had.

The next day, she'd hoped to be able to sneak off to see the couple when Judy was doing the paperwork, or whatever job she had planned. But unusually, she'd decided to help Nancy outside. Their job was to extend the fruit garden. The raspberry canes needed thinning and there were enough new bushes to make a separate bed.

That kept them busy for most of the day, but at least it gave Nancy an excuse to go out later to check on the livestock while Judy cooked their tea. Nancy never got to go near the food. Not on her own. Just in case she was tempted to eat more than her share.

She checked her watch as she left, knowing she didn't have long.

As fast as she could, she hurried up through the woods, arriving at the field over the adjoining wall and surprising Ty and Jade, who were lying on the grass staring at one of the devices. They glanced up as she approached.

'Hi, Nan. Come and join us. We're just watching the end of this programme.'

Nancy sat behind them, peering over Jade's shoulder. It was a programme about reuniting long-lost relatives. Ten minutes later, when it was finished, she realised tears were rolling down her cheeks.

Jade's eyes were red-rimmed too. In fact, they'd all been crying, the reunion scene at the end so moving you'd have to be a robot not to be touched by it.

'Oh, I love that programme,' Jade said. 'We had something like that in our family not so long ago. My mum was adopted – she'd been given up by her birth mum when she was a baby. Anyway, she had a happy childhood, but then when she had me, she started thinking about her own mum and tried to find her, but no luck.

Then last year, out of the blue, her mum got in touch. She'd been living abroad and the Salvation Army, who'd been helping, had managed to track her down.' Jade sighed. 'Honestly, it was mad. They look so alike and have all the same mannerisms and the same sense of humour. It's just been the best thing that could have happened.' She grinned. 'And I've got a second nana now, which is lovely.'

She pulled an apologetic face then. 'I'm sorry about yesterday. I got mixed up with your name. I realised when the woman was calling you that you're Nancy. That's what Nan's short for. I'm sorry for implying you're a grandma. You're way too young for that, aren't you?'

Nancy smiled, but she wasn't really listening. Jade's story had made her think about her own life again.

'I want to find my dad,' she said, the thought forming into words before she could stop it. 'I haven't seen him for twenty-four years.'

Ty whistled between his teeth. 'That's a long time.'

Nancy pulled at the grass, wishing she hadn't said anything.

'The Salvation Army are the people to go to.' Jade's eyes lit up and she put a hand on Nancy's arm. 'I can help you. I love a project, and you've been so kind letting us stay here.' She crawled over to the tent and came back with a little notebook. 'Okay, give me your details.'

Nancy opened her mouth, then shut it again. She couldn't do that. *Think about the police.*

'What happened?' Ty asked. 'Did he leave you and your mum? That happened to my mate, not seen his dad since he was five.'

Nancy shook her head. 'No, it was me who left. My mum died.' She sighed. 'It's a long time ago. I don't know what was going through my head. In fact, I'm really confused about what happened. I did try and ring him after a while, but he'd moved, so I've no idea where he is now.' Her throat tightened and she looked down at the grass, sweeping a hand over it, letting the stems tickle her palm.

'You can do all sorts of research on the internet,' Ty said, swiping at his screen. 'Come on, let's see what we can find out.'

'Oh yes.' Jade wriggled next to him, notebook at the ready. 'What's his name? Tell us about him, Nancy. He's bound to be on the internet somewhere.'

'You really think so?' Nancy felt herself ripping in two. Her heart was telling her to go for it, because when was she ever going to get an opportunity like this again? The other half of her was shouting, no, there were consequences. What if these people found out who she really was?

With her head feeling like it might burst with the internal racket, she stood and brushed the grass off her clothes. 'I'm sorry, I've got to go.' It wasn't a lie. Judy would come and look for her if she took too long. She glanced down the field, then back at the couple.

Jade looked disappointed. 'Just give us his name,' she said. Nancy bit her lip to stop herself from blurting out the details. 'Hey, whatever happened between you, we're not going to judge. Not with our background.' They looked at each other and laughed. 'We got arrested for having sex in a car park. Apparently it was lewd behaviour, but we were so pissed we didn't really think about where we were.' Jade's face reddened and Ty grimaced. 'Not our finest moment, but we got off with a caution.'

Nancy's cheeks flushed. But it struck her that these two didn't seem to be worried about the police and being arrested. And if they were happy to tell a stranger about that, then would they really think badly of her?

'I ran away from home and left a suicide note so they'd think I was dead.' She looked up at the sky as she spoke. 'I suppose I wanted to punish my dad for not taking much notice of me after Mum died, but then… Well, it's complicated.'

Jade looked sympathetic. 'Families *are* complicated and you're not the same person you were twenty-four years ago. He'll be different too.' She smiled. 'I bet he'd be delighted to see you.'

Nancy frowned, not convinced. 'I've always been worried that I'd be arrested.'

'Arrested?' Ty gave her a puzzled look. 'What for? You'd be closing a cold case, so I'm sure the police would be happy to know you're still alive. The Salvation Army would respect your need for privacy, you know. It would be your decision if you wanted to be in touch with him, but if we can find his contact details, then at least you've got the option, haven't you?'

Uncertain, she started to walk away, but then turned and retraced her steps. This might be her one and only chance. 'My dad's name is Mike Gordon. He used to be a teacher. And we used to live in Blackpool.' She gave them her old address and phone number, and her dad's date of birth, together with her own details, with a promise that she'd see them the following day.

What if they found him? She could ring on one of their phones. Her heart flipped; the possibility felt real. This was happening. Two days before her fortieth birthday, her life was about to change.

CHAPTER TWENTY-SEVEN

She hardly slept that night, and in the morning she was jittery, chewing at a nail as she waited to find out Judy's plans for the day. Then she could work out when she'd have the opportunity to sneak out to visit Jade and Ty.

'What's wrong with you?' Judy snapped, when Nancy managed to knock her mug of tea onto the floor. 'You're all jumpy today, aren't you?' Her frown turned to concern. 'You're not ill, are you?' She studied Nancy's face. 'Hmm, you're looking a bit pale. If you think you're going down with that bug I've just had, you'd be better off resting today. Do something inside.'

Nancy flashed an apologetic smile, her eyes dipping to the mess on the floor. 'I'm fine, really I am. I just… I didn't sleep very well.' She got up and found a cloth, started to clear up. Judy hated it when she broke things, always reminding her that everything cost money and money was something that was in short supply. 'Anyway, I thought I could finish off the fruit beds today and get the weeding done. Would that be okay, or is there something else I need to be doing?'

'That's fine. Those need finishing. I've got the accounts to deal with, so I'll see you at lunch.' Judy finished her tea. 'I have to go out later.'

'Again?' Nancy knew from the expression on Judy's face that she'd made a mistake.

'Yes. Again.' She stood and started clearing the table. 'I'll be back late afternoon, I expect.' There was a flash of a smile on her face as she turned, like she had a secret. Maybe she did.

Nancy noticed then that Judy was wearing her smart clothes and make-up, her hair twisted into a chignon at the back of her head. She knew better than to ask where she was going. Anyway, she didn't really care. Judy was free to live her life as she wished. Nancy just wanted to be able to do the same.

She got the tools together, put them in the wheelbarrow and made her way to the orchard. It would be wise to wait until Judy had gone, she kept telling herself, but she itched to know what Ty and Jade had found out. Unable to contain her excitement, she dug the spade into the ground and dashed up the fields to where the couple were camped.

Her heart sank when she saw they'd gone.

All that was left was a flattened oblong of grass and the platform of stones they'd used as a base for the stove. She sank to the ground. So close. She'd been so close. *Maybe they've only just left?* It was still early. Perhaps she could catch them up. Frantically she scanned the field, then peeped over the wall. She stopped and listened, wondering if she might hear them chatting in the distance, cracking through piles of twigs in the woods, but the only sound was the whispering of the breeze in the trees.

Disheartened, she turned to go, but stopped when she noticed something yellow poking out from under the stones. She bent to look, and found it was the notebook Jade had been using the day before.

She looked inside. Lots of pages had been ripped out, but on the first page, in large, rounded letters, Jade had written: *Nancy Gordon. Dad – Mike Gordon.* This was followed by the old address and phone number Nancy had given her. Underneath, she'd written: *Current contact details: 142 Jacobsen Mount, Nottingham.* Followed by a phone number. She'd also written: *insurance salesman*, and there was a phone number for his work.

A sob caught in Nancy's throat. She could hardly believe what she was looking at. But her spirits fell as fast as they'd risen. Without the young couple, she had no way of calling him. There was no phone in the house anymore, Judy deciding they couldn't afford it.

'Nancy! Nancy!'

The sound of Judy's voice seared through her. She stuffed the notebook in her back pocket, glad that her top was long enough to hide it. Her mind started to work out an excuse as she hurried back to the orchard, her heart racing. Judy hated it when she wasn't where she was supposed to be.

'Where have you been?' Judy snapped. 'You've been acting weird these last couple of days.' Her hands settled on her hips. 'What's going on?'

Nancy tried to smile, her chest heaving with the exertion of running full pelt down the hill. 'Nothing's going on. I thought I heard the pigs squealing. Thought maybe one had got stuck again, so I went to check.'

Judy stared at her. Nancy held her nerve and gazed back.

'Did you now?'

She swallowed, feeling a need to elaborate. 'I think it was just some people walking through. I heard voices, but I couldn't see anyone. It probably just unsettled the pigs.' She cursed herself as soon as she'd said it. She'd been trying to make her lie close to the truth, so it wouldn't feel so bad and she might sound convincing, but why put that notion of other people being on their property into Judy's head?

Judy frowned. 'What are you talking about? Nobody walks through the woods. Where would they be walking to, for goodness' sake? It's not like it's a right of way or anything.'

Nancy shrugged. 'Probably just hearing things again. You know me.'

Judy gave an impatient sigh. 'Look, I have to go out sooner than I'd planned. I have a meeting with…' She stopped herself. 'Doesn't matter. I won't bore you with the details.'

Nancy gave her a broad smile. 'Okay, well… see you later then.' She walked over to the wheelbarrow and started unloading the tools.

As soon as Judy was gone, Nancy stopped what she was doing and went to sit on the bench. Her heart was thudding so hard she felt light-headed, needing a moment to calm down.

She pulled the notebook out of her pocket and read the details again. There he was, her dad. Contactable. After all these years. Would he be pleased to hear from her? Did she dare ring him?

Her mind was dragged back to the past, and she cringed now at the behaviour of the girl she'd been. How much hurt she must have caused, so soon after her mum's death, by pretending to be dead herself. And then there was the confusing matter of how her mum had actually died. How the accident had happened. The chronology of the day and the time immediately after was so blurry, she found it impossible to bring it into focus in her mind. Whatever had happened, would her dad have forgiven her, or should she just leave him in peace?

He'd want to know I'm alive. She was sure of it. He must feel some element of guilt for her disappearance, suicide or not, and she wanted to relieve him of that burden if nothing else. She didn't have to be part of his life, not if it wasn't what either of them wanted.

I wonder if Linda is still around. And what about my sister? So much she didn't know about her family. Could she be part of it again? She closed her eyes, dreaming of a different future, away from hard labour and Judy's particular set of rules.

The sound of footsteps made her eyes flick open. Then the notebook was wrenched from her hands.

Judy stood in front of her, staring at the first page. Her eyes met Nancy's.

'Do you want to tell me what this is, then?'

Nancy blanched, felt herself start to shake as the ramifications played themselves out in her mind. She braced herself, so tense that she couldn't reply; knew that she wasn't supposed to reply, but wait and listen and then take what was coming to her. That was the quickest way for it to be over. She said a silent prayer, while Judy's eyes sparked with rage.

'You ungrateful bitch. What were you planning to do? Are you running back home? Imagining a happy ending?'

The slap made Nancy's head spin to the side, wrenching a muscle in her neck and blurring her vision. She gasped, the searing pain bringing tears to her eyes. Was it better to let Judy know how much she'd hurt her, or take her punishment in silence? She'd never known the answer, never knew what Judy was looking for in these situations.

'Let me remind you of a few facts, shall I? Without me, you would have been living on the streets, probably picked up by a gang for prostitution. That's what happens to young girls living rough.'

Nancy had heard this before, of course. Many times. But after meeting the young couple, she wondered if the world out there was quite as scary as Judy had made her believe. *They* weren't scared. Far from it. They seemed carefree. They'd even made a joke out of being arrested.

Another switch flicked inside her brain. It was as though an optician had just changed the lens in her mind's eye. Ever since she was sixteen, she'd trusted Judy completely, this woman who'd given her refuge and initially been so kind. When her dog had died, the way she'd viewed her life had altered. But now, as Judy carried on with her rant, the same old arguments she'd heard a thousand times, Nancy's life spooled out in front of her with a clarity she'd never experienced before.

Another slap sent her head flying in the other direction, so hard she couldn't help crying out.

'You're not even listening, are you?'

'I am,' she sobbed, unable to stop the tears now, her ears ringing, face stinging like she'd been attacked by a swarm of wasps. 'Honestly I am. I was just feeling dizzy.'

'Bloody wimp. I had this at boarding school just about every day. Taught me to look after myself, I can tell you.'

'I'm sorry,' Nancy murmured, although inside she felt different. Inside she felt the opposite of sorry.

'Where did you get this?' Judy demanded, waving the book in her face. 'It's not your writing.'

Nancy swallowed. She'd never imagined the book would be found, hadn't prepared an excuse, and now she was stuck for words.

Judy's face darkened and she started hitting Nancy with the book, slicing blows to her head and arms and torso, speaking through gritted teeth while she meted out the punishment.

'You want to leave? That's what this is about, isn't it? Have you learned nothing?' Her words were staccato, timed with each blow. 'You have no money. There's nowhere to go. Nobody to help you.' She tapped her own chest with a finger. 'I am all you have. Your father won't want you after what you did.'

'But I didn't actually *do* anything wrong. I was grieving and vulnerable and—'

'I'm not talking about pretending to commit suicide,' Judy snarled as she continued to whip her with the book. 'Although that's bad enough. No, I'm talking about the fact you killed your mother. Remember that?'

'I did not. I didn't.' She was sobbing uncontrollably now, unable to stop, the words more painful than the blows. 'It was an accident. She died in an accident.'

'Tell the police that. Or shall I make this easy and ring them for you? I'm sure they'd love to speak to you about it. Then you can be tried for murder and thrown in jail for the rest of your miserable life. Is that what you want?'

'No! No, Judy, please. I'm sorry, I'll make it up to you.'

Judy stopped, her face red and blotchy. 'Yes, you will.' The tone of her voice left Nancy in no doubt that there were going to be consequences. 'You definitely will.'

Her heart was pounding as she told herself she was okay. It would all be okay. She just had to weather the storm, then they'd be back to normal. What she needed to do now, though, was a bit of grovelling. Show that she was sorry, not just say it.

'I'll get the new fruit bed done today, I promise, and weed all the other vegetable plots. I'll work really hard.' She didn't even dare look at Judy in case it set her off again.

Judy stepped back and slotted the notebook into her handbag. Then she turned and left.

Nancy closed her eyes, her body throbbing with the many blows, a heavy weight landing in her stomach. That was it. Now Judy had the notebook, her chance to reconnect with her family had gone.

CHAPTER TWENTY-EIGHT

Nancy busied herself with some weeding while she waited for Judy to go, listening for the sound of the engine as the Land Rover roared down the track. Then she sat back on her heels and allowed the tears to come.

Get out. Come on. Now's your chance to get away. A little voice in her brain was shouting at her.

Could she? Of course she could. Hadn't Judy said many times that she wasn't a prisoner?

Ah yes, but those were weasel words. It was the opposite of what she'd meant. Over the past few months, ever since her brain had changed into a different gear, Nancy had come to understand how Judy had manipulated her over the years. Saying one thing but meaning the opposite. Undermining her confidence in her memories, her feelings. Making her believe that the farm was a paradise to be grateful for, instead of a prison with bars of her own making. An emotional bunker that she'd been tricked into thinking was a safe haven. All the dangers of the outside world amplified, making her fearful to go out.

She stood and dusted the soil off her jeans, hardly able to believe how her thinking had flipped on its head. But now the thoughts had gathered together and laid themselves out in front of her, it was all that she could see.

What she could also see was the fact that she could walk out of the farm right now and Judy wouldn't have a clue where she'd gone. Her eyes widened. Freedom. It could be hers. It really could.

Her heart raced. And so did her mind.

What about the police? The fact she had no money? If she walked out, which direction would she go in? And how would she get anywhere if she couldn't pay for transport? Dare she hitch a ride? But what about all those women who'd been kidnapped over the years when they were hitching? Raped and murdered. Or had Judy made that up?

The questions flooded into her mind, settling like quick-setting cement so she found she couldn't move. She felt like she was suffocating, unable to breathe. Drowning in panic.

It doesn't have to be now, she reassured herself, desperate to get her panic attack under control. Not right now.

Gradually she managed to calm her breathing and unblock her thoughts. *I have to try.* She owed it to herself, didn't she? But still she couldn't move.

If she was more prepared, the thought of being out in the world on her own might not feel so terrifying. Perhaps it would be better to let the plan percolate, prepare herself mentally and get a bit of money together. Surely she could sneak some from Judy's purse? And get the notebook back with her dad's address. And pack a bag. Give herself a couple of days to prepare rather than dash off.

Her heartbeat started to slow. That was better. She was more likely to be successful if she waited and got together what she needed. Just like she had when she'd left home in the first place. And look how well that had gone. Like clockwork. Judy would go out again in a few days, and Nancy would be ready. She had one chance to get this right. One chance to get away from here for good, and she had to make sure she didn't mess it up. *Proper planning.*

Now that her mind was made up, she felt a new energy surge round her body. *I can manage for another couple of days.* Of course she could. As long as she did nothing to upset Judy or make her suspicious. Which meant getting all the work done as she'd promised.

With renewed determination, she went back to the weeding. It was a job she found quite relaxing, turning chaos into order, and it would be good to get her bruised muscles moving again.

Her mind drifted as she worked, thinking about the young couple travelling around with no worries. Why couldn't her life have been like that? All those wasted years. Judy's words wormed their way into her head, and she bit her lip as her thoughts dragged her back to the day of her mum's death. It hadn't been her fault. It hadn't. But there was something troubling her about that day. Was she in denial, as Judy insisted? Or was this something else, something she was only now starting to see – Judy's mind games at work, making her doubt her own memories?

She sighed and stood up, rubbing her back as she surveyed the newly weeded bed. One down, nine more to go. Her hands were shaking after her beating and the shock of being found out. She knew that wouldn't be the end of it. Things were never that simple. She'd probably have Judy ranting at her when she came back, threatening all sorts of consequences. Some of which would actually happen, while some wouldn't, meaning that she lived in a state of uncertainty. This time, though, things would feel different.

I'm leaving.

Her hand covered her mouth as if she'd spoken the words out loud. The very thought was thrilling and almost too scary to contemplate.

She sprang up from the seat, pulled the spade out of the ground, ready to get back to work. There was no way she could do everything today, so she decided that making the new bed for the fruit bushes would look more impressive.

They'd done a row the other day and she was going to dig a new bed in front of that one. But wherever she dug, her shovel kept hitting a band of rock, and she decided it wasn't going to be possible. She'd have to try somewhere else.

Scanning the area, she spotted a patch next to the bench that looked as though the soil would dig more easily. It also appeared to be more fertile, judging by the healthy growth of nettles and other weeds. She remembered Judy telling her it would be too much work to get all the nettles out and to leave it for the wildlife, but now she didn't have another option. She set to work, cutting the turf round the edges first to mark out the shape before pulling out the worst of the weeds. It wasn't as difficult as she'd imagined; the roots lifted easily, leaving her hopeful that she'd get the job finished before Judy returned.

When she started to dig the trench for the first row of plants, her spade hit something with a crunch, a barrier that meant she couldn't go deeper. Not a rock; this was different. Puzzled, she tried a bit further along, but the same thing happened, and this time, she uncovered something. Cloth of some sort. Light-coloured. She scraped away the soil, her heart jumping in her chest as she suddenly understood what she was seeing. It was a shirt, and now that she looked back to where she'd made her first attempt, she could see that the soil had fallen away from an object further down. She could make out the tip of something that looked horribly like a boot. And attached to it was… a bone?

A body! Oh my God. She dropped the spade, her hands flying to her mouth as she backed away. *It's a body.*

Her stomach convulsed, bile burning the back of her throat, but she couldn't look away. She stared at the remains in the soil as her mind tried to work out who it could be. They'd made many changes to the beds in this area over the years. In fact, when she thought about it, there'd been a wood pile here until this winter. Perfect camouflage for a grave. She'd never have known what was under it, would she?

Is it Ryan? He'd disappeared surprising quickly, along with the rest of the shearers. And there had been a lot of blood; Judy had been covered in it when she'd come and woken her up. She only had Judy's version of what had happened that night, and that stain on the bedroom floor… What if the fight hadn't been between Ryan and Levi? What if it had been an argument between Judy and Ryan? Could she have buried him here without Nancy knowing? It was perfectly possible.

Her stomach convulsed again, and she turned and ran back to the house, unable to look at the remains any longer.

Panic gripped her brain, like a fist squeezing juice from a lemon, her thoughts spurting out in an uncontrollable stream of internal chatter. *She killed him. Oh my God, she actually killed him.* When she reached the kitchen, she gulped down a glass of water, pacing up and down.

There was only one course of action open to her, however panicky it might make her feel. *I've got to leave now.*

She grabbed a rucksack that she used to carry a packed lunch and waterproofs when she worked out in the fields. It was small but would have to do. She dashed upstairs and started pulling clothes from her drawers, stuffing them in the bag, wondering what she'd need if she was going to be on the road for a few days.

Her heart thundered in her chest as her mind scurried around putting a plan together. Although she couldn't remember her dad's phone number, she could remember the address. *I can hitch.* She'd done it before. The young couple were hitching. It just needed a bit of patience and a kindly driver to take pity on her.

She went over to the window and glanced outside, checking the weather.

'What are you doing?'

She jumped at the sound of Judy's voice and turned to see her standing in the doorway.

Nancy's mouth fell open. Her eyes flicked to the rucksack on the bed, clothes spilling out of the top. It was very obvious what she was doing. She swallowed. 'I… um… didn't hear you come back.'

Judy gave a sly smile. 'That's because I never went.'

'But… the car.' Nancy glanced out of the window but there was no sign of the vehicle in its normal parking place.

'It's at the bottom of the track.' Judy glared at her. 'I knew I couldn't trust you. Running back home to Daddy, are we? Someone's been talking to you, haven't they? Turned your head?'

Nancy swallowed, adrenaline firing round her body. That was when she noticed the rolling pin in Judy's hand, slapping against her leg.

CHAPTER TWENTY-NINE

Nancy scanned the room, looking for a weapon, something to use to protect herself, but of course there was nothing.

The air fizzed with tension, Judy's eyes never leaving Nancy's face.

Sweat gathered under Nancy's arms while the rolling pin slapped against Judy's leg in a hypnotic rhythm.

Nancy could feel her mouth filling with saliva. You could do a lot of damage with a rolling pin. She knew that from experience. It had been three broken bones in her hand the last time. Judy had wrapped it in a splint while she sobbed her apology, telling her she hadn't meant to hit her and it wouldn't happen again. Even thinking about it made the old wounds throb.

She swallowed her fear, her thoughts speeding up as though she was watching a movie on fast-forward. As soon as Judy took a step into the room, Nancy knew what to do. With her heart pounding, she grabbed the rucksack, jumped onto the bed, then leapt off the other side. Before Judy could work out what was happening, Nancy crashed into her, the rucksack acting as both a cudgel and a shield. The momentum knocked Judy off her feet, sending the rolling pin spinning out of her hand and under the bed.

Without a backwards glance, Nancy stumbled towards the door, dragging the rucksack with her, until Judy grabbed one of the straps and gave a sharp tug, pulling her backwards. She let go of the bag, the release of tension sending Judy's head smacking against the door, disorientating her for a moment.

Go, go, go! Nancy hurtled down the stairs and out through the kitchen, not even thinking where she was going, just instinctively running. But she knew Judy was quicker than her. Ever since she'd broken her foot, running was something she would never do by choice.

Outside, her eyes darted around the yard, frantically searching for inspiration. *Where to go?* If she tried to run down the track, Judy would surely catch up with her, and she had the car down there somewhere. There was no escape that way. But going the other way wouldn't lead her to freedom either – once she'd left their land, she'd be on rough, rocky mountainside, which was impossible to run over. Not fast enough anyway. Not when Judy had a gun.

Hide.

With no time to debate whether it was a good idea or not, she skidded into the barn and scrambled up the ladder into the loft. Hopefully Judy would think she'd run off into the fields somewhere. Her heart thundered in her chest as she lay on the floor, peering through a gap in the boards. Her ears strained, listening for any sounds, but all she could hear was the clucking of the chickens beneath her. It seemed unnaturally quiet. She held her breath.

What was that?

A scuffling noise. Her heart skipped, her breath catching in her throat. She put her eye to the gap, but it was so dark down there she couldn't see anything. A chicken squawked, the sudden sound making her tense like she'd been tasered. It was no good; she had to get closer to the edge, so she'd have a better view. As quietly as she could, she inched her way towards the ladder, peered over the edge.

It took her a couple of second to realise she was staring right into the barrel of a gun.

She reared back just as Judy pulled the trigger, the sound so loud in the confined space that she was deaf for a moment; then a shrill ringing filled her ears, blocking out everything else. She thought she might be sick, knew she'd been millimetres away from being shot.

It's an airgun, she reassured herself. It won't kill you. *But it might*, a frantic voice whispered in her ear, if she was shot in the right place – and Judy was an expert with it. Even if it didn't kill her, she could be maimed for life. It wasn't just a weapon for shooting; on a couple of occasions, Judy had lashed out with it to give her a beating.

She halted her panicky thoughts and gritted her teeth. This was crunch time, the difference between life how it was and life how she wanted it to be. Or possibly no life at all. Come on, take the initiative, she urged herself. Don't just bow down to her; fight back for once. In reality, she had the advantage here, even though Judy was armed. She had the high ground. Judy was perched on a ladder. Precarious when you had a gun in one hand.

Like a coiled spring, she launched herself forward, leaning down the ladder as she screamed as loudly as she could. A war cry so shrill and piercing, it would surely be the last thing Judy was expecting.

She watched the gun waver in the air, only a foot away from her face. She snatched at the barrel, ripping it from Judy's hands. Saw the horrified expression, Judy's arms windmilling before she toppled backwards, landing with a thump on the packed earth of the barn floor.

Jubilant, Nancy pushed herself back to the safety of the platform, the gun at her shoulder, ready to use if Judy moved. But she didn't move. She was completely still. And quiet. No groans or moans, her body laid out flat on her back.

After a few minutes, with no movement from below, Nancy put the gun down and laid her head on the floor, exhausted by the rush of adrenaline, the certainty that she'd been close to death.

It was strange what thoughts came into your head when you believed you were about to breathe your last breath. Hers had been of when she was a child and she was at a fair with her parents, maybe the first fair she'd ever been to. She recalled the feeling of wonder at the different rides, the air full of the cloying smell of candyfloss and fried onions, the sound of screaming children, their faces alight with excitement. And her mum and dad holding one hand each. In that moment, she'd felt secure. She'd felt loved.

The urge to see her father filled her heart. All those things Judy had said were wrong. He'd loved her, she was sure of it. He'd be pleased to see her. Whatever had happened all those years ago, that bond of love would still exist and could be built on into the future. She belonged with her real family, not here with this woman who had bent her mind and body out of shape so that she no longer had an opinion.

She wanted to be like the young couple. Her jaw clenched. *I will be like them.*

When she peered over the edge of the platform again, Judy was still lying there. Lifeless.

Her eyes widened. *What if I've killed her?* Her stomach lurched at the thought.

Tucking the gun under her arm, she started to descend the ladder as fast as she could, needing to know that Judy wasn't dead, but she was shaking so much, she missed a rung and slithered to the bottom. With a loud *oomph*, she landed in a heap next to Judy, the gun jabbing her in the ribs as she fell. She heard a crack, felt a sharp, stabbing pain, all the breath going out of her with the shock of falling.

Get up, get up! With a groan, she rolled onto her knees and grabbed the ladder to heave herself to her feet. Every movement hurt and her hand went to her chest. She winced, guessed she might have a cracked rib. *Breathe through it, come on, get moving.* Cursing under her breath, she glanced at Judy, her face pale, completely calm, as peaceful as she'd ever seen her.

She remembered the cheerful young woman who'd picked her up when she'd been hitching out of Caernarfon; how kind she'd been, the fun they'd had in those early years. She'd genuinely loved her as a friend and felt sure the feeling was reciprocated.

For a split second, she wavered. Then she remembered how Judy had changed, her moods flipping in an instant. The start of the beatings, the change from being a guest to becoming a slave. She had no money, no rights, no freedom, and even though Judy didn't keep her locked up, the fears she'd planted in Nancy's mind served as an invisible cage, keeping her here.

Well, now she was going. This was over. Done with. She was ready to face her fear, because staying here with a murderer was unthinkable.

As she bent to pick up the gun, a swift kick to the back of her knee sent her sprawling face first into the ladder, her nose smacking against a rung as her legs crumpled beneath her. The pain was instantaneous, an explosion of blood spurting from her nostrils, filling her throat so she struggled to breathe.

'You stupid bitch,' Judy snarled, aiming a kick at her back.

Nancy grunted, and for a moment she was tempted to behave as she always had: submissive, waiting for the abuse to end. But she knew this time things were different. This time it was a matter of life or death. Now that she'd seen what surely was a body in the orchard, she knew what Judy was capable of.

Her brain fired to life.

From the corner of her eye, she saw Judy stoop to pick up the gun. She kicked out, a donkey kick that caught Judy's thigh and sent her staggering sideways, slamming into the tractor. The effort sent a searing pain through her ribs, but she had to ignore it. She turned to pick up the gun. Judy lunged for it at the same time, trying to shove her out of the way. They both had a tight hold of it, and they spun and tugged and tussled across the floor of the barn as though they were taking part in some deadly dance, neither of them willing to let go. Because whoever got that gun was surely the one who was going to live.

Nancy was beginning to tire, her fingers starting to lose their grip. Judy writhed, elbowing her, trying to bite at any part of her body that came close. A final twist, and she wrenched the gun from Nancy's grasp. Nancy staggered backwards against the mesh of the chicken pen, knocking against the shovel they used for cleaning out. Her survival instincts brought the implement to her hands. Just as Judy was putting the gun to her shoulder, she swung it with all her might, like an athlete throwing the hammer. It hit Judy in the chest, sending her tumbling to the floor.

She was already on her knees, trying to get to her feet, when Nancy reached her. She picked up the shovel and brought it down on the back of Judy's head.

With a grunt, she sprawled face down on the floor.

Nancy grabbed the gun and ran out of the barn, towards the woods, as fast as her injuries would allow.

CHAPTER THIRTY

When she could run no more, Nancy slowed to a halt, leaning against a tree. The pain in her ribs was almost unbearable. Her nose felt like it was four times its normal size, her face on fire. A little stream ran through the woods, and using a handful of moss as a sponge, she gently tended to her wounds with the icy water. All the while she listened for the sound of footsteps, Judy crashing through the undergrowth after her. But the only noise was the grunting of the pigs as they snuffled about, the singing of the birds and the rushing of the water as it tumbled over rocks.

She sat down on a large boulder under the canopy of an oak tree and wondered how much damage she might have done to Judy. To be honest, she hadn't looked closely. But the noise as the shovel had made contact with her head was on repeat in her brain. Like the cracking of an egg. She shuddered, tears springing to her eyes.

What if I've killed her?

That on its own was a terrifying thought, along with all the possible consequences, including having Judy's death on her conscience for the rest of her life. It was a while before the panic settled and she realised something important. *Nobody knows I live here.* In all the years she'd been at the farm, few people had ever come to the door, and when they did, she hid away out of sight. She'd never had a letter. No official documents to confirm she was a resident.

If Judy was dead, there was nothing keeping her here. The best thing would be to try and find some money and leave. Maybe call it in from a public phone box so the animals would be looked after and Judy would have a proper burial. And then Nancy would be free. She hardly dared believe it was possible, but she had to try and find out.

It took an hour for her to pluck up courage. With the gun under her arm, she made her way back to the house and peered into the barn.

No Judy.

The hairs stood up on the back of her neck. *Be careful now.* She could be hiding anywhere, waiting to pounce. Adrenaline pumped round her body, her pulse going at a frantic rate. Slowly she turned in a circle, the gun to her shoulder, and froze when she saw people through the kitchen window. A man and a woman in uniform. Creeping to the end of the barn, she spotted the corner of an ambulance parked in front of the house. As far as Nancy had been aware, Judy had no way of calling for help. *She must have bought herself a mobile, kept it hidden.* It was the only possibility. She remembered all those times when she'd heard her talking to herself and realised that she'd actually been on the phone. *How stupid am I?* She gave an annoyed grunt, astounded at her own naivety. Not even questioning Judy's behaviour, trusting that she was always honest with her because they'd agreed right from the start that their friendship would be based on the truth. Now she could see that was another of Judy's manipulations.

A man came running out of the door, one of the paramedics. Nancy couldn't allow herself to be seen but she needed to know what was happening. *Is Judy still alive?* The urgency of the paramedic suggested that she was. She crept back to the kitchen and peeked through the window. Judy was lying on the floor. She didn't look conscious and there was a big bandage on her head. The woman who was tending to her suddenly looked up. Nancy ducked down, slipping round to the side of the house again. There was a water butt on this corner, and she slid behind it, so she'd be able to make out what they were saying but would be hidden from sight.

Finally she heard the clatter of the trolley as the stretcher was pushed towards the ambulance. The paramedics' voices were indistinct as they loaded Judy into the vehicle, but then she heard them say something about calling the police, and her heart stuttered in her chest.

The police!

What if they brought dogs? They'd surely find her. She couldn't stay. But she wasn't in any fit state to go far either. The light was starting to fade now and she wondered how hard the police would look. Whether they'd come at all.

Once the ambulance had left, she went into the house to get herself a drink and something to eat. She'd had nothing since breakfast and was feeling too light-headed to think straight. But she did know that even if the police were called now, it would be a while before they could get anyone to a remote location like this. She had a little bit of breathing space to work out what she was going to do.

Her face looked a mess, staring back at her in the hall mirror. A purple bruise was forming on her swollen nose and spreading across her cheeks where she'd hit the ladder. How could she think about hitching a lift anywhere looking like she'd just come out of a boxing ring? That was a non-starter as plans went. And she'd never learnt to drive, Judy had made sure of that, so even if she could find the keys, she couldn't take the car. Her only option was to hide and recuperate for a little while, then make her move when she felt stronger and didn't look quite so scary.

She was weary and sore, the pain throbbing through various parts of her body like toothache, but she forced herself on. Freedom could be hers if she could just get through this.

Ten minutes later, carrying her rucksack and wearing a full set of waterproofs so she could stay out as long as she needed to, she set off up the back fields to a place where she could look down on the farm but wouldn't be seen. If the police did turn up, she could keep an eye on them from here and escape over the wall into the woods if they decided to come near.

She lay on the cool grass, finding it hard to get comfortable with her injured rib, but eventually she found a way, her head propped on her rucksack. Exhausted, she closed her eyes, and soon she was asleep.

The sound of voices woke her. It was pitch black now. She blinked, trying to focus, reaching for the binoculars she'd brought with her. A dot of light moved about the yard. There was someone in the house as well. She had to assume it was the police.

Half an hour later, after they'd had a good look round the house, the barn and outbuildings, they went away. She waited another hour before making her way back down the hill.

She pushed the back door, but it wouldn't open. Locked.

Her heart sank. *Of course it's locked. The police wouldn't leave a house open, would they?* She trudged round to the front door, but that was locked too. The idea of spending a cold night outside brought tears to her eyes. What she longed for was a hot bath to soothe her battered body, some bandages to strap her ribs, a plaster for her nose. Food. Then she'd feel better.

She'd just decided she'd have to make do with the barn when she remembered the window by the washing machine. It was always open. Could she crawl through it? Then she could grab the spare set of keys that hung in the utility room.

It was awkward, and not a little painful, but with lots of cursing, she managed to wriggle inside, pushing her rucksack through first. She was safe. The police wouldn't be back tonight. She could make sure she was up and out at the crack of dawn, just in case they returned in the morning. For now, though, she could eat her fill, patch herself up and plan what her next move should be.

CHAPTER THIRTY-ONE

On the third day after the fight, Nancy was starting to feel a little better. Her face, however, told a different story. She now had two black eyes, and her bruises were a rainbow of garish colours. Her body ached like she'd been kicked by a horse and it still hurt every time she breathed. The swelling had gone down a bit, though, and she'd been able to examine her ribs. She felt it was probably a crack rather than a break, so should heal okay, given time. Of course, what she needed most was rest, but it was unlikely she'd be able to do much of that.

The last two days had been spent running on adrenaline, jumping at the slightest sound, on constant alert for the return of the police. She was in no shape to make her escape, her only desire being to sleep and eat, lethargy weighing down her limbs. It was her body's response to the trauma, but she wished she could think straight.

Instead, her mind took her round a never-ending circle as she tried to pin down a definite plan. The walk to the bottom of the track seemed too far, the idea of it overwhelming her before she'd even started. Even if she did make it to the road, she'd have no chance of a lift and a very long walk to any sort of civilisation. She hadn't been able to find any money to pay for a bus or a taxi. And then there was the matter of the police. Judy had been taken to hospital, and whether she lived or died, Nancy had caused her serious harm and would therefore be accused of committing a crime. She had to get away, but quite how she was going to do it was a problem still to be solved.

Round and round her thoughts went as she lay in bed listening for signs of trouble, unwilling to move unless she really had to.

I've got the gun.

Her eyes flicked open, her heart skipping at the thought.

I'm in control now, if Judy comes back.

That was a very alien concept – being in control. Maybe she could hang on here a bit longer, until she was fully recovered.

But what if Judy's dead?

Would the old man, the owner of the farm, be informed? Would he come back? Would the police return to gather evidence, check everything in more detail? Then she'd have to leave. But not yet.

A plan evolved. If Judy came back, Nancy would take charge. She could lock Judy in her room and have a free run of the place while she got her strength back. That way, she could take the process of leaving more slowly, at a pace that wouldn't be quite so frightening. More manageable. Having not left the farm for twenty-four years, it was going to take a lot of courage to face the outside world. At the very least, she needed her bruises to die down. Then she'd be more likely to get a lift.

With a clear plan in mind, she felt a spurt of energy. Enough to get herself out of bed, have a refreshing shower and make a late lunch. She'd just fed the chickens and was about to collect the eggs when she heard the crackle of tyres on the stony track: a car approaching.

The police! She hurried out of the barn and up the back field to her spying place, wishing she had her binoculars. She heard the car doors bang shut. Then nothing. No search party, no police dogs. After an hour, she crept closer to the house. Maybe it was just Judy, not the police at all. Perhaps the car had been a taxi, although she hadn't heard it leave. She had to check, then maybe her heart would stop pounding so hard.

She crept into the yard, thought she saw movement in the kitchen and peered in. A young woman with a dark ponytail was unloading shopping bags onto the table. She turned, and Nancy ducked down, creeping under the window and round the side of the house. The car didn't look like a taxi. The woman came outside and got a bag from the back seat. It looked like she was staying. *Is she a carer, maybe?* But she wasn't wearing a uniform.

Puzzled, Nancy went back to the kitchen window, standing out of sight but where she could hear. After a while, when her legs had become too tired, she slumped down to sit on the ground, shivering in the gathering dusk. She heard Judy's voice, faint as though she was calling from upstairs.

'Eva…'

Nancy frowned. The name caught hold of a memory: a baby called Eva. *My little sister.* But she supposed a lot of people shared that name. Something stirred inside her, though. Could it be? It would be very odd if it was. She told herself to stop being fanciful.

Her leg started cramping, and she got to her feet, had a little walk around, risked a peep through the window. The kitchen was empty, the food still on the table. *Look at it all. So many treats.* Saliva filled her mouth. *Could I sneak in and get something?* Her stomach was rumbling at the thought of food. She could be quick. In and out the back door while the woman was upstairs. But when she tried the handle, the door was locked. She pulled the spare keys from her pocket, thankful that she'd thought to grab them on her way out. But although the key turned, the door had been bolted.

Christ! It looked like she was locked out now. Then she remembered the window in the utility room was still open. She could get in there. Should she risk it? She decided to check the kitchen again first. It was still empty. *I've got to eat.*

As quietly as she could, she climbed inside and sneaked into the kitchen, grabbing the first things she saw. A quiche and a loaf of bread. Perfect. She stopped and listened, could hear voices and thought they must be upstairs. She knew there was a big lump of cheese in the fridge, so she took that as well. Then, unable to stop herself, she crept into the hallway to see if she could overhear anything that would give her a clue as to who the stranger was.

The young woman was talking. Did she just call Judy 'Nancy'?

Hearing footsteps above her head, she crept back into the kitchen and struggled out of the utility room window. Pain from her ribs spiked through her, making her bite down on her lip so she didn't cry out. She crept into the barn and up into the loft, enjoying her stolen food, stashing the rest for later, secured in an old tin away from any rodents.

When it was almost dark, and light spilled across the yard, she sneaked back to the kitchen window. The young woman, Eva, was reorganising the shopping on the table, looking for something. Nancy cringed. She must have spotted that some of the food was missing. Taking it had been a bad idea, she realised now. But her hunger had been gnawing at her insides and it had been instinct, without thinking of the consequences.

Eva came and stood by the window, looking out. From her place by the wall, Nancy could just make out her profile. *She looks like Dad. Is this my sister?* Then it dawned on her – the only possibility that made sense. *Is Judy pretending to be me?*

She made her way back to the barn, deciding that she would spend the night in the loft. She had her sleeping bag up there and tarpaulins that would give her some warmth. In the gathering gloom, she settled down for the night, her mind racing.

How did Eva get here?

But that wasn't important. The really important thing was whether she could help Nancy get away. *She has a car.* Suddenly, the possibility of escape had become real.

The following day was stormy – the barn wasn't the best place to be with lightning around. She moved downstairs, away from the steel girders and metal sheeting of the roof, and sat on the tractor, watching the rain hammering in the yard. It sounded so loud in here. Today, she felt weak and sore, her resolve crumbling. The clambering in and out of the window had been a really bad idea on a number of levels; every breath brought a sharp pain in her chest. Her head throbbed, as did her nose, which she'd managed to knock on her way out of the window; the throbbing keeping her awake half the night.

She was in no state to try and talk to Eva, not when she looked like this – the poor girl would probably run a mile or scream the place down and alert Judy to Nancy's presence. No, better not to rush. Eva had brought bags into the house, so was clearly planning on staying. She'd still be here tomorrow. Better to wait and have a proper think about the right way to approach her. She'd get one chance. That was all. *I've got to get it right.*

Patiently, she waited in the barn, sneaking behind the tractor when Eva came in unexpectedly. Now that the possibility of talking to her was real, she found she couldn't do it, scared that the sight of her beaten-up face would frighten her sister, that she wouldn't believe her.

Scared. That was her permanent state of mind, and she cursed herself for reverting to type. She had to break out of that way of thinking if she was ever going to leave this place. She had to dredge up some courage from somewhere.

I've got the gun, she reminded herself. Judy can't touch me. I'm in control.

With that thought in mind, she pondered how she should approach Eva. But before she could come up with an answer, she watched her sister run out of the barn towards the orchard. Ten minutes later, she came running back into the yard. It looked like she was crying, a horrified expression on her face.

The body! She'd seen the body. Nancy's heart missed a beat. *Now what?* Surely she'd leave. *Without me.*

Panicked, she started to run after her. Then turned and went back into the barn. She wasn't going anywhere near Judy without that gun in her hand.

Once she was armed, she crept behind the water butt, where she could keep an eye on Eva's car. If the girl decided to go, she could jump in and go with her, leaving Judy to do whatever she wanted. It would no longer matter because Nancy would be free.

The sound of shouting made her leave the safety of her hiding place, sneaking round the front of the house towards the noise. It sounded like banging on wood.

'Let me out!' she heard Eva shout.

In that moment, she understood what had happened. Judy had locked Eva in her room. And the only reason she'd do that was if Eva had told her she'd found the body.

PART THREE

Now: Nancy and Eva

CHAPTER THIRTY-TWO

Eva

Eva sat on the bed, hardly able to believe that she'd allowed herself to be cornered like this. She gritted her teeth and thumped the pillow. *I shouldn't have come back in. I should have just driven away, let the police get my stuff back.* Hindsight was a wonderful thing, though, and she'd been sure she'd be able to nip in and out before she was seen. Never had she imagined the woman who'd been pretending to be Nancy would be up and about, let alone lock her in her room – that hadn't been anywhere in her thinking. She seemed so much better today. A remarkable improvement, now she thought about it. *Was she just pretending to be frail?* It now seemed a distinct possibility.

None of it made sense, though. What was the woman hoping to achieve? Surely Linda would realise that Eva hadn't been in touch and would get the police involved? But then it would be easy to hide Eva's car and… She quickly shushed her thoughts before they could say 'body'. That really was taking things too far. But there *was* an actual body in the orchard, there was no doubting that. No doubting it at all. She shivered at the memory.

Her thoughts chattered on, deafening her to the voice of reason, until she realised she had an escape route. A risky one maybe, but she could get out of the window, couldn't she?

As she stood, she felt the woman's phone in her back pocket and blew out a relieved breath. Things were not as bleak as she'd imagined. She found her phone charger, selected the right fitting and plugged it in. It would only take a few minutes to get some charge, then she could call the police. She tried to calm herself, clear her brain of the fanciful imaginings, the possibilities of what might happen next. As usual, she'd been getting way too far ahead of herself.

While the phone charged, she went over to the window and peered out. *Could I jump?* She'd be landing on slate slabs, an unyielding surface that would send shock waves through her body and there was a high risk of breaking bones. But maybe if she hung by her arms, that would make the distance manageable. *Bend your legs to absorb the force.* Her dad used to tell her that at the climbing wall when she got stuck and wanted to jump off. She sighed at the memories, longing to get home where she belonged, and felt a new surge of determination. *Dad would do it.* She stared at the drop, trying to channel his courage, which must be in her DNA somewhere. *Can I manage it without hurting myself?*

She swallowed.

Or just wait for the police to come.

That seemed like a more sensible option. She'd just have to be ready for the woman if she came back. There was still a chance she could take her by surprise and overpower her. Now she knew she had options, she was feeling better by the minute and her pulse started to slow to something approaching normal.

The phone buzzed as it finally came to life, and she smiled at it like it was her new best friend. She turned it on, the screen lighting up with a couple of new notifications. It also showed a keypad, asking for a PIN – no chance on earth of guessing that. But below it was another button to be used in an emergency.

She pressed it, working out how to explain her predicament to an operator as succinctly as possible. It took a few seconds to realise there was no ringtone – the connection didn't seem to be working. Then she remembered the woman's words about there being little signal in the house. Perhaps she's wrong, she thought, desperate now. She walked over to the window, holding the phone in various places, but it made no difference. With a strangled scream, she understood that she wasn't going to be making a call to anyone.

Beyond disappointed, she leant her head on the window. Plan A was a non-starter; there was no waiting for the police to come and rescue her. She sank into the chair, trying to control her fear, her body curling in on itself like an armadillo seeking safety from a predator. *You don't think straight when you're frightened*, her dad's voice told her. *Take a few deep breaths and calm down.*

Gradually she straightened up, her fear a tight knot in her stomach. Her mind started to clear. There was always plan B. *Jump*. It was worth taking a proper look.

She stood and put the phone back on charge, just in case there was a better signal once she got the window open and leant out. The plug was next to the chest of drawers and couldn't be seen from the door, but she tucked the phone underneath just to be on the safe side.

With that done, she turned her attention to the sash window. She studied it for a moment, uncertain whether to push the top down or the bottom up. In the end, after trying both, she managed to create a gap at the bottom that was just wide enough to slide a hand through, but that was it. Even putting all her strength into it, she couldn't make it budge any further.

She stood, panting after her exertions. It was no good. There was no way to escape… not until the door was opened. So that was plan C. She'd wait for the woman to come into the room, then overpower her and make a run for it.

The sound of footsteps on the stairs would be warning enough – she could be ready for her. If only she had a weapon. What could she use? The room was pretty bare. She had her bag – that would work, wouldn't it? If she hit her full in the chest or head, it would surely tip her off balance. It was definitely worth a try.

After an hour of silence, her mind was running out of control. *What if she doesn't come back? What if she leaves me here to starve to death?* In fact, why *would* she come back? She had no need for Eva now she was feeling better. She was totally dispensable. In truth, she was a liability, because she knew the woman's secret. Knew that she had a body buried in the orchard. Wouldn't it be much better for her if Eva was dead?

By the time her thoughts had reached this point, she'd worked herself into a state bordering on hysteria.

A sudden brainwave made her jump up from the bed. *Break the window. Yes!* Why hadn't she thought of that before? She'd have to be ready, though. It would make a lot of noise and the woman would hear it. She scanned the room, and that was when she realised she'd overlooked the chair. That would be a handy weapon if the woman came in but would it be strong enough to break the window?

She picked it up and was about to slam it into the glass when she stopped herself, put it down. She needed to have her valuables ready. She slipped the phone and keys into her handbag and slung it across her body so it wouldn't get in the way, then got her holdall ready to throw outside before she jumped. *There'll be jagged glass.* Hmm, she needed something to put over that so she could climb out without ripping herself to shreds. Her gaze landed on the duvet, and she pulled it from the bed, dropping it under the window.

Now she was ready. She picked up the chair and did a couple of practice swings before slamming it into the glass as hard as she could. She screamed as it bounced back at her, smacking her in the face and sending her sprawling on the floor. The metallic taste of blood filled her mouth, the grit of a broken tooth on her tongue. She spat out the tooth, tears streaming down her cheeks as her whole face throbbed with pain, her mouth feeling like it was on fire.

The sound of footsteps thumped up the stairs. The woman's voice outside the door. 'What are you doing in there?'

She didn't come in and look. Eva decided to stay quiet. Then maybe she would come and check to see if she was all right. At which point she could try and make her escape.

The chair had lost one of its legs, she noticed; it had slid under the bunk bed and she could just make it out in the gloom. If she shuffled closer, she thought she'd be able to reach it.

'Eva? Are you okay?'

Her throat was choked with blood and she was desperate to cough. She spat on the floor, so at least she could breathe, then reached for the chair leg. As weapons went, it wasn't the most threatening, but a whack on the face or hands or even the shins would really hurt – enough to shock the woman. Enough for Eva to get past and out of the house.

She gripped the weapon tighter.

The sound of footsteps walking away.

She slumped back onto the floor, blinking back tears of disappointment. *When you're in a tough situation, you just have to look at the positives,* her dad used to say when he'd been talking about adventures gone wrong. Being stuck out in the mountains overnight, or when his tent had been wrecked by cows, or his car broken into and all his gear nicked. If he'd got through those situations, she could get through this.

She tried to dredge up a positive and gave a satisfied smile at the chair leg still in her hand. Even though she hadn't managed to break the window, at least she had a weapon.

CHAPTER THIRTY-THREE

Nancy

Nancy heard a commotion, a loud bang at the window making her glance upwards. She frowned, even more concerned for Eva's safety. She knew the window didn't open, so there'd be no escape that way. If Eva was locked in, Nancy would have to go inside and unlock the door herself.

Her heart was racing, hands slick around the gun as she held it to her shoulder. In truth, she'd never been allowed near the weapon, had no idea how to shoot, and her hands were shaking so much, she wondered if she'd be able to hit her target. *If it comes to that.* Hopefully the threat would be enough to keep Judy at bay.

The back door had been bolted, and she expected the front door might be too, but it swung open in a lazy arc. Her heart flipped, her body tensed, ready to run away, but she made herself move forward. Scarcely daring to breathe, she advanced into the hallway. Judy could be in either of the front rooms, waiting to ambush her. Or hiding in the kitchen, waiting for her to start up the stairs, at which point she'd sneak up behind her.

She has no idea where you are, she reminded herself. Come on, you've got the advantage.

She ran her tongue round dry lips, tasting the sweat.

Her heart was racing so fast she could hear herself gasping, each breath shaking her injured ribs and sending shards of pain through her torso. She closed the study door and turned the key.

The same with the sitting room. There. If Judy had been inside, she was contained for now.

Feeling more confident, she crept further into the hallway, glancing up the stairs, listening. Nobody there. She had to be in the kitchen, she decided. If she could force her into the utility room, she could lock her in there, run up and release Eva and they could be on their way. She held her breath as she inched forward.

'You're going the wrong way,' Judy's voice said from upstairs.

Nancy froze, then turned and retraced her steps, her back against the wall, the gun wavering in front of her as though it had a life of its own.

'You should put that thing down before you hurt yourself.' Judy was standing on the top step, dressed in her usual jeans and sweatshirt. She had a mug in her hand. Just an ordinary day. The normality of it shook Nancy for a moment and she had to fight hard to keep her focus.

'Let her out of that room,' she said, her voice shaking as much as the gun.

Judy snorted. 'Or else?' She smiled and moved down a couple of steps. 'Come on, Nancy. I think this has gone far enough.' She was using her wheedling voice, the one that created doubt. 'You really going to shoot me?' She pulled a face, trying for comedy.

Nancy swallowed. 'If you make me, yes, I will. Go on, let her out.'

Judy continued to descend the stairs, her hand on the banister. One step, then two, and before Nancy could decide what to do, she was already halfway down.

'Don't come any closer,' she said, her voice unsteady. 'I'll shoot, I mean it.'

'You couldn't hit me if you wanted to,' Judy laughed. 'Now put that gun down and let's see if we can sort out this misunderstanding.'

Nancy's grip tightened. Judy was doing it again. Befuddling her, trying to make her believe there was nothing wrong, that this was normal.

She pulled the trigger, reeling as the butt of the gun kicked into her shoulder and pain sliced through her.

Silence.

She stared at Judy, wondering if she'd hit her, but then she saw the splintered hole, where the pellet had embedded itself in the wall.

Judy pulled a face of mock horror and sat down on the step. 'Nice try,' she said, taking a sip from the mug.

'I want you to come down here.' Nancy tried to put a bit of authority in her voice, but in truth she was shaking even more now. She beckoned with the gun. 'Come on. Now. Down here.'

Judy leant against the banister.

'This is all your fault, you know. Eva being here is down to you.' She nodded as if to confirm that what she was saying was true. 'If you hadn't spoken to whoever it was who gave you that notebook, if you hadn't let them poison your mind, none of this would have happened.'

Nancy bit her lip, wondering now if maybe she *was* to blame.

'The hospital found the notebook with your name and your father's contact details in my bag when they were looking for identification, and assumed it was mine.' Judy gave a derisive snort. 'Well, they would, I suppose. I have no ID of any sort in there. I make sure of that. Those stupid people put two and two together and made five.'

'Why didn't you tell them? Why did you let them ring?'

'I had no choice in the matter.' She flapped a dismissive hand. 'Well, they said they asked permission, but I don't remember.' She leant forward, her voice getting louder, anger sparking in her eyes. 'Because a certain somebody cracked my skull open with a bloody shovel.'

Nancy jumped at the sudden sharpness of her voice, the force of her glare. An instinctive reaction, as it was usually a precursor to a wallop at the very least. You've got the gun, she reminded herself, holding it a little tighter, her finger on the trigger. Her heart thundered in her chest, all her senses on high alert as Judy carried on talking.

'I wanted to get home and they didn't want me to be alone. I decided not to put them right.' She gave a sly smile. 'A means to an end. And anyway, I was curious. A younger version of you could come in handy. And to be fair, she's looked after me very well.'

'So you pretended to be me.'

Judy shrugged. 'Not really, I just didn't deny it. Let them carry on assuming.' She finished whatever was in her mug.

Silence filled the air, pressing down on Nancy. She wiped the sweat from her brow with the back of her hand, summoning her courage.

'You've got to let Eva go. Let me go. Just allow us to walk away and that will be the end of it. We'll keep your secret.'

Judy's eyebrows inched up her forehead. 'And what secret would that be?'

Nancy swallowed, hardly able to speak about her find. 'The body in the orchard. It's Ryan, isn't it?'

Judy tossed her head back and laughed. Nancy stared at her. What was so funny about killing someone?

Nancy's head snapped back down. 'You're such a silly billy,' she said, all nice now, as if they were talking about a cake recipe. 'That's not Ryan. See what happens when you try and think for yourself? You get it so wrong, it's…' She left her sentence hanging, chuckling to herself.

Nancy had been so convinced she was right, for a second she was distracted from her task, the gun barrel dropping from its target. A pain exploded in her forehead as Judy hurled the mug at her, scoring a direct hit. She staggered backwards, and the gun dropped from her hands, clattering onto the quarry tiles.

Quick as a flash, Judy was down the rest of the stairs and scooping the gun into her hands.

With a satisfied smile, she fired a shot into Nancy's leg.

It was so sudden, Nancy had no time to think, no time to anticipate. The blast hit her like a hammer blow, making her fall to the floor, taking her breath away.

Judy stood over her, the gun still at her shoulder, her finger on the trigger.

'Okay, get up.' She waved the weapon. 'It's time for you to meet your little sister.'

Nancy struggled to her feet, screaming out when she tried to put weight on her injured leg.

'Don't be such a baby,' Judy said with a shake of her head. 'It's only a flesh wound.'

Nancy's teeth clamped together, silent tears rolling down her face. *She's going to kill me.* If not now, then soon. Because why wouldn't she? Why would she let them live when they knew about the body in the orchard?

Her only thought was to save her sister. Little Eva, who she'd abandoned all those years ago. Dismissed as a problem, a distraction from her own needs. She was appalled at her younger self, but at least she might have a chance to make up for it now. She had to hang on to the hope there was still a possibility of escape.

'Get a move on, or I'll give you something to really cry about.' Judy was getting impatient and jabbed at Nancy with the rifle. 'Come on, up the stairs.'

'It doesn't have to be like this,' Nancy whimpered, as she hauled herself step by step towards Eva's prison.

'Oh, I'm afraid it does.' The barrel of the rifle landed in her kidneys, making her gasp. 'Just remember, you did this to yourself. All of this… it's all your fault.'

CHAPTER THIRTY-FOUR

Eva

Eva could hear voices and rushed to the door, ear pressed against the wood to try and hear what was being said. Who else would be here? Then she remembered the doctor's warning, her conviction that the woman had been attacked. The police hadn't found anyone, but that person could still be at large. Had they come back to finish the job? In which case, was she in more or less danger?

Her heart raced as she strained to hear what was being said, the chair leg gripped firmly in her hand.

The sound of the first shot made her jump away from the door, hand covering her mouth. *Was that a gun?* Her brain froze. The voices were louder now. Another shot made her heart miss a beat. She heard a cry. Then the woman's raised voice.

The sound of footsteps plodding up the stairs.

She pressed herself against the wall at the side of the door, ready to ambush whoever was going to come in. It was her only hope of escaping from this nightmare.

There was a loud thump on the door, like someone had fallen against it.

'For God's sake!' she heard the woman snap. 'Do you want a shot in the other leg? Because that's what's going to happen if you don't sort yourself out.'

'I can't help it.' A female voice. 'My leg's gone dead. It's not working.'

If this person had been the woman's attacker, then it sounded like she was her prisoner now. *The same as me.* Eva readied herself, trying to work out the best thing to do. If she swung the chair leg as soon as the door opened, she might hit this other woman and her chance would be wasted. She had to wait, get her timing just right.

The key rattled in the lock. 'I'm coming in,' the woman shouted. 'You try anything and Nancy gets shot in the back.'

Nancy? My sister? But… the body in the orchard?

Her mind flew along at a hundred miles an hour until she forced it to stop. They were both in danger, and she was the only one who could do anything about it. She had to focus all her attention on getting this right.

The door opened; she held her breath. Someone stumbled into the room. Eva let her pass, then swung the chair leg with as much force as she could muster, catching the woman standing in the doorway full in the throat.

The sound of the shot rang in her ears, but she knew she couldn't hesitate, knew she had to end this. She swung again, grunting with the force of the blow. It seemed to happen in slow motion, the chair leg whipping through the air and connecting with the side of the woman's head. The startled expression, just for a split second, before she crumpled to the landing floor like a puppet whose strings had been cut, the gun tumbling from her hands.

Eva snatched the gun from the floor, pretending that she knew what she was doing, that she really would fire it at a living human, whilst knowing that she never could. Then, with her chest heaving, she surveyed the scene. It looked like the woman was out cold. She turned her attention to the other woman – Nancy. She was sprawled on the bedroom floor, but Eva could see her ribs moving up and down with every breath. She crouched beside her, a hand on her back.

'Nancy? Are you okay?'

Her body was shaking and Eva realised she was sobbing.

'It's over,' she murmured. 'She's out cold, but we need to get her in here, then lock her in so she's secure.'

Slowly, Nancy rolled onto her side. Eva winced when she saw her bruised face and the angry red gash on her forehead. But there was no doubting this was her sister, her face a copy of their mother's, her hair the same vibrant colour. Her chest felt tight, tears gathering in her throat, filling her eyes. She couldn't speak.

'Did that shot get you?' Nancy asked. Eva shook her head, and Nancy carried on. 'I thought if I fell into the room it might give you a chance to get out. But I didn't know if Judy had tied you up or hurt you. Or…' her voice dropped to a horrified whisper, 'if you were dead.'

The sisters clung to each other for a moment before Eva let go and clambered to her feet. She glanced at their attacker where she lay on the floor. 'I don't want to push our luck. We've got to get her locked up.'

She held out her hand and hauled her sister to her feet. 'Tell you what, you sit on the bed. You're looking ever so pale, and my God, you're shaking like a leaf.' She gave Nancy's shoulder a reassuring rub. 'I can drag her in here.'

With Nancy safely on the bed, Eva's hand tightened round the gun while she gingerly advanced towards Judy. Not a flicker of movement. She poked her with the barrel. Still nothing, although she was definitely breathing.

She put the gun down and scooted round to the woman's feet, tying her legs together with her fleece jacket in case she came round and started struggling. Then she started hauling her into the bedroom.

'Nancy, you've got to get out of here,' she grunted as she inched backwards, the woman's weight so much harder to manoeuvre than she'd imagined. Sweat was beading on her forehead, trickling down her spine, but she was determined to finish the task she'd started.

Once she'd pulled her into the middle of the room, she dropped her legs. Her chest was heaving with the effort, but she knew there was no time to stop and get her breath. She grabbed Nancy's arm and tugged her out onto the landing, slamming the door behind her and turning the key. The banister formed a welcome support as the strength seeped out of her legs, and she burst into tears.

Nancy hesitated, then came and stood next to her.

'Hello, little sis,' she said, putting a gentle arm round her shoulders, pulling her into an embrace.

CHAPTER THIRTY-FIVE

Judy

Judy lay on the floor, quite motionless. The click of the lock confirmed her fate. She was the prisoner now, the fabric of her carefully constructed existence unravelling so quickly she couldn't quite understand how it had happened.

There was a terrible throbbing in the side of her head, spreading now to join with the ache in her throat. Tears tracked down her cheeks, but these were born of regret rather than physical pain. So many things had gone against her in her lifetime, so many bad people she'd encountered along the way. But given the coldness of her parents, she was cursed the minute she'd been born. She'd been a must-have accessory rather than a person to be loved and nurtured and as soon as she developed a mind of her own, she was pushed further to the edges of her parents' lives. *It's all their fault.*

Her mother should never really have been allowed to have children. So distant emotionally, it wasn't even pleasant on the rare occasions she gave Judy a hug. Her father was the opposite, so tactile that she couldn't bear to have his hairy hands near her. He tickled her too hard, smoothed her hair in a way that felt gross rather than comforting. The smell of him – a combination of whisky and tobacco – turned her stomach. Thankfully she'd had some nice nannies, and the house they'd lived in was huge, with plenty of space for her to roam and hide when she wanted to be alone and pretend she belonged to somebody else.

Boarding school had been a mixed blessing. At least she got to go somewhere different, rather than prowling the grounds of her home like a caged animal, rarely allowed off the premises. But the other girls could be so stupid, and they had no sense of humour. Still, that was something she often used to her advantage to get revenge when someone had been mean to her. So many ways to wind up those hysterical females without the finger being pointed her way.

She'd always assumed that she'd finish school and then find some sort of job, though she had no ambitions, no real direction and nobody interested enough to encourage her. So she didn't try with her school work, saw no point in exams, and left at sixteen with no qualifications whatsoever. In her mind, she was a rebel, aware that her parents would be mortified.

She sighed. That had backfired, hadn't it? Bloody teachers should have tried harder, but they didn't like her; she didn't fit in because she questioned things. In those sorts of places, you weren't supposed to question, and in all honesty, the teachers weren't that bright. She could run rings round them, and often did.

She smiled to herself as she thought about her school days. She'd had a lot of fun in her own way, playing people off against each other, setting teachers up to look stupid, embarrassing them, thinking up practical jokes to amuse her peers and maybe gain some favour with them. She'd done so well with the art teacher, the poor man had a breakdown and left. A few of her least favourite class-mates disappeared after holidays as well, moving to other schools.

Ah yes, it had kept her entertained and made sure that people left her alone unless she recruited them as her helpers. She'd had a few of those. Little mice. That was how she'd thought of them. The scared girls who were afraid of her and would do whatever she asked of them. It made sure they were protected. They were the clever ones really. They understood the transaction they were entering into.

Her mind tracked through the chronology of her life. It had been sort of bearable until her parents had made a disastrous decision to acquire another company, overstretching themselves financially. In a matter of months they were bankrupt. But the worst thing was, they didn't even think to tell her. Not to her face.

Her jaw clenched tight. It still made her furious, even now, after all these years.

She'd been at a private college at the time, sent there to retake her failed GCSEs. The college secretary had come into her classroom to take her to see the principal. He'd had an expression on his face that said he had something to tell her that she wasn't going to like.

'Please, take a seat, Judy.' He indicated an armchair by the window instead of the usual telling-off chair in front of his desk. That one she was familiar with. This one was a new experience. Gingerly she perched on the edge of it.

'I've had a message from your parents.' He wore a pained expression on his face. 'I'm afraid they are withdrawing you from the college.'

Judy's mouth dropped open. It had been their idea that she should come here in the first place, and it didn't make sense to withdraw her now. 'But it's only a few months until exams.'

He gave a sympathetic sigh. 'I know. Very unfortunate timing. They've asked me to pass on this letter. You can have a read in your room while you're packing.'

Her breath hitched in her throat. 'You mean I've got to go now? Right now?'

He nodded. 'That's correct.'

She'd stormed off to her room and ripped open the letter. Her parents were sorry, but the money was gone, and the house had been repossessed. They were starting a new life abroad, but she was an adult now and it was time she became independent. Oh, and her trust fund had a bit less in it than she might expect. Essential costs. Five thousand pounds would give her a start until she found a job, wouldn't it? There was no address, no way of contacting them. She'd been dumped.

Flabbergasted, she'd packed in a daze and resolved to do everything they wouldn't want her to do. Bring the family name into disrepute? Yeah, she could do that. Big time. She ran away from the foster home she was placed with, got herself arrested for being drunk and disorderly, was cautioned for shoplifting, charged with possession of class B drugs. She even spent a few months at a youth detention centre. All for nothing. Her activities went unnoticed and she failed to get what she'd yearned for all her life – their attention.

Now, on the bedroom floor, she coughed and gave a silent scream at the pain that ricocheted through her head, her throat so bruised she could hear her breath rasping in the stillness of the air. It was all her parents' fault. Everything that had gone wrong in her life, right up to this moment, had spun out like a thread that could be traced back to their selfishness.

It was a lucky break when she'd caught up with one of her mice from school. Zara had agreed to Judy joining her for a few weeks on her travels round festivals in her camper van. That lasted a couple of years, until the girl stupidly took an overdose. Well, Judy supposed she'd been the one who had persuaded her to take the drugs, as a bit of sport, pretending that she herself had already taken some and was having a great time – why didn't Zara join in? It had been Zara's choice to put the things in her mouth, hadn't it? At first, it had been hilarious as she'd watched the tablets take effect, like giving alcohol to a puppy, but then the girl went floppy and her breathing funny, and it all went pear-shaped.

Of course she'd had to scarper after that, reinvent herself. Lots of people had seen her and Zara together. The police were probably looking for her and it was possible she'd be treated as a murder suspect. That had been a very scary time. Probably the worst time of her life. Wales, she'd decided, was a good place to hide. All those mountains and valleys, miles and miles of emptiness. Nobody would think of looking for her there. She raided her account, took all the cash and got rid of her bank card. That meant she could live off the grid and the authorities would be unable to track her.

It was a stroke of luck when Marj and Bill had picked her up when she was hitching. It was a few weeks after their son's funeral. He'd been mad keen on off-roading in his Land Rover and had died in an accident. Poor Marj was distraught that she'd lost her only son and Bill was all silent and sad. Oh yes, the gods had been smiling on Judy that day. Immediately she saw an opportunity. It didn't take long to wheedle her way into Marj's affections, and to be honest, she did genuinely care about the woman. She was the best cook, always kind, and she protected Judy from Bill's impatience to see her gone.

Judy became Marj's surrogate daughter and made herself indispensable. She could see that Bill's joints gave him a lot of pain, so she ran around doing the work he could no longer do, and found she was quite enjoying herself. Who knew she'd find comfort in the physical work of farming?

She gazed round the room from her position on the floor. The same old bunk beds that were here when she'd arrived. In fact, that bottom bunk had been hers for a while. She'd put up with the squeaky springs because at least here she was well fed and cared for. Anyway, she was playing the long game. That required sacrifice at the beginning to see rewards further down the line.

The pain in her head had moved again, stabbing behind her eyes. She squinted against the brightness of the light, but even that became too much effort. She turned onto her side, tucking her hands together under her cheek like a pillow, legs curled to her chest. Ah, that was better.

She was right back where she'd started now. No, she was probably further back than that, even. Of course, good things never lasted, did they?

After Marj had died, Bill had turned quite hostile. Obviously he'd been grieving, but he seemed to take everything out on Judy. They'd had row after row and the whole atmosphere became unbearably sour. The turning point came when a strange car drove up to the house and a young woman in a suit stepped out. As usual, Judy kept out of the way. Nobody knew who she was here, and she liked it that way. Even Bill and Marj didn't know her real identity. To them she was Judy Holt, a name she'd made up on the spur of the moment, along with a tragic backstory guaranteed to make them feel sorry for her.

She watched from behind the curtains in the study, saw how the woman was looking at the house, a clipboard in her hands, taking notes. Later that evening, when they were eating their supper, she questioned Bill about it.

'I was wondering… who was the woman here earlier?'

He wiped his mouth with the back of his hand, pursed his lips before replying, like he was working out whether to tell her the truth or make something up. 'She's an estate agent,' he said, looking her straight in the eye. 'I'm putting the place on the market.'

Judy gasped. She couldn't believe what she was hearing. 'So what happens to me if you sell?'

He shrugged like he really didn't care. 'I don't know. Look, you've been a great worker, and Marj did love having you here. But you've got to admit that it's different now she's gone. With my knees I can't keep doing this work. It's too much and I've had enough. So I've decided to sell up and go down to the south coast, where it's warmer. Get myself a little bungalow by the sea in one of those retirement villages.'

In a burst of fury, she bounced to her feet. 'You selfish bastard!' she yelled.

Before she could think about what she was doing, she'd smacked him across the face. Obviously, she hadn't meant to hit him that hard. It was years of frustration concentrated in that one act.

Years of having to be nice to this smelly, bad-tempered old man. His head spun to the side, his chair rocked backwards, and she watched silently as he fell, wincing as his head crunched on the floor. Quarry tiles were a very unforgiving surface.

It had been a blessing in disguise, though, and when she'd checked for a pulse and found that he was dead, she'd smiled. On one level, she'd known it was wrong to be happy that he'd died, but on another, her future was secure, the farm as good as hers. Who would even know he was dead? She managed the farm accounts and had long ago mastered his signature. Now she would tell anyone who asked that he'd gone to live down south, because that was what he might already have told people. She could utilise his bank accounts and do whatever she pleased.

The next day, she'd buried him in the orchard, covered the plot with a big pile of branches. She'd written a letter to the estate agents saying that he'd changed his mind. Judy was renting the farm while he retired to the south coast. And that was it. Sorted.

Bill had been old school in his approach to farming, and there were opportunities that he'd refused to consider. Now Judy could go ahead with her plans for getting cheap labour to help her run the place, so she could actually make enough money to live on – no mean feat with a hill farm. The old couple had been using savings to keep the place going – they'd had a payout from the insurance company after their son's death, a windfall that came at a very fortuitous time. There was still a chunk of that left for her to dip into, but she wanted to stretch it out for as long as possible. Her idea was to recruit volunteers who'd work for free in return for board and lodgings.

Then she'd picked up Nancy and another idea blossomed. As a child, her family had always had staff. She'd grown up in that environment and the novelty of hard graft was definitely wearing thin. Nancy was a perfect little mouse. Young enough to be vulnerable and easily influenced, and as a runaway she was the ideal candidate for the job. Over the years, Judy had moulded her into a shape that had worked very well, and not a penny paid in wages. She'd also liked her, though. As a worker and companion, she'd fitted the bill exactly.

At one time, she'd thought things might take a different turn. When Ryan had proposed, that had been a surprise. Stupid of her to take him seriously, of course. She knew that now. Thank goodness she'd overheard him and his cousin arguing over the payout for his dare. Well, she'd soon sorted him out. Made sure his cousins and his dad were out drinking when she'd confronted him. Not that it had worked out according to plan. She'd probably hit him a bit too hard as well, the gun bursting his lip, blood pouring all over the place. But he'd been only too happy to leave. She'd driven him to the end of the track, dumped him there for his dad to pick up later. Let him explain what he'd done.

After that, she vowed she was never falling in love ever again, and poured all her energy into the farm. Obviously she had… needs, and she'd found men to fulfil those over the years. But she never let them come to the farm. Afternoon delight, that was all it ever was. Never serious, and if the men got too clingy, she dumped them and found someone else.

Yes, it had all worked until recently. Getting rid of the dog had probably been a mistake. Nancy had been a bit sullen since then, a strange look in her eye. And this last week she'd been different again. Clearly somebody had been talking to her, putting ideas in her head. The notebook was evidence of that. Yes, she thought now, as her breathing slowed, it was all their fault. If they hadn't turned Nancy's head, she would never have thought of leaving.

Her mouth was dry, each breath causing her pain, but that wasn't her main concern. Her main concern was that she couldn't blame anyone but herself for leaving Nancy alone at the farm and giving her the opportunity to actually meet people. That had been a serious miscalculation. But then how could she have foreseen it would end like this?

The consequences of one little slip didn't bear thinking about. Would it all come out now? Would they find out her real name and trace her back to Zara and that drug overdose? Or find out what had happened to Bill?

She tasted salt in her mouth; a tear had slid down her cheek without her realising.

Until this year, Nancy had been willing and compliant and most of the time had actually seemed content with the status quo. What was it about turning forty that made people act out of character, want something different? She'd seen it happen to several local people, and now Nancy. It was like an infection.

This pain in her head. Nancy had done that to her. And Eva. *I'll tell the police they attacked me.*

Despite her discomfort, she managed a satisfied smile. She'd be the winner. She was always the winner. And once she'd made her decision to tread the path of revenge, her breathing slowed.

CHAPTER THIRTY-SIX

Nancy

'I thought this day would never come,' Nancy said, as she hugged her sobbing sister outside the bedroom. How strange to have this human contact, the feel of another person in her arms, a mingling of breath, a touching of cheeks. It was intoxicating and she didn't want to let go. At last she had something that was hers. A missing sister, a person who had only existed as a screaming memory but was now this grown woman full of grit and determination.

They clung to each other until Eva managed to stop crying and pulled away.

'I'm sorry,' she said, wiping her eyes on her sleeve. 'Making a fool of myself. Honestly, I've never been so scared in my life. I thought I was going to die.'

Nancy nodded. 'Me too.' She stared at the closed door, thinking about the woman who lay captive behind it. The Jekyll and Hyde character she'd shared her life with. 'It's not the first time I thought she might kill me. When she had the gun, though, I was sure it was all over. And it would have been if you hadn't had that chair leg ready.'

Eva gave a little snort. 'Well, if you hadn't ducked down, it would've been you I'd hit.'

Nancy caught her eye and found a little part of herself staring back. The same-shaped nose, a little dink in the chin. It really was quite strange.

'Teamwork.' She smiled, just starting to understand that a new life might be possible. 'I know this sounds odd, and please don't take it the wrong way, but I'd sort of forgotten I even had a sister. My world is this place. Literally, just the farm. Judy convinced me that I'd be arrested if I ever set foot outside the boundaries. Or I'd get lost and die of hypothermia. Or I'd be picked up by a murdering rapist. She had me living in fear, thinking the farm was the only safe place.' She frowned and hung her head. 'I feel so dumb, like I've been sleepwalking through my life all these years. Hypnotised. And then, a few days ago, I met these people and… I suddenly woke up.' She cringed. 'Does that make me sound stupid?'

Eva gave her shoulder a squeeze. 'The mind is a weird thing, isn't it? We believe what we need to believe to makes our lives palatable. It sounds to me like you were a prisoner here.' Her voice was gentle, compassion in her eyes. 'Is that what it was like?'

Nancy gazed at the floor, studying the grain of the wood, the intricate patterns of waves and knots. 'At first I was grateful to Judy for taking me in and looking after me. I was in a really bad place after Mum died. Judy was protective, and honestly, I thought of her as a friend. It was only as the years went on that I saw another side to her. A nasty temper. But it was always my fault when we argued and I suppose I just lost sight of myself.' She sighed. 'I was naive. There's no two ways about it. Still a child really. And I believed everything she told me.'

She shrugged. 'I had no money. No transport. And you can see how remote this place is. You'd have to walk miles to get away, and it would be easy to catch up with you in a car before you'd got very far. People die in these mountains. They get lost, out on their own, or they hurt themselves and can't call for help.' She blinked away tears, understanding how she'd allowed Judy to take so much from her without even realising. 'She convinced me that my family wouldn't want to hear from me. That the police wanted to question me about Mum's death. That I'd told her I was responsible. All sorts of things.'

Eva frowned. 'Why would the police think you were involved in Mum's death?'

'Well…' Nancy tried to picture the events in her mind, squinting as she peered into the past. 'She fell off a ladder and broke her neck. The police were investigating if it was an accident or if foul play was involved.'

Eva's jaw dropped, her voice hushed, as though she hardly dared say it. 'They thought you pushed her?'

Nancy traced a knot of wood on the banister with her finger. 'We had a bit of a tricky relationship. I was a horrible teenager. Well, I suppose I'd been an only child and then this baby was coming along, and it was just when I was about to take my GCSEs, so I was worked up about those.' She glanced at her sister. 'There was going to be a massive change in my life. I had so many mixed emotions, I didn't know what to do with them.'

'Is it true that Mum wanted to leave?' Eva studied her face. 'Judy told me all sorts of stuff and I don't know what to believe.'

Nancy sighed. 'Mum did want to leave. Dad had been seeing someone for years. Then she found out she was pregnant with you and they decided to stay together.'

Eva nodded, sadness in her eyes.

'Dad was useless after she died. I remember that. Well, he was worse than useless. I was alone and frightened and angry and…' Nancy gasped as a pain shot up her injured leg, making her feel sick. 'Christ, this hurts.' She put a protective hand on the wound, but that just made it worse. She grabbed the banister. 'I really need to sit down.'

Eva put an arm round her shoulders. 'You're looking ever so pale. You're not going to faint or anything, are you?'

Nancy glanced down the stairs, eager to be outside in the fresh air. Maybe then she'd feel like she could breathe properly again.

'Let me help you,' Eva said. 'We can't have you falling down the stairs. Not after all this.'

Slowly they made their way out of the house, and Nancy pointed to the bench under the living room window. 'Let's sit there.'

'I'm going to call the police and an ambulance,' Eva said, pulling a phone from her back pocket. 'I've just got to get a signal.' She walked away, towards her car. Nancy studied her back as she made the call, thinking that the way she stood was just like their dad; they had the same build. It really was uncanny. Her dad who she'd loved and despised. Admired and derided.

Memories from the past flooded into her mind. It seemed that now she'd invited a couple of them in, they all wanted to come out of hiding. Things she'd forgotten. Things she'd hidden in the hope they'd fade to nothing, cease to exist.

She stared at the mountains, trying to push the thoughts away. It was a long time ago. Her mum was dead. Did any of that matter anymore? Wouldn't it be better to move forward instead of trying to go back and repair what couldn't be mended?

Eva finished her call and they sat in shocked silence for a while, Nancy keeping her gaze focused on the distant view, making sure she didn't catch Eva's eye, hoping she was sending out the signal that she didn't want to talk.

In all honesty, she was too dazed to speak, and nervous that Eva would start asking questions again. The pain in her body was amplifying now the adrenaline had ebbed away. Her head throbbed in time with her pulse. Her leg felt like it was on fire where the air pellet had punched through the skin. She couldn't believe what had just happened. Or that she was now sitting beside her sister. Desperate for comfort, she reached for Eva's hand, and they sat like that until they heard the sound of tyres crunching on the track, the revving of an engine, signalling the arrival of a vehicle. An ambulance.

Eva jumped up and Nancy let her take control. She was feeling light-headed now, the world spinning. She let her head lean back against the wall, watching from a distance. After a quick conversation, one of the paramedics came over to her, while Eva led the other upstairs to see to Judy.

'Hello, Nancy. I'm Ann. Let's see if we can patch you up, shall we?'

Nancy was compliant, subdued as the paramedic checked her over, answering her questions but not offering anything in the way of explanation about how she'd come to be injured. She was too exhausted now and just wanted to sleep.

Twenty minutes later, she had a bandage on her leg and a large plaster on her head where the mug had hit her. A cut that might need a stitch. She hadn't even noticed it had been bleeding.

'We'll just see how the other patient is, then we'll take whoever is most urgent.' The paramedic glanced at the car. 'Could your friend bring you? It's just there's been an RTC on the A55 and it could be a while before another ambulance can get here.'

'She's my sister.' It was the first time Nancy had said the word out loud, and it felt very odd, like it wasn't hers to use.

The paramedic turned as her colleague approached, and Nancy followed her gaze. He had a grim expression on his face, and behind him, Eva was ghostly pale.

He sat down beside Nancy. 'I'm so sorry to have to tell you this, but the lady upstairs has passed away.'

CHAPTER THIRTY-SEVEN

Nancy gulped. Dead? *No, no, no. She can't be dead.* Her heart stuttered in her chest. *Does that make me a murderer?* Or was the deadly blow Eva's? Her mind whipped itself into a frenzy, lining up all the consequences for her to see. Just when she'd thought she was free, her life was going to be snatched away from her.

Ann frowned. 'I'll call it in, shall I? See what the police want us to do?'

The man said nothing, but followed her to the ambulance. Nancy watched them huddled together, having a whispered conversation.

Eva sank onto the seat beside her and grasped her hand. 'I killed her,' she murmured, a sob catching in her throat. 'Oh my God, I can't believe it. I didn't mean to. I was just trying to—'

'Now you listen to me,' Nancy said, as firmly as she could. 'None of this is your fault. It's down to me. I came here. I stayed here. I found Dad's address and decided I wanted to leave. That's what caused me and Judy to fight in the first place. I put her in hospital. That's what started the whole thing off.' Her jaw clamped tight. 'I'm going to say I did it.'

Eva looked horrified. 'No! No, I won't let you.'

Nancy fixed her with a stern look. 'I've spent my life in a virtual prison. A few more years isn't going to make much of a difference to me.' She squeezed Eva's hand. 'I won't be able to live with myself if you end up being charged for this. Please. I'm going to say it was me.'

Eva's eyes sparked with defiance. 'Well, I'll say I saw her attacking you and it was self-defence.'

'We don't know which injury killed her. Maybe it was me anyway.' Nancy sighed. 'That *was* self-defence, but there were no witnesses.'

'Well then. You've got to let me help you.'

Eva's insistence was wearing Nancy down. She'd had no practice at asserting herself. 'I don't want you telling lies.'

'Is it a lie, though? If I hadn't hit her, what would have happened to the two of us?' Their eyes met. 'I think... she was going to kill us.'

The thought of how close they'd been to death robbed Nancy of any reply. Her eyes dropped to her lap, focused on her sister's hand held in her own.

The paramedics had finished their little conference and the woman was talking on the phone, the man listening in.

Eva leant her head towards Nancy. 'We'll get through this. If we stick together, tell the same story, we'll be okay.'

'The story is that I hit her. Not negotiable. That's what we're saying. Then you aren't implicated in any of it. It's my mess. I started this when I ran away. That was my decision.'

'Okay,' Eva said eventually. 'Okay, we'll do it your way. But only if you answer this one question. Why did you really run away? Why pretend to be dead?'

Nancy knew it was time for the truth. 'Because I found out who Linda was.'

CHAPTER THIRTY-EIGHT

Eva

Eva frowned, nerves stirring up the contents of her stomach. 'I'm not sure what you mean,' she said cautiously, as though she was watching a scary programme from behind a cushion, ready to hide.

Nancy sighed. 'Look, I'm not saying this to be mean or hurtful, or in any way…' Her grip on Eva's hand tightened as if she was afraid that Eva would somehow fly away if she didn't hang onto her. 'If we're going to have any sort of relationship, it's got to be based on the truth.'

Eva's frown deepened. 'Even though you want me to lie about what happened up there?' She was fast deciding that her sister could be infuriating. *Can I trust her to tell the truth when she's just told me I have to lie?*

'That's not the same. I mean being honest with each other. Agreed?'

Eva nodded, biting her lip, unsure if she wanted to hear what Nancy had to say. The things Judy had told her when she was pretending to be Nancy were bad enough. Did she want to know more? She took her hand from Nancy's grasp, about to stand up, but her sister had already started to speak.

'Basically, Linda was Dad's bit on the side.'

Eva's eyes widened, a weight dropping into the pit of her stomach. So Judy had been telling the truth about that as well.

'As far as I understand it, he used to be a teacher, and he met and fell in love with a sixth former from a different school to the one he taught at.' Nancy sighed. 'Mum found out he was seeing someone called Ellie. They had a massive row. He told Mum it was all over, but she'd had enough and was planning on leaving him anyway. Then she found out she was pregnant with you and decided to give him another chance. A little while later, the house next door came up for rent and Linda moved in.' She gave a derisive snort. 'Turned out that Ellie – Elle – was short for Linda.'

Eva swallowed, her whole world as she knew it turned upside down. With mounting horror, she remembered that her dad often called Linda 'L'. 'Wait a minute… You're saying that Linda had been seeing Dad since she was at school?' Her voice rose to a disbelieving squeak. It hardly seemed possible. Her mum wasn't that sort of person. She just wasn't. 'Are you sure?'

'One hundred per cent sure. I overheard them talking over the garden fence. She was asking him when he was going to tell Mum. He said once the baby was born he'd sort everything out.' Nancy's face was clouded with anger. 'He was going to leave us. Then Mum died and Linda moved in. Like a couple of days later.'

Eva felt lost, cut adrift from her own life. *Would Mum do that?* She was no longer sure.

'Anyway,' Nancy carried on, 'I couldn't live in the same house with them. I wish I hadn't told Mum, though. It was the day she died. I can't remember what we'd been rowing about, but we had a shouting match and I told her what I'd overheard, just to hurt her. Then I flounced out and slammed the door behind me.' Her voice cracked. 'Those were the last words I spoke to her. I know she was upset and I can't help feeling it was my fault she fell. Getting her worked up and distracting her from what she was doing.'

Eva looked at her sister, could see the guilt etched on her face. What a horrible thing to have to live with. 'I don't see how you can blame yourself,' she said gently. 'I didn't even know she'd had an accident until Judy told me. Imagine that! I just assumed she'd died in childbirth, and felt guilty all my life, thinking my birth had caused my mother's death.'

Nancy took her hand again. 'She was decorating the bedroom that was going to be your nursery. Dad said he'd do it, but he hadn't got round to it and she was all restless. So she was up a ladder and fell off. I'd stormed off to a friend's house and Linda had to come and get me and take me to the hospital. That was awful because I knew Linda had been cheating with Dad.' She closed her eyes. 'It was just… the most terrible day of my life.'

'I can see why you'd want to leave.' Eva's eyes dropped to their hands, clasped tightly together. 'You won't know this, but… Dad's got dementia.' She glanced at her sister. 'Poor Mum… Linda… finds it a bit of a struggle.'

Nancy huffed. 'Really? That's karma for you. But she's a lot younger than him. I don't suppose she thought she'd be spending this part of her life nursing her husband.'

'No. It's hard for her.' Eva caught Nancy's eye. 'Will you come home with me? Come and see Dad? I don't know how long he's got left, and he still recognises me. I'm not sure how much longer that will last.'

Nancy was quiet for a moment. 'I do want to see him. But I don't want to see her.' She pulled a face. 'It's going to feel really awkward.'

Eva was struggling to match the mum she knew with the Linda Nancy had described. They seemed like two different people.

After a pause, she said, 'I think you should give her a chance. She's obviously not perfect. But she's been a lovely mum to me. You know, I've always counted myself as one of the lucky ones.'

Nancy stared at her. 'How on earth can you say that when she's lied to you your whole life?'

Eva pressed her lips together, tears not far away as Nancy's words hit a truth she'd been trying to deny. 'I didn't even know you existed until Judy was in hospital and they rang to see if someone could look after her for a little while. Imagine that.'

Nancy shook her head. 'See. Doesn't that just prove what I was saying?'

Eva looked away. Was Nancy's version the truth? She had to ask herself that. Then again, what did Nancy have to gain by lying? The answer was nothing, whereas Linda…

Could she really go back and live with her parents after what she'd learnt? Her trust in her mum had been snapped in two, and even if they managed to stick it back together, it was permanently damaged. There would always be questions, uncertainties about everything she was told. Wondering if it was another of Linda's little white lies.

She grasped Nancy's hand a little tighter. *My sister.* At least she wasn't an only child anymore. And as long as they had each other, they'd be okay, wouldn't they?

The crunch of tyres signalled the arrival of another vehicle. A police car.

CHAPTER THIRTY-NINE

Nancy

Murder. The word rumbled round Nancy's head. *Self-defence.* Eva's voice in her mind. She watched the police officers as they huddled with the paramedics, obviously getting an update, the odd furtive glance being directed their way.

It took a little while before a plan of action was agreed and the group broke apart. One of the police officers spoke into his radio, while the other headed in their direction. Eva's hand was still in hers the sweat on their palms sticking them together. She peeled her hand away, readying herself for handcuffs. She had no idea what to expect, no experience to call upon. Fear clenched the back of her neck, the sound of her pulse loud in her ears.

'Hello. I'm Sergeant Roberts,' the man said when he stopped in front of them, his gaze resting on Nancy, then shifting to Eva and back again. He was a stocky man and had obviously put on weight recently, as his uniform strained at the front, over his belly. His voice was deep, with a strong local accent. 'I just wanted to tell you what's going to happen next. As you both require hospital treatment, we're going to send you in the ambulance, and our colleagues will meet you at the hospital and take your statements.' He looked up at the house before his eyes settled on Nancy again. 'This is now a crime scene, so I'm afraid nothing can go into or come out of the building for the time being.'

'What about my car?' Eva asked.

'That will have to stay here for the moment. But once we're finished with it, we can get it to the station and you can pick it up from there.'

Nancy nodded. Eva said nothing.

The officer walked back to his colleague, and the paramedics came over to help the sisters into the ambulance. Nancy's leg had decided not to work now she'd been sitting for a while, and it was a relief to get settled on a stretcher inside, a shot of morphine allowing her to float above the pain.

It was early morning by the time they'd been processed through the hospital system and their injuries dealt with. Nancy felt weary beyond belief now the adrenaline had worn off, but the police still wanted an interview.

She'd had a lot of time to think it over while she'd been waiting and decided that honesty was the best policy. Once she was in the meeting room, two officers sitting opposite, the whole story came tumbling out, right from the day she'd run away. She told them about Judy's manipulation, the way she'd been coerced into thinking she was wanted for her mother's murder, the way she'd been moulded into a slave, based on a premise of friendship that appeared now to be a mere fabrication. She admitted hitting Judy with the shovel. She also said it was she who'd hit her with the chair leg. Self-defence, she asserted, on both occasions. Did she see the police officer give an imperceptible nod when she said it? She had no idea, too tired to care but keen to make sure that she took the blame so Eva would be in the clear.

Of course she had to give an address where she could be located and questioned further as the investigation progressed. With the farm out of bounds for now, there was one choice and one choice only for Nancy – to go to Nottingham with Eva.

'I told them it was me,' she said once they were in the car and on their way. She glanced at her sister. 'What did you tell them?'

Eva let out a huge sigh. 'I… I told them it was you.' Her voice wavered. 'It was horrible. I felt awful doing it.'

Nancy rubbed her shoulder. 'Good girl. It was the right thing to do. You know it was.'

'I've always been an awful liar, though. I'm pretty sure they didn't believe me.'

Nancy hadn't really considered that. Had her efforts to save Eva from blame been in vain? She frowned, trying to remember what had happened, whether the evidence would support her version of events. 'I think they'll find my fingerprints on there as well as yours. I'm pretty sure I took the chair leg out of the room, didn't I? So there was no chance of Judy using it against us.' She pulled a face, unsure. 'It's all a bit of a blur.'

'I can't remember either.' Eva glanced at her. 'What if they only find my fingerprints? They'll know I was lying.'

A burst of panic brought Nancy's hands to her chest, the implications too dreadful to consider. 'Let's just face that if and when it happens,' she said, trying to sound calm, reassuring. It was a surprise to her how quickly she'd taken on the mantle of big sister, desperate to protect Eva. 'We've just got to let them get on with it and answer any questions as honestly as possible. Except for the question as to who hit her on the side of the head. I've told them I hit her with the shovel, so they already know I've caused her serious harm once.' She smoothed out the fabric of her jeans. 'Makes sense that I might do it again.'

'You sound very philosophical,' Eva said. 'Honestly, my heart is still racing and my hands are all sweaty. That's the scariest thing I've ever had to deal with.'

'Me too.' Nancy shook the vision of Judy with the gun out of her mind, not wanting to relive the horror again. 'Thank God it's over.'

She looked out of the window, revelling in the view of the sea to her left as they approached Llandudno along the coast road. How long since she'd seen the sea? 'Can we stop here?' she asked, seeing a junction coming up. 'Let's have a walk on the beach and calm down a bit. I don't want you to have to drive if you're not feeling up to it.' The sea looked so enticing, the surface still and calm, waves gently lapping on the sandy shore. How good would it feel to have a paddle? Feel the sand between her toes.

'Great idea,' Eva said as she swerved off the dual carriageway. 'I'm not sure I'm safe at the moment. We'll find a café, shall we?'

For Nancy the idea of a café was quite daunting with her face looking so battered. *I can sit in the car. I don't have to go in.* In all honesty, she felt like an alien who'd just landed on earth, seeing everything for the first time. She gave Eva a quick smile, her eyes drawn to the sea. 'I've no money. So that's up to you. But I haven't seen the sea for twenty-four years and I really just want to get my feet wet.'

Eva laughed. 'Okay, let's do that, then we'll stop further on for something to eat. And don't worry about money, I can pay for us.'

She found a parking space and they clambered out of the car. Nancy closed her eyes and took a deep breath, filling her lungs with the salty air, relishing the briny scent in her nostrils.

'Come on,' Eva said, taking her hand and pointing to a gap in the sea wall, steps down to the beach.

It was lovely, Nancy thought, to have a sister. She watched Eva's face, as she allowed herself to be pulled along, enthralled by the familiarity of her features. There was no doubting she was her father's child, but her personality was all their mum. She'd been tactile and playful when Nancy had been young. That had worn off as she'd got older and they had less in common. She thought about all the years of Eva's life that she'd missed, and a sadness filled her heart. Time she'd never get back, memories that she'd never have.

How she regretted the rash and thoughtless actions of her sixteen-year-old self. If only she hadn't run away, she would have known Eva completely, been a central part of her life. Maybe she would have been married and had children of her own by now. These were things she hadn't let herself consider, knowing they were out of her reach. But now? Was it too late for her to live the second part of her life in some sort of normality?

She watched Eva pull off her shoes and socks. 'Come on,' she said, urging Nancy to do the same.

'I need something to lean on. My leg's sore as hell where they gouged that pellet out, and my body feels like it's done ten rounds in the boxing ring.'

Eva stood next to her. 'You can lean on me.' She had that determined look in her eyes again. 'You can *always* lean on me.'

Her meaning was clearly deeper than just the practical offer. The sisters looked at each other, Nancy blinking as tears welled in her eyes. She wrapped Eva in a hug. 'I'm so sorry I left you when you were a baby,' she sobbed, years' worth of emotion pouring out in a torrent of tears. 'It won't happen again, I promise.'

'You bet it won't,' Eva said, her words catching in her throat.

'Oh God, I'm a blubbering mess.' Nancy laughed through her tears when she pulled away. She found a scrunched-up tissue in her pocket and wiped her face, blew her nose. She noticed Eva doing the same and her heart swelled with love. Perhaps the future could be different. She could allow herself to hope for that, couldn't she?

She hung onto Eva's arm while she fumbled to take off her shoes and socks, sighing at the coolness of the sand between her toes. With their jeans rolled up, they stood in the shallows, letting the waves ripple over their feet.

Nancy smiled, joy blossoming in her heart. 'It tickles, doesn't it?'

Eva screamed as a larger wave splashed over them. 'It's bloody freezing.'

Nancy reached for her sister's hand, not knowing how long she'd have this luxury of human contact. Maybe the police would come and arrest her when they'd done further investigations and decided they didn't believe her actions were self-defence. She pondered the situation as she scanned the view, watching the seagulls soaring above the waves. Who was there to contradict her? Eva had backed her up, so on balance she was hopeful.

What was really important, though, was seeing her dad. However she felt about him and his cheating, for her own peace of mind she needed to apologise. She knew he must have gone through a terrible time when she'd faked her own suicide just after her mum's death. That had been a horrible thing to do. Shame burned her cheeks just thinking about it.

She liked to think she wasn't that person anymore. If she had anything to thank Judy for, it was knocking that selfish attitude out of her. Giving her time to think about things on the deepest of levels. At the age of forty, she thought she knew herself pretty well, at peace with herself, despite the limitations of her life.

The thought of being cut from the routine of that life with Judy was quite unnerving, as it had been the pattern of her existence for so many years. But at least she wasn't on her own. At least now she had Eva.

When they got back to the car, Nancy felt revitalised, her skin tingling from the cold sea. Simple pleasures, she thought as she sat in the passenger seat, trying to get the sand off her feet before she put her socks and shoes back on. Eva was pacing a little distance away. She'd bought a new phone from the supermarket and was talking to Linda to let her know they were on their way home. Nancy couldn't hear what was being said, but there was a lot of gesticulating and irritated body language going on. Tension pulled at her shoulders. Was she going to be welcome, or was it all going to be horribly awkward? Once again her bad behaviour was coming back to haunt her. The nasty things she'd said to Linda. The awful names she'd called her. Would she be forgiven?

They took their time on the journey home, having plenty of stops for food and drinks. After their paddle in the sea, Nancy felt they were bonding as sisters rather than strangers. With each of them curious to find out about the other, the conversation flowed freely, as they compared and contrasted their likes and dislikes, finding things in common. Eventually it moved to the more emotive subject of their upbringings.

It seemed to Nancy that her father had done a better job the second time round, Eva's memories of him quite different to her own. And Linda did sound like a more hands-on mum, doing so much with Eva that Nancy would have loved their mum to do with her. She couldn't help feeling jealous, a twist of envy souring her mood as they got closer to Nottingham. It wasn't fair, this half-life she'd lived, and the root cause of it had been her dad. If he'd been the father to her that he'd been to Eva, she might never have run away, would never have met Judy and wasted her life. That thought left a bitterness in her mouth that wouldn't go away.

Do I even want to see him again? She wasn't sure now. Didn't know what it would achieve. How could she not despise him for moving his lover in next door? Having an affair while her mother was pregnant, right under her nose. And how was she going to forgive Linda for her part in the deception? Her stomach churned and she started to regret her decision to come back with Eva. *You didn't have a choice, remember?* The police had insisted on an address where they could be contacted. *You've nowhere else to go.*

She fell silent, lost in her thoughts, trawling through her memories of her dad. Snatches of conversation echoed in her head, fleeting images. Had he really been so bad or was it Judy's influence that had skewed her view, accentuating the negatives, making her feel he didn't care? Convincing her that he'd been a terrible father.

As the memories gathered, she allowed herself to inspect them one by one. The time they'd been in the playground and a dog had been snarling at her and he'd picked her up and kept it at bay with an umbrella until someone came to help. Or when she'd been crying with frustration over some homework and he'd sat beside her and patiently explained it until she'd suddenly understood and could answer the questions on her own. She could still remember how much confidence that had given her. The freedom she'd felt out on bike rides, the wind in her hair as they sped down hills. His melodious voice as he sang while they tidied up the garden. When he'd been at home, she'd followed him round like a puppy, always ready to join in with whatever he was doing.

That was the reality of her childhood. Not too different to Eva's if she looked at it without Judy's filter of spiteful comments. It was the last year at home that had been horrible, her loyalties torn as her parents' relationship had degenerated and she was stuck in the middle. First thinking she was moving out with her mum, then having to ready herself for a new baby, at the same time as she was coping with the stress of exams and knowing that her father was a cheater. That was where the root of the problem lay. It was understandable, wasn't it, that she'd had a meltdown?

It was early evening by the time they arrived in Nottingham, the undulating suburban landscape so different to the mountainous terrain of Snowdonia. Do I belong here? Nancy wondered. It certainly wasn't the place she'd known as home, and she'd feel like a visitor, rather than part of this family, unfamiliar with both the city and the house. Unfamiliar with her dad, come to that. After all, she'd lived apart from him much longer than she'd ever lived with him. Her heart rate sped up, her instincts telling her to turn and run.

You've got to do this, she told herself, her hands finding each other in her lap, fingers knotting together. Even if it's just the once. Tie up the loose ends, decide which way is forwards.

They entered an estate, all the houses very similar, Nancy noticed, as they slowed to go over speed bumps. After a few turns, Eva pulled into the paved driveway of a large dormer bungalow on a corner plot, with a garden all the way round. A high wooden fence ran from the corner of the house to the garden wall, creating a private area at the back. At the front was a small lawn with a neat flower border around it, a cherry tree in the middle. It was very different from the three-bed semi of Nancy's childhood. It felt pristine and not altogether welcoming.

She struggled out of the car, Eva running round to give her a helping hand.

'I know you're worried,' Eva said, giving her shoulder a rub. 'You've been ever so quiet, and I can see it on your face.' She gave her a reassuring smile. 'Whatever Linda thinks, Dad's going to be delighted to see you. He lives in the past a lot, and I'm sure your disappearance has been preying on his mind.'

Nancy knew this was probably said to comfort her rather than being based on reality. Hadn't Eva said that she didn't know she had a sister until the hospital had rung? She didn't think she'd been on anyone's mind. Not for a very long time.

She looked at Eva, saw that her jaw was set, her mouth pinched, and understood that she was nervous too. After all, she'd learnt some difficult truths about her parents in the last few days. She linked arms with her, as much for emotional support as physical, and Eva steered her up the path and round to the side door.

Nancy stopped walking, her heart fluttering in her chest like a bird trapped against a window pane. 'I'm not… I'm not sure about this.'

'What do you mean?'

'I don't think it's a good idea. I mean, maybe…' She looked back at the car, wishing they could get in and drive away. You've nowhere else to go, she reminded herself. She sighed, her body trembling with nerves. 'I don't think I'm ready. Maybe I should wait until my face has healed up?'

Eva squeezed her arm. 'Look, we're here now. If it goes pear-shaped, I promise I'll take you wherever you want to go.' She pulled a face. 'We could get you a room at a Travelodge or something. Just give it a try. Please? For me.'

Nancy pulled her arm from her sister's grasp and turned to go, the impulse to get away and be on her own stronger by the minute, but Eva grabbed her hand and pulled her back.

'No you don't. There's nothing to be scared of. Honestly. I'll be here.' She looked into Nancy's eyes. 'I promise I'll look after you.' She squeezed her hand. 'If you're going to move forwards with your life, it's time to confront your past, isn't it?'

Nancy nodded, fear snatching her ability to speak. Eva tightened her grip on her hand, like a mother holding onto her child next to a busy road. Then she opened the door and drew Nancy inside.

Nancy felt a bit sick. She was going to be face to face with the woman she'd hated for so long with a ferocity it was impossible to describe. The woman who'd jumped into her dead mother's shoes. Whose actions had made her run away in the first place. Could she really forgive and forget?

CHAPTER FORTY

Eva

'Mum. We're home,' Eva called as they entered the kitchen. It was a large open space running from the front to the back of the house, with the units at one end, a dining area in the middle and a couple of two-seater settees by the back window, overlooking a well-tended garden. It was modern and slick, duck-egg blue and white, quite the opposite of the ancient kitchen at the farm. She was nervous now, really not sure how this was going to play out.

It's the right thing to do, she told herself. Doesn't matter what Linda thinks, this is about Dad and Nancy.

Her sister's hand felt clammy, and Eva held on tight, giving her no chance to change her mind and run away.

Linda appeared in the doorway. She was only six years older than Nancy, her figure still trim in jeans and a long-sleeved navy top. Her eyes widened when she saw them, her hands flying to her mouth.

'Oh my God. What happened to you? Eva, sweetheart. Your face!' She came rushing forward, her hands cupping Eva's face as she studied the damage, ignoring Nancy completely.

Nancy let go of Eva's hand, but Eva snatched it back, gently pushing Linda away. 'I'm okay, Mum. But Nancy has had a really rough time of it.'

She watched as Linda studied her sister, could see a flicker of uncertainty on her face. Was that fear? Her eyes met Eva's. 'I thought we'd agreed—'

'No, we didn't, Mum. We didn't agree anything.' Eva's voice was sharp, annoyed. She put a protective arm round Nancy's shoulders, could feel her trembling. 'Don't you think it's time for the truth? Before Dad...' She swallowed. 'Before it's too late.'

She marched past her mum and into the living room, pulling a reluctant Nancy in her wake. Her dad sat in his usual chair, looking out over the garden at the back. Watching the birds at the feeder stationed on the patio outside. He'd spend hours just sitting there, and Eva wondered what he was thinking, where his mind was taking him. Was he remembering her mum, his missing daughter?

He turned when they entered, still with that faraway look. His gaze travelled past Eva to her sister. Then something changed; a light ignited in his eyes and his face broke into a huge grin.

'Janine! Oh my God. I knew it. I knew they'd got it wrong.'

Eva frowned. He'd obviously mistaken Nancy for their mother, and she could see why.

His hands clasped the arms of his chair so tightly his knuckles were a row of white dots against his tanned skin. He laughed. 'I knew it. I knew it!' He pushed himself up to standing, stretching his arms out to Nancy, who tore her hand from Eva's grasp and ran out of the room. Moments later, she heard the back door slam shut.

Her dad's face fell as fast as it had lit up. He looked around, puzzled. 'Where's she gone? She was just here.' Confusion and fear clouded his eyes, taking the place of the joy that had been there when he'd seen Nancy. There was no point in trying to reason with him, tell him it was his daughter not her mother. Eva knew it would only cause more upset. She turned to run after Nancy, but Linda grabbed her shoulder. She hadn't seen her come in and scowled, wanting to get past.

Her dad sank back into his chair, mumbling to himself, his hands wrapping themselves round and round each other. Linda pulled her into the hallway and closed the door behind them.

'I told you not to bring her. I told you.' Eva tensed, could see by the set of her jaw that Linda was seething.

'Mum, you've no idea what she's been through. What we've both been through these last few days.'

Linda tried to pull her into a hug, but Eva pushed her away, anger flaring.

'Don't you come near me. I found out some things from Nancy and—'

'You can't believe a word that girl says,' Linda snapped, arms folding across her chest. 'She always was trouble. Always. Imagine pretending you've committed suicide. What sort of person does that? Hmm?' Her face was pinched with annoyance. 'She put your dad through years of anguish. Torture it was for him.'

'You were having an affair with him before Mum died, weren't you?'

Linda ran her tongue round her lips, her mouth opening as if to speak, then closing again.

It was all the confirmation Eva needed. 'That's right. You were. Nancy overheard your conversation. She ran away because of you.'

Linda's face crumpled. 'It's not my fault. Your dad got me that house to rent. I didn't know it was next door. He said it was temporary, until you were born and he could sort everything out properly.'

'I don't believe you.'

'You don't have to believe me, but it's the truth.'

Eva huffed. 'You and the truth have a very tenuous relationship at times.'

Linda's jaw dropped, her hands falling away from her chest as she leant forward. 'Don't you dare talk to me like that, you little madam. Don't you dare.'

Eva stepped away, closer to the kitchen door and escape. She longed to join Nancy outside. Hoped she'd just gone to the car.

She was torn between finishing her conversation with her mum and running after her sister, making sure she was okay.

'You and Dad. You've never been honest with me. Glossing over the truth so you didn't look bad.'

Her mum lost all her defiance then and leant against the wall, eyes closed. 'I didn't want to lie to you but your dad thought… he thought it was best. You were his child.' She gave a little snort. 'I was barely more than a child myself. He was all I'd ever known, and I trusted him, went along with what he wanted.' She looked at Eva, her face full of sadness. 'As I got older, I knew it wasn't right, but it wasn't up to me.'

It struck Eva then that her mum had been very young when she'd met her father. Still at school. And it seemed that Linda was similar to Nancy, living her life according to someone else's rules.

They stared at each other across the hallway, Eva's mind shooting off in myriad directions. She wanted to go and make sure Nancy was okay. Wanted to try and talk to her dad, get more information from him. Wanted to ask her mum so many questions. Wanted to leave here and not come back, not have to face this emotional quagmire.

It's time to sort this out, she told herself. No running away. No more lies. But she knew that getting to the truth was going to take time.

'I'm going to go and get Nancy and bring her back, and however hard this is, we're going to talk to each other. You're all my family. Nancy included.'

Her mum pursed her lips. 'I honestly don't think we're going to achieve anything today. I think it's going to be too much for your dad. A bit too much for me as well, if I'm honest. It's been a heck of a shock, Nancy turning up again, and he's going to be a handful now, not knowing which decade he's in.' She glanced up the stairs. 'Look, why don't you and Nancy go out and get something to eat, and then by the time you get back, he'll have gone to bed. The guest room is made up, so Nancy can sleep there, and you'll just be next door to her. We're down here out of your way if he starts wandering.' She sighed, clearly not sure if it was a good idea having Nancy to stay. 'Let's start afresh tomorrow.'

Eva realised it was the best they could hope for, and an early night was going to be good for all of them. She was dead on her feet and was sure Nancy must feel the same. She managed a fleeting smile. 'Sounds like a plan. Right, well I'll be back later.'

She hurried through the kitchen and out of the back door, relieved to see Nancy sitting in the car. Where else would she be? Their only option was to stay, and Eva hoped that if she was patient, things would settle down.

The next morning, Eva woke to the sound of her mum screaming. She jumped out of bed and dashed downstairs in her pyjamas, worried that Nancy had got up before her and there was some sort of argument going on. She stopped when she reached the kitchen and saw her mum in the garden, her dad slumped in a chair on the patio, still wearing his pyjamas.

Her heart leapt up her throat and she dashed outside.

'Mum, what's going on?'

Linda glanced up at her, tears running down her face. 'He's gone, love.'

Eva gasped, finding it hard to speak. 'But... I don't understand.' She touched her dad's cheek with the back of her hand, recoiling at the chill of his flesh. It was obvious he'd been dead for a while. 'How did he get outside?'

'I don't know. I was sure I'd locked the door, put the key in the bowl on the sideboard like I usually do. But maybe I didn't. I was so flustered last night, and your dad was confused about Nancy being Janine.' She looked at her husband. 'He must have let himself out. Gone looking for her or something and the door shut behind him.' She started sobbing, her hands covering her face. 'You know how he gets all confused about door handles these days. He must have forgotten how to get back in. And this handle sticks a bit. Maybe he thought he was locked out.'

Eva studied her dad's face, his expression peaceful. He didn't look like he'd suffered and for that she was grateful. Perhaps he hadn't wanted to get back in, content to sit outside in his natural habitat until the chill night air sent him to sleep for ever.

She glanced at her mum, the bad feeling between them forgotten as they hugged. She was crying for her father, but also for herself, because the truth had died with him. She'd wanted him to tell her about her mum's accident, but now she'd only have Linda's version and she supposed that would have to do.

CHAPTER FORTY-ONE

Nancy

Eighteen months later

Being free from Judy had taken a bit of getting used to, Nancy thought, as she sat on a boulder next to the Glaslyn river, only a few miles from the farm. She watched the water rushing over the rocks on its journey down the rapids, troubled by a decision she had to make. A decision that could potentially ruin her relationship with Eva.

What a journey they'd been on these last eighteen months. She hoped that like the river, they'd come through the rapids and were now gliding through calmer waters. She wanted it to stay like that for ever, but there was no avoiding the fact that ultimately the river meets the restless sea. That was where she was right now in her life. About to launch herself into the waves, unsure if she'd sink or swim. Because she held a secret that was destroying her. Could she bring herself to tell the truth?

Her mind floated as she watched the water eddying behind the big stones, thinking about how she'd come to be at this moment in time with this decision to make.

Eventually, with no other witnesses or evidence to suggest otherwise, the authorities had accepted Nancy and Eva's version of events, and no charges were presented against either sister. The hospital confirmed they'd been unhappy that Judy had chosen to discharge herself before all their tests had been completed and against their recommendation. The autopsy concluded that the bleed on her brain that had caused her death had resulted from her original injury and could have been the result of not being careful while she was still suffering from concussion. If she'd stayed in hospital, as advised, there was a strong possibility she would still be alive.

Nancy still blamed herself. She was the one who'd hit her with the shovel in the first place. But if she hadn't done that, surely Judy would have maimed or even killed her. In her mind she'd discounted the blow dealt by Eva, not willing to entertain the possibility that it had in any way contributed to Judy's death.

After their father's funeral, she'd wanted to go back to the farm. She couldn't explain it even to herself, but she knew that she would never be at peace if she didn't let go of the place and her history there in her own good time. Anyway, she felt claustrophobic in the city and yearned for the wildness of the mountains. Where else was she going to go? To her, the farm was still home.

Eva had come with her, and it had been wonderful having her sister to help deal with all the official paperwork. The police had found Judy's passport hidden in the house. Her real name was Cara Hetherington. All her close relatives were now deceased, so there was nobody to inform of her death. She was buried in a common grave. Karma, Nancy thought, throwing a stone into the water and hearing it sink. At least she didn't have to worry about Judy anymore.

A therapist was helping her come to terms with everything that had happened since she'd run away from home. Bit by bit she was starting to accept things and let them go. Instead of worrying about the past, she was learning to embrace the possibilities of the future. In therapy sessions, she'd been told about Stockholm syndrome, how it was a coping mechanism, her mind's way of making her captivity acceptable to herself. In spite of the explanation, she still found it hard to understand how she could have let herself be manipulated in that way for so long. But as her therapist pointed out, Judy's coercive control had been progressive, gradually undermining Nancy's sense of self, making her believe everything was her fault, that she'd said and done things she hadn't, that the outside world was a dangerous place. It was hard to keep your thoughts straight in such a toxic environment.

It was clear that although Judy could be charming, she had a thoroughly nasty side to her personality. Nancy hadn't caused her to behave like that, the therapist kept reminding her; it was a combination of nature and nurture that had made her that way.

Nancy felt sorry for the old farmer who'd taken Judy in. It was his body she'd found in the orchard. He hadn't left a will, so the state had sorted out disposal of his assets. It had been a long and meticulous process, which had allowed the sisters to stay and keep the property in order and see to the welfare of the animals while the legalities were dealt with. The National Trust had bought the farm, as it adjoined land they already owned. It seemed like a fitting result.

Nancy let her mind drift back to the time, just over six months ago, when they'd said goodbye to the place. She still found it hard to explain the mixture of sadness and relief that had overwhelmed her. There was nothing stopping her going to visit, though, if ever she felt the need, and Eva had started to do voluntary work up there, surveying the wildlife and contributing to the conservation plan that was being put in place.

They had a bit of money now their father had died. Linda had sold the family home and bought an apartment in the same block as her best friend. Their dad's estate was split between Linda and Eva, because his will had been written before he could be told that Nancy was still alive, but Eva insisted on sharing her inheritance with her sister.

There had been arguments, Nancy not sure if she even wanted her dad's money, especially after their final encounter. But Eva had pointed out that they needed to find somewhere to live once the farm was sold. Her suggestion was that they buy a place to share, so that was what they did. A little miner's cottage on the edge of Beddgelert, a beautiful village in the heart of the mountains, the closest village to the farm and an area familiar enough for Nancy to feel at home.

Eva had fallen in love with northern Snowdonia, with its abundance of wildlife and fabulous scenery. She'd found work at one of the hotels in the village, which was suiting her fine for now. She said she didn't want to look too far ahead, but had started learning Welsh, so that in time she could find a job that related more closely to her qualifications. Her enthusiasm was infectious, filtering into Nancy's own view of the world. She actually felt hopeful now that she could live a normal life.

Nancy herself wasn't working yet, her anxiety still causing problems with everyday interactions. Eva had told her not to worry about earning money, happy for her to concentrate on her recovery. So for now, she spent her time wandering the mountain paths, pottering about in the garden, looking after the house and getting used to being master of her own destiny. She was feeling stronger by the day, more open to new experiences, and getting braver at being around strangers. Eva had suggested she should open her own Etsy shop to sell the garments she'd been knitting, and she thought she might give it a go. It sounded like fun.

The trickiest thing now was finding a solution to this last problem without ruining her relationships with Eva and Linda.

To be fair, Linda had been very keen to make everything easy for the sisters, and now that Nancy had spoken to her more, she found she couldn't hate her like she used to. Linda had been a child herself when she'd met their dad. He was the one at fault. He was the one who'd moved her next door. He was the one who'd been planning on leaving the family, who'd caused all the turmoil in her life.

Eva was probably struggling with her relationship with Linda more than Nancy was, after all the lies that had been uncovered. It had got to the point where Nancy felt a bit sorry for Linda. She knew that Eva missed her, so they'd organised a visit the following week.

Nancy had a dilemma, though. Should she tell Linda and Eva what had really happened the night her father died? Or was it better for them not to know?

She threw another stone into the water, then another, as the events of that night flooded into her mind.

She'd woken in the middle of the night feeling sore and restless, confused as to where she was. Her mouth was dry, and after tossing and turning for a while, she padded downstairs into the kitchen to make a cup of tea.

She drifted into the lounge, and decided to go and sit outside, where she wouldn't feel so hemmed in. There was a table and chairs on the patio, so she let herself out of the patio doors and sat for a while sipping her tea and listening to the sounds of the suburbs. She could hear a pair of cats fighting. The distant hoot of an owl. A car door slamming. The hum of an engine.

'Janine. There you are.'

Startled by the sound of her dad's voice, she turned to see him standing in the doorway in his pyjamas. He shuffled over to the table where she was sitting, pulling up a chair beside her.

He was beaming at her and took her hand in his, raised it to his lips. 'I knew you weren't dead. She told me you were…' he chuckled, 'but I never believed her, you know.'

Nancy gazed at him for a long moment, hardly recognising this man. And he obviously didn't recognise her. She didn't exist to him except as a mirror image of her mother. Anger flared in her chest. 'Why would you think I was dead?'

He looked bewildered for a moment, and she wondered if she'd get an answer.

'It was just a little push. That was all. Not enough to kill anyone.'

Her breath caught in her throat. Her dad was gazing at her, a distant look in his eye.

'That's right,' she said, playing along. 'You did push me, didn't you?'

'I'm so sorry, love. I didn't mean to hurt you. I just wanted to stop you from attacking Linda.'

She struggled to contain her anger, but forced it down, needing to know more. 'Why would I be attacking Linda?'

He looked down at his hand clasped around hers. 'Well, after you thought you saw us kissing in the garden, I came up to explain, but I didn't realise Linda had followed me.' His thumb caressed the back of her hand. 'You've always had a bit of a temper, haven't you? Didn't I say it would get you in trouble one of these days?'

'I'm sure you did,' she said, understanding for the first time what had happened on the day her mum had died. She pulled her hand away, not wanting to sit with this man a moment longer.

'Where are you going?' He looked confused. 'Don't leave, Janine. Stay with me.'

She patted his shoulder as she walked past. 'You stay here. I'll go and get you a cup of tea.'

He smiled at her, happiness shining in his eyes. She gritted her teeth, feeling nothing but hatred as she walked into the house, hearing the door click shut behind her before she made her way upstairs and back to bed. *He killed Mum! Dad killed her.* Well, he could stay outside all night then. That had always been her punishment when she did something Judy was angry about. Now it was his turn to be punished.

In the morning, he was dead.

At first she'd been horrified – it was her fault that he'd died. How could she tell Eva and Linda what had happened? They were grieving and she didn't want to make life any more complicated than it already was. She'd felt numb, unable to summon any tears for the man who'd killed her mother.

She threw another stone into the water. Was it time to tell Eva and Linda the truth, get that burden off her shoulders? But perhaps it was her burden to bear. She just couldn't decide. Was it her place to tell Eva that their father had killed their mother? Their relationship was strong, but would it cope with this terrible revelation? And if she told her, she'd have to explain how she knew, and how she'd left their father outside.

Karma's a bitch, said Judy's voice in her head.

She went home still undecided. Later that week, the phone rang while Eva was at work. It was Linda.

'Eva's not here, I'm afraid.'

'It's you I wanted to speak to.' Linda sounded nervous.

'Okay, fire away,' Nancy said, assuming that she wanted to discuss arrangements for their visit at the weekend.

'I need to say this before you come and stay because I want this to be a fresh start for all of us.' Linda took a deep breath. 'I know you shut him out, Nancy. That's what happened, isn't it?'

Nancy felt the earth fall away beneath her feet, and she sank into a chair. There was no point denying it and in a way, wasn't this what she'd wanted? To get rid of this terrible secret?

'How do you know that?' she whispered.

'There was a mug on the table. Black tea. Nobody in our house drinks their tea black, so it had to be you who'd left it there. And he couldn't open those patio doors on his own. Kept forgetting how to do it.'

Nancy couldn't speak. She'd known about her dad's difficulties with doors. Eva had told her on the journey, listing the many ways he was losing everyday functions.

'I think you were sitting out there and he did his usual wandering about and saw you. He came to talk to you. And you shut him out.'

Nancy could feel her eyes stinging, horrified by her own behaviour. She hadn't been thinking straight. Hadn't meant for him to die. But however hard this conversation was going to be, at last she could admit the truth.

She sniffed back tears, her voice shaky. 'You're right. He thought I was Mum. And he told me that he pushed her. That he was responsible for her accident.' A sob caught in her throat. 'I couldn't be anywhere near him, so I came back inside and left him out there.'

Linda was quiet for a moment. 'I thought it was something like that.'

'I'm so sorry,' Nancy said, between sobs. 'I was behaving like Judy and it was completely wrong. She used to shut me out when I'd done something wrong, and…' She caught herself trying to justify her actions. 'I didn't mean for him to die.'

Linda's breath crackled down the line. 'That's the thing, love. In his lucid moments, all he would talk about was *wanting* to die. Your dad was such an active man, he hated what was happening to his body and his brain. He was so frightened, so confused a lot of the time; it was heartbreaking to watch, so goodness knows what it was like to actually *be* him.'

There was a long silence, then they both started talking at the same time.

'Sorry – after you, Linda.'

'I wanted you to know that I'm not angry with you. It wasn't deliberate. Just… well, an accident really. Like your mum's accident. That wasn't deliberate either.'

Nancy's brain screeched to a halt. 'He admitted it, though. He said he pushed her.'

'Well, sort of…' Linda sighed. 'Janine was going to attack me with a paint scraper and your dad got between us, pushed us apart. We both went flying.' Her voice cracked. 'It was a horrible accident and I've lived with it ever since. He said we should keep our relationship a secret, that it wouldn't look good if I'd been there when she fell.'

Nancy knew that nothing could change the facts. Her actions had contributed to her father's death, just like her father's actions had caused her mum to die. It was a tough one to come to terms with. 'It's probably best if I don't come this weekend.'

'No, love, no, I want you to come. Please. I want us to be a family. I want us to put all our tragedies behind us. See if we can start again. Eva… and you, Nancy, you're all I've got now.'

After Linda had rung off, Nancy sat for a long time, thinking about secrets and lies and how they weighed you down and ruined lives. But could they repair lives as well?

It was only when Eva came home that she moved from her seat.

'Eva,' she said, nerves fluttering in her stomach, 'I've got something to tell you.'

Eva raised an eyebrow. 'Wow, why so serious?' She gave her a hug, rocking from side to side, her breath warming Nancy's cheek. 'I don't think this is ever going to get old,' she said, holding her tighter. 'Coming home to my big sis.'

The answer to Nancy's dilemma became clear then. Nobody was perfect. They'd all made mistakes, she as much as any of them. And Linda's lies weren't all of her own making. She'd been under the influence of their father. Now she wanted to keep a secret to protect Eva, the most precious person in each of their lives. Someone who'd had a hard enough time through no fault of her own. She was the only innocent in the whole messy situation – what purpose would the truth serve, except to rip their relationships apart again, leaving them all torn to shreds?

Eva pushed away, staring into Nancy's eyes, an infectious smile on her lips. 'So what do you need to tell me?'

Nancy smiled back, her decision made. 'Oh… um… Linda called. We've cleared the air, and I think… well, I think we understand each other now.' Eva beamed, tucking a strand of Nancy's hair behind her ear. 'Everything's going to be just fine.'

The truth about their parents' deaths was something Nancy would willingly keep to herself in return for the love of her sister. Perhaps, in time, it was something else she'd come to terms with.

We all make mistakes. That would be her mantra.

A LETTER FROM RONA

I want to say a huge thank you for choosing to read *The Liar's Daughter*. If you enjoyed it and want to keep up to date with all my latest releases, just sign up at the following link. Your email address will never be shared, and you can unsubscribe at any time.

www.bookouture.com/rona-halsall

I always think it's quite magical the way a premise for a story evolves from the first nugget of an idea to the finished article. I wanted to write about sisters, as this is a dynamic that is different in every family but that many of us can relate to. I wondered how the relationship would develop if there was a big age gap. And what if the younger sibling didn't even know she had a sister? How on earth could that happen? It was fun to play around with the possibilities until I settled on a final scenario.

I also wanted to write about modern slavery, and how vulnerable young people can easily be taken advantage of, mistaking manipulation for kindness. This idea came from a news story about homeless youngsters; I was appalled at some of the stories they had to tell. I wanted to explore how coercive control can be used to create a virtual prison, rather than using the force of violence.

I hope you loved *The Liar's Daughter*; if you did, I would be very grateful if you could write a review. I'd love to hear what you think, and it makes such a difference helping new readers to discover one of my books for the first time.

I love hearing from my readers – you can get in touch on my Facebook page, and through Twitter, Instagram or Goodreads. I also have a new website if you fancy having a look!

Many thanks,
Rona Halsall

RonaHalsallAuthor

@RonaHalsallAuth

18051355.Rona_Halsall

ronahalsall

www.ronahalsall.com

ACKNOWLEDGEMENTS

There are so many people to thank who have helped in the development and publishing of this book.

As always, I'd like to thank my agent, Hayley Steed of Madeleine Milburn TV, Film and Literary Agency, for her enthusiastic support and wise words, helping to shape the initial idea. I am proud to be part of team MM!

My publishers do a fantastic job of turning a rough idea into a finished book. I have to thank my editor, Isobel Akenhead, for her creative input and astute observations, which often make me laugh and make the process a pleasure. Big thanks to editorial manager Alex Holmes for organising Jane Selley to do copyedits and Jon Appleton to proofread. Thanks as well to Alba Proko for sorting out the audio production. And then there's Kim Nash, Noelle Holten and Sarah Hardy in the publicity team, who shout about my books and get them noticed – you guys are the best! Supported by Alex Crow and Hannah Deuce in the marketing team, who produce wonderful graphics and do all sorts of magic with adverts behind the scenes. There are many other people within Bookouture who will have had an input at some stage, so I thank you all for your dedication and hard work in making my book the best it can be.

My little team of early readers deserve a massive thank you for reading a rough second draft, pointing out the mistakes and giving me ideas to make the book better. Big thanks to Kerry-Ann Mitchell, Gill Mitchell, Sandra Henderson, Wendy Clarke, Chloe

Jordan, Dee Groocock and Mark Fearn – your feedback was very much appreciated.

Thanks also to Jules Swain, who took time out of her busy shift as a paramedic to answer my questions – you are an amazing woman! And Stuart Gibbon of GIB Consultancy, thanks as always for help on the police procedural elements.

I also want to give a shout-out to all the people who read and review early copies and post all over the place. You guys are awesome and I am grateful that you are willing to take the time to do this. In particular, I'd like to thank members of The Fiction Café Book Club, who are always such enthusiastic and lovely readers. I would also like to give a special thanks to book bloggers and bookstagrammers for all your wonderful pictures and carefully considered reviews.

Finally, I want to thank family and friends for their support in what has been a very difficult time.

Made in the USA
Las Vegas, NV
20 March 2022

46026388R00157